The Dancer's Choice

ALSO BY JUNE TATE

Riches of the Heart
For Love of a Soldier
No One Promised Me Tomorrow
Better Days
Nothing is Forever
For Love or Money
Every Time You Say Goodbye
To Be a Lady
Talk of the Town
A Family Affair
The Dressmaker's Girl
The Dancer's Choice

The Dancer's *Choice*

JUNE TATE

JOFFE BOOKS

Revised edition 2025
Joffe Books, London
www.joffebooks.com

First published by Severn House Publishers Ltd in Great Britain in 2010 as *Born to Dance*

This paperback edition was first published in Great Britain in 2025

ISBN: 978-1-80573-343-0

For the lovely Tracy Brooks, a foxy lady with a great sense of humour who is very special to me.

CHAPTER ONE

Southampton, 1934

Bonny Burton had started dancing almost as soon as she was able to walk. As a child, whenever her mother had turned on the wireless, Bonny would beam with delight and sway to the beat, taking unsteady steps, yet keeping in time with the music, which was extraordinary in one so young. Her mother Millie and her father Frank, a bank clerk, had crowed with parental pride and encouraged her. At five, they'd paid for her to attend the local dancing class on a Saturday morning, where she'd learned tap and ballet. Throughout her childhood, Bonny had always told anyone who asked what she was going to do when she grew up that she was going to be a dancer.

So when, at eighteen, she told her parents that she had decided to audition for the chorus line at the Palace Theatre, in Above Bar, they did not hesitate before giving their blessing. After all, this was what their daughter had trained for, and it was locally situated, which meant she would be staying at home where they could make sure she was not being led into temptation at such a tender age. Had they known a little more about life in the theatre, they may not have been quite so happy with the idea!

* * *

The interior of the Palace Theatre in Above Bar was not brightly lit when Bonny arrived for the audition, only the stage area. In the gloom of the auditorium, the musical director sat with the producer, watching the hopefuls do their stuff.

'Next!' a voice boomed out and another girl took the stage, handing her music to the pianist.

Bonny watched from the wings. The girl on the stage was obviously nervous and made several mistakes in her tap routine.

'Thank you. Next!'

Taking a deep breath, Bonny walked over to the pianist and, with a shy smile, handed him her music. She wore a short practice skirt in black, a plain white blouse with short sleeves and, of course, her tap shoes. Her long auburn hair was tied back in a black bow.

As soon as the first notes of 'Alexander's Ragtime Band' started, Bonny went into her routine. Her long legs tapping out the steps to the music in perfect time. As usual when she danced, Bonny lost herself in the music, and she forgot about the two people who were watching and just enjoyed the moment. At the end, she stopped and waited. She could hear the two talking.

'Untie your hair!' she was told.

She did so, shaking the long luscious tresses loose.

'Thank you, take a seat in the front row and wait.'

There were two other dancers sitting there. They smiled at her, but no one said a word. The audition continued.

Two hours later, twenty girls were sitting in the stalls when the auditions finished. The rest were dismissed.

'Right, you girls, up on the stage please.'

As they stood in line on stage and waited, a tall slim figure of a man walked down the centre aisle, up the steps to the stage and stood staring at them individually. The girls looked back with interest.

Rob Andrews was tall with short brown hair and piercing blue eyes. He wore trousers and a white singlet; his muscular arms and trim waist showed his supreme fitness. There was no look of welcome on his clear-cut features. If anything he looked angry.

'You were the best of a bad bunch!' he informed them. 'We have a lot of work to do. Be here at eight thirty tomorrow morning, and don't be late or you won't be employed!' Then he walked away.

The blonde girl standing next to Bonny said, 'Bloody hell, I bet he's hard on his girls.'

'This is my first job,' Bonny confided.

'Well, darling, it would seem that you're in for a baptism of fire. I've seen his type before. Mind you, they usually know their onions, but you'll be worked to death to get the routine right.'

'I want to do well, so I will be pleased if he's good at his job. He'll be able to teach me a lot.'

The other girl laughed heartily. 'You just be careful he doesn't want to teach you more than dancing.'

'Whatever do you mean?'

'These dancers are either randy buggers or they're queer, and believe me that one is all man! I wouldn't kick him out of bed, that's for sure. My name's Shirley, by the way.'

'I'm Bonny. Bonny Burton.'

'That's a great moniker for a dancer, love. Let's go and find a place for a good strong cup of tea and get to know one another. You can tell me about Southampton. I've never been here before.'

Shirley Gates was twenty-three and came from Clapham in London and had been dancing for the past five years, Bonny learned as they sat drinking tea at a small cafe.

'I've been all round the country in my time, but I want to work in a good variety show in the West End. That's my ambition, but so far I've failed the auditions. I have made it to the callbacks, but in the end, when they whittle the girls down to the final selection, I've never made the final cut. But I will one day,' she declared firmly.

'It must be great to be on a West End stage,' said Bonny wistfully.

'You should think about it,' said Shirley. 'I watched your audition, you're a great dancer.'

Bonny was delighted. 'Do you really think so?'

'I do, and I'll tell you why. Apart from being a brilliant hoofer, you love what you do and it shows. Some of the others were just going through the motions, but not you. You are a natural, my girl!'

'My dream is to be one of Mr Cochran's young ladies, then I would be in the West End. I'd love to be in a musical.'

'Blimey, girl! If we got in with his lot, we'd be made.'

They finished their tea and Shirley went off to find some cheap digs. 'The doorman gave me a couple of addresses to try,' she told Bonny. 'See you in the morning and for God's sake don't be late!'

As Bonny walked home, she couldn't help but smile to herself. What a great day! She'd been hired to join the chorus and had found a new friend. She couldn't wait to tell her parents the good news.

* * *

At home, Bonny's mother, Millie, had been on pins wondering how the audition was going. As the hours passed, she told herself that had to be good or Bonny would surely have been home by now. She cleaned the house from top to bottom, to help calm her nerves. When she heard the key in the lock of the front door, she flew down the stairs. 'How did you get on?' she asked.

'I'm in, Mum. I got the job, I start tomorrow morning!'

The two of them danced around the narrow hallway together.

'Come into the kitchen and I'll make us a cup of tea and you can tell me all about it,' said Millie, flushed with excitement.

Bonny regaled her with the happenings of the morning, how she'd been picked with nineteen others and about her new friend Shirley. 'She's such a laugh, Mum, and she's been in the business for some time. She can show me the ropes.'

'What about the musical director, is he all right?'

Bonny paused and with a frown said, 'I'm not sure. He looked pretty fearsome but if he's good, he can teach me a lot.' She didn't share Shirley's view of the man. After all, there was nothing to indicate that he was a ladies' man. Shirley could be wrong. Secretly, Bonny thought his brooding looks were fascinating. Tomorrow she would certainly find out more about him as he put them through their paces. She couldn't wait.

* * *

The following morning, Bonny joined the other girls as they filed through the stage door for their first morning.

Jack, the middle-aged stage doorman greeted them warmly. 'Morning ladies. I hope you are full of energy because by God you're going to need it with young Mr Andrews!'

They all hung up their coats and changed their shoes, then the girls gathered on the stage, murmuring nervously among themselves as they waited.

Rob walked on to the stage and without hesitation said, 'We'll practice the opening number.' He split the girls into two lines according to their height and proceeded to show them the routine.

As Bonny watched him, she was filled with admiration. This man was amazing to watch. His expertise and grace as he tapped out the first steps was a joy to watch and Bonny felt her heart race with excitement.

She was quick to pick up the steps, whereas one or two others had some difficulty, which did not please Rob Andrews.

'You're going to do a hell of a lot better than that by the end of the day,' he told them, 'or I'll have to replace you!'

The girls looked stricken. Shirley looked over at Bonny and grimaced. She, like Bonny, had mastered the steps without difficulty.

By the end of the morning, they were all exhausted, but now all the girls had almost mastered the opening sequence.

'Break for lunch and be back in an hour,' Rob told them, 'but don't stuff yourselves. We have a lot of work to do and you can't possibly dance on a full stomach!' He marched off the stage without a backward glance. The girls all breathed a sigh of relief.

'My mum packed up some sandwiches for me,' Bonny told Shirley. 'There's more than enough for two, would you like to share?'

'That'd be great, thanks. Let's sit out on the fire-escape steps; there we'll at least get some fresh air.'

As they tucked into their food, they discussed the morning's workout.

'There's one girl there who'll never make the grade,' Shirley stated.

'Which one's that?'

'The girl with the mousy pigtails.'

Bonny knew immediately; she'd been one who had found the routine very difficult.

'She's strictly an amateur and is way out of her league.' Shirley took a bite out of her sandwich and then gave a quiet smirk.

'What?' asked Bonny.

'You know the girl with the long black hair and legs up to her armpits? You just watch her over the next few days.'

'Whatever for?'

'I've seen her type in every show I've ever done. She thinks she's better than she is, thinks she's more attractive that she is . . . and you wait, she'll make a play for our Rob Andrews before the day is out.'

'No!' Bonny looked amazed. 'What makes you think that?'

'Oh, Bonny love, you are such a bleedin' innocent. Just watch and learn.'

Now Bonny was intrigued. 'If you're right, what do you think Mr Andrews will do?'

Cocking her head on one side, Shirley contemplated her answer. 'Well, it depends how much sex he's had lately and if he's gone without his oats.'

'Oh, Shirley, you are dreadful!'

Ignoring her friend's outburst, Shirley continued: 'But if he's the man I hope he is, he'll cut her down to size very quickly.'

In the short time she'd spent with Rob Andrews, Bonny was in awe of the man and she sincerely hoped he was above being seduced so easily. It would have destroyed her admiration for him.

It was time to return to the stage. Rob Andrews was waiting for them. 'Right! Now watch me very carefully,' he ordered, 'because this is the next bit of the routine and it will prove to me just how much you have learned this morning.'

His short routine was sharp and tricky and he did it with perfection and style. Bonny watched him carefully, memorizing every step. She loved the complexity of it.

One by one the girls came forward to try out the routine. Several almost did it correctly, the girl with the mousy pigtails made a complete hash of it and stepped back in line almost in tears, and when the girl with the black hair stepped forward, she smiled confidently at Rob and managed every step, but without the grace it required. He made no comment as she stepped back in line.

'You next, Red,' he called and Bonny stepped forward. She did it to perfection.

'Well done!'

She beamed with pride.

Shirley, too, managed without a mistake.

At the end he called Bonny and Shirley forward and said, 'Right, the rest of you watch. Thank God I've at least got two dancers who know their left foot from their right!'

Lily, the girl with the black hair, looked sullen. 'I got the steps right, Mr Andrews,' she wheedled.

Shirley gave Bonny a quick nudge. They both waited.

'You did and it was soulless. For Christ's sake, woman, dancing is far more than getting the steps right, you have to feel it in here!' He banged on his chest. 'You two ready?'

They nodded and he gave the pianist the signal to play.

The two girls went through the routine, faultlessly.

Glaring at Lily he said,' See what I mean?' and to the others, he told them to do it again.

At the end of the day, tired though they were, both Bonny and Shirley were elated. But as they left they saw Rob Andrews take the girl with the pigtails, aside.

'She's for the chop!' Shirley declared. Then with a grin she looked at Bonny and said, 'Told you about that Lily, didn't I? She didn't get very far with her so-called feminine wiles after all. Good for him, I say.'

Bonny laughed. 'No, she didn't, and I'm glad. I would have been bitterly disappointed with Mr Andrews if she had.'

Shirley cast a glance in her direction. 'Don't you go falling for that bugger,' she warned. 'Business and pleasure never mix. You remember that, my girl! See you tomorrow. I'm going to soak my aching bones in a hot bath and I advise you to do the same, else you'll be as stiff as a corpse in the morning. Ta ra.'

Tired though she was, there was a spring in her step as Bonny walked home. Rob Andrews had praised her dancing and that was good enough for her.

CHAPTER TWO

Rob and Sammy Kendrick, the producer, sat having a beer in Sammy's office, discussing the day's work.

'I have to find a replacement for the girl I fired,' said Rob and read through the list of dancers who had auditioned originally. He put a tick beside a name, picked up his glass and drank thirstily. 'Shirley the blonde and the redhead have what it takes, thank God. Especially—' he looked at his notes — 'Bonny Burton, that's her, the girl with the red hair. Now, she has real talent and the nice thing is she doesn't realize how good she is.'

'Unlike the one with the fluttering eyelashes,' laughed Sammy.

Rob shook his head. 'Stupid bitch! She's not nearly as good as she thinks she is. Anyway, I've no time for such tricks. Bloody women! Why do they try it on?'

'I only wish they'd try it on with me more often.'

Rob stared straight at his colleague. 'You keep away from my dancers this time, Sammy. You get involved and before I know where I am they are trying to tell *me* what to do, just because you've bedded them. You know what happens in the end: I fire them and lose a good chorus girl.'

Sammy Kendrick drew on his cigarette and blew the smoke out slowly and deliberately. 'Lily might prefer an older man now that you have put her in her place.' He started laughing when he saw the look of anger on Rob's face. 'I'm only joking, dear boy. I hate a woman who is that easy. Besides, Belle Carlisle is in the next review and we go back a long way.'

Rob gazed at Sammy with both affection and censure. They had worked at the Palace together for the past four years and had a good working relationship. Sammy was an excellent producer and was well known and liked in theatrical circles. He had the good sense to appreciate the professionalism and talent of his musical director. Only occasionally did they fall out and that was always over Sammy's weakness for women.

'A good screw would do you the world of good, my boy,' Rob was told. 'Release some of that nervous tension!'

With a hearty laugh Rob raised an eyebrow and asked, 'Are you so sure my tensions haven't been released lately?'

'Not as far as I know.'

Rising to his feet, Rob said, 'You don't know everything, you old lecher.'

'Cruel words, Rob! Cruel words,' grinned Sammy.

The musical director rose to his feet. 'I need to go and practice for an hour. I'll see you in the morning at some time.'

Once inside the theatre, Rob stood centre stage, going through the steps practised that day and then through the whole routine, followed by the further two routines needed for the show. He heard the musical number in his head as he tapped around the stage. During the day, the theatre was his to use as a practice area. He liked the girls to work on the stage from the beginning, if possible, rather than a practice room in some hall, as it immediately gave them the feel of the size of the area they had to work with. And as the current variety show was all turns without dancers, he wasn't treading on any toes.

In the evenings and Saturday afternoons, those in the show took over the theatre, which worked well for Rob. After a full day's practice, he and his dancers needed the time to recuperate.

He came from a theatrical family. His father was a musician. He had played the trumpet with various bands and was currently with Jack Hylton. His mother had been a dancer and it was from her that Rob had inherited his love of tap. She had retired after she became pregnant, but had encouraged him from the start of his career. He began his teenage years in a school for dance and drama, then became a chorus boy, and later their lead. Eventually, he became a musical director.

Rob was fanatical about his work. He practised for hours until he was satisfied with a routine, and his innovation put him near the top of his profession. His goal was a company and show of his own in London's West End. But, for this, he would need a financial backer, or angel, as they were known in theatrical circles.

His total dedication meant that he had little time for relationships of a personal nature. He'd had girlfriends earlier in his life, mostly from amongst his fellow dancers, but there had never been anyone special. During his theatrical life, he'd moved from town to town, which didn't leave time to build a lasting relationship. He didn't feel deprived; he was too busy to need such ties. Now he'd reached the position of musical director, the production was his only love.

* * *

The following week was hard work for the dancers, with having to learn three routines to Rob's exacting standards, and then there were the costume fittings, which thrilled Bonny. Now she felt a real professional.

'At least our Mr Andrews doesn't skimp on quality,' Shirley remarked during a fitting.

'What do you mean?' Bonny asked.

'I've been in some shows where money was short, so old costumes just hanging by a thread were handed out to us.

Many a time my modesty has only been saved by the strength of a few safety pins I'd used, but these costumes are first rate.'

Bonny twisted round in her silver skimpy sequinned pants and boned bodice. Her red top hat glittered in the lights. She stopped in front of a mirror. Was this really her? She looked so glamorous, so sophisticated. She couldn't wait for her parents to see her perform. They had booked tickets for the Saturday evening show. Her father, Frank, a quiet and industrious man, hadn't said a great deal, but Bonny knew he was pleased for her, and she hoped, after seeing her perform, he would be proud too.

* * *

Dress rehearsal had been a nightmare! Rob Andrews had all but torn his hair from its roots in frustration.

'What the hell's wrong with some of you?' he'd said. 'It's as if you had just walked in off the streets this morning! If you want to be professionals, you can't afford to let nerves spoil your performance. We will go through this until it's perfect or I'll fire those who can't cut the mustard and make do with those who can.'

He had been relentless. Some had been reduced to tears, but he hadn't stopped. Eventually, he'd been satisfied — and had sent them home.

Bonny and Shirley collapsed in comfortable chairs in the nearest cafe. 'I think I feel sick!' Bonny said, wiping her forehead with a handkerchief. 'I have *never* worked so hard in all my life.'

'It was because of Amy and Hazel. They suddenly realized that this was it. The final rehearsal. It happens. They'll be all right tomorrow and then they'll be so bloody pleased with themselves, they will hardly be able to wait to do it again.'

'Don't you suffer with nerves, Shirley?'

'Not any more. I do get an adrenalin rush as I wait in the wings to go on. The excitement of it helps me, I find. You will too.'

Bonny's eyes brightened. 'Oh, Shirley, I can hardly contain myself until tomorrow night.'

'Just be prepared for the bustle and air of mayhem backstage when the other acts arrive,' her friend advised. 'We have three changes to do, so try not to get flustered. Just keep focussed on what you have to do. In time it will be automatic.'

'How can life in the theatre be automatic? It's far too exciting!'

Laughing, Shirley said, 'A couple of years down the line, I'll ask you if you feel the same.'

'You're just an old cynic,' Bonny teased.

'No, love, just an old hand.'

* * *

It was opening night! Backstage was a scene of great activity, unlike the days when the girls had the place to themselves to learn their routines. Now, the building was alive. Other artists arrived and made their way to their dressing rooms. The footlights lit up, stage lights and spotlights were set, the musicians in the orchestra pit tuned their instruments, the call boy checked the list of performers pinned up on the notice board against his own, noting what time each artist was to make an entrance.

In the long dressing room, inhabited by the chorus line, the noise was like a flock of caged birds, all twittering together. Nervous tension filled the air as they applied their stage make-up and changed into their first costumes, with the aid of the wardrobe mistress.

'Fifteen minutes to curtain up. Keep the noise down now please, ladies!' ordered the call boy. 'And when you hear the overture, take your places, *quietly*, in the wings.'

Bonny could feel her heart racing and glanced at her friend Shirley, seated next to her. Shirley looked back at her and winked. Then the first notes of the overture began and, 'Beginners please!' was called. The girls, suddenly silent, made their way to either side of the wings to wait for their music, as they were to open the show with their first number.

The curtains parted as the music for the chorus began, and the girls tapped their way on to the stage from either side, meeting in the centre of the stage amidst applause from the audience in appreciation for their costumes and precision dancing.

Bonny was in her element! She looked to the front with a smile that lit up her face and tapped out the routine. As the last note died, the chorus, as one, bowed to the audience and danced off. As they left the stage, the sound of applause rang in their ears.

Scurrying back to the dressing room, all the girls were filled with elation. No one had made a mistake. Now, with a feeling of success, they changed into the next costume and waited, listening to the show over the loudspeaker in the dressing room. They heard the laughter as the comedian told his jokes, the change of music as the juggler went on, followed by a company of tumblers.

'Five minutes, ladies,' the call boy said from the doorway. 'Start heading for the stage, please. And make sure you stand aside to give the previous act room to get by.'

Standing at the back of the stalls, Rob Andrews watched his girls perform with a critical eye. Although no one took a wrong step, he saw the weakness in one or two of the girls and mentally made a note to work on them, but Bonny stood out from the rest. She had a certain air about her. She was loving every step and it showed in her performance. Next week he'd give her a solo spot. He had some speciality numbers in mind which she could do standing on her head.

The final dance number closed the show. Then, as the cast of solo performers took to the stage one by one in front of the dancers, the applause was heartening.

Sammy Kendrick stood beside Rob and puffed contentedly on his cigar. 'Good show, Rob, wasn't it? You dancers did well after all your yelling and screaming!'

Rob grinned at him. 'My direction, I think you're alluding to.'

'Come into the office and we'll have a drink. The bookings for the week are healthy, so I feel the need of a little celebration.'

'I'll be there after I've had a word with my girls,' he replied.

Rob knocked on the dressing-room door and walked in. There were a few squeals from some of the girls who were half undressed.

'Oh, for goodness' sake,' he snapped, 'I've seen it all before. Now, I just want to say well done. There is a little work still to do, so I'll see you at rehearsal at eleven o'clock tomorrow morning. Get a good night's sleep; there are still five evening shows and a matinee to go.'

As he left the room, Shirley nudged Bonny. 'Praise from the master. We must have done all right!'

'Oh, Shirley, I loved every minute and can't wait for tomorrow to come.'

'Make sure you rub some cream into your feet, they're not used to such hard work. By the end of the week, they'll hurt like hell if you don't look after them.'

But nothing could mar the euphoria that Bonny was feeling.

Later, as she sat on the edge of her bed after a bath and rubbed the cream into her feet, as instructed, she wondered just how far her career could take her. Would she ever be good enough for a West End show? Would she perhaps one day see her name in lights? These were heady dreams. She turned back the covers and climbed into bed, going over the music and the steps of her numbers — and was soon asleep.

CHAPTER THREE

The week seemed to fly by, and the work was harder. Apart from their nightly show, the girls were rehearsing every day for the new numbers to be used in the following week. Bonny had been given a solo spot, which delighted her. 'I'm terrified I'll get muddled and start dancing the new routine by mistake,' she admitted to her friend.

'No, you won't,' Shirley assured her. 'When you hear the music, the dance steps fall into place automatically. Think about it, the new routine just wouldn't fit, would it?'

'No, you're right. It's just so much to remember.'

'Get used to it, love, this will be your life from now on. Your solo spot looks good,' she added.

'Thanks, but I don't think Lily agrees with you.'

'Ha! That silly bitch isn't good enough for a solo spot, anyway. She's strictly chorus and will always be so.'

'She doesn't think so. I heard her asking Rob when she would be picked to do one.'

'Really?' Shirley was bemused. 'What did he say?'

'Don't hold your breath! She hurried off muttering obscenities that would make a sailor blush.'

Shirley thought this highly amusing. 'Just watch your step with her, Bonny,' she warned. 'That girl has a wide jealous streak in her.'

'Whatever do you mean?'

'I've seen it too many times with her type. They have false hopes, and when someone other than them is picked out for a special number, they will do their damnedest to spoil it somehow or another. Just watch your back, that's all.'

* * *

It was the Saturday evening performance and Bonny's parents were in the theatre. When the girls made their second entrance, they watched their daughter's every step, filled with pride. Millie squeezed her husband's hand and whispered, 'She's really good, isn't she?'

'Nodding, Frank said, 'Splendid.' A man of few words, who kept his feelings hidden, Frank Burton saw the talent in his daughter. She was better than any of the other girls, except for the blonde, and he wondered if her talent would be recognized. Could she go on to greater things or would she remain in the chorus? And if she rose to greater heights, where would this lead? Although he wanted Bonny to be successful after all her hard work, he couldn't help feeling somewhat trepidatious about the future.

* * *

The following week, Belle Carlisle arrived early to rehearse with the orchestra. There was a buzz of excitement among the entertainers and chorus girls, as Belle was a well-known singer, appearing mainly in the West End, but was now touring and Southampton was her first stop.

She brought with her her own dresser and a trunk packed with exquisite gowns. The aroma of expensive perfume wafted behind her as she swept along the corridor to Sammy

Kendrick's office. Her tall elegant figure was clothed in the latest stylish suit in dark grey, and on her head was a black hat with a short veil. She wore matching bag and gloves — and, over her shoulders, a fox fur.

'Sammy, darling,' she cried as she threw open the door and stood poised, waiting for his greeting and admiration.

The producer beamed from ear to ear as he rose to welcome her. He took her into his arms. 'I can't tell you how much I've longed to see you again. You look wonderful.' And he kissed her.

'Down boy,' she teased. 'I'm here for a whole week.'

'That's not nearly long enough,' he said as he led her to a chair and opened a bottle of champagne from the ice bucket standing on the desk. Handing her a glass, he said, 'To a great reunion.'

She gave a seductive chuckle, sipped her drink and said softly, 'No one moves me quite like you do, darling.'

'I've booked you in your usual room at the Dolphin Hotel,' he said. 'I suggest after your rehearsal you have a rest, and I'll come and take you out to dinner.'

'That will be wonderful,' she said. 'Now tell me, who's on the bill with me this week?'

Whilst this discussion was taking place, Rob was working with Bonny, running through her solo routine. They worked well together and she was able to follow his every move.

'Well done, Bonny. In a couple of week's time, we are having a musical week with songs from the shows and I have some great numbers worked out for the chorus. I'll use you again, and I have a duet ready for you and Shirley to do together. But I warn you, it means extra work.'

'I don't mind, Mr Andrews,' she told him breathlessly.

There was something about her expression, her eagerness, the brightness of her eyes as she talked about her work, that touched him. Here was someone who felt as strongly as he did about the performance, which was heartening. 'You keep this up, young lady, and I can see you reaching the top of your profession.'

'Honestly?'

He laughed. 'Honestly! You are really talented, Bonny, and I intend to see that you get there.'

The rest of the chorus joined them to go through their routine until Belle Carlisle walked on to the stage.

'Take a break, girls,' Rob called. 'Sit in the stalls until the stage is free.'

They all scurried to their seats, knowing they were able to watch a star at work.

Belle Carlisle was known for her voice, her body and the love songs that she chose — many which came from the States, sent over to her when first they came out in Tin Pan Alley, and some before they even hit the British market, which made her repertoire modern and sophisticated. As she sang the words in her deep husky voice, and with great feeling, her sex appeal was always apparent to every man who watched. Each one wishing that they could be the one for whom the song was meant.

The girls could overhear her conversation with the conductor, and from it, it was obvious the singer knew what she was talking about and was intent on getting things done her way.

'I bet she's a first-class bitch!' whispered Shirley to her friend.

The opening bars of Cole Porter's 'Night and Day' began, and Belle stood centre stage, clutching the mike like a lover. As the star started to sing, Bonny was mesmerized. The woman had such stage presence. Not a sound was heard from those who watched, but towards the end, Belle glared at the trumpet player who came in a half a beat late. At the end of the number she berated the man and the conductor, and they started again until she was satisfied.

Shirley nudged Bonny. 'Told you she was a bitch.'

At the end of the rehearsal, Belle marched off the stage with barely a nod to the conductor. There were angry mutterings among the musicians.

As the girls assembled, Lily cannoned into Bonny. 'Look where you're going, can't you!'

'I was thinking the same about you,' Bonny retorted.

The other girl looked disdainfully at her. 'Teacher's pet!' She spat out the words with great venom and took her place.

At the end of the session, the girls made their way back to their dressing rooms, passing Belle Carlisle on the way, who was complaining loudly to Sammy about the inadequacies of the band. He was doing his best to placate her as they left through the stage door.

* * *

With the afternoon free before the evening performance, Shirley and Bonny took their sandwiches and a flask of tea along to the park and sat near the bird aviary, watching the variety of birds flitting about, feeding and twittering.

'Reminds me of our dressing room!' Shirley remarked drily.

With a chuckle, Bonny agreed. Then, glancing at the flower beds bedecked with summer flowers, added, 'A few of these would brighten it up a bit.'

'All you need to do is get friendly with one of the men who wait at the stage door at night and maybe they would send you flowers!'

At the end of each show, the stage door was besieged with flirtatious young men who each had a favourite in the chorus and begged them to let them take their chosen girl to dinner. Neither Shirley nor Bonny had accepted, but several of the girls had.

'I saw Lily going off with a much older man last night,' Bonny said. 'I was surprised.'

'I wasn't. She's a schemer, that one. She probably thought he had more money to spend than the younger men.'

'That's a bit harsh,' Bonny remonstrated.

'No, love, I know her type. She'll get what she wants, any way she can.'

'Not with Rob Andrews.'

'Ah,' said Shirley knowingly, 'she'll keep trying; I'll put money on it.'

Little did Shirley know just how close to the truth her comment was.

* * *

After rehearsals ended, Rob Andrews chatted with the conductor of the band, then made his way to his small office. He was tired after working and planned to do some paperwork before leaving the theatre to have a light lunch and a rest before tonight's performance. He was therefore very surprised to see Lily sitting in his office waiting for him.

'What are you doing here?' he asked, lowering himself into his chair behind the desk.

'I thought you might need a little relaxation after your morning workout,' she said with a slow smile.

His eyes narrowed as he looked at her. 'That's precisely what I intend to do when I've finished here, so get to the point, Lily.'

She rose slowly from her seat and perched on the edge of the desk, facing him. 'I just thought I might help in that direction.' The invitation was blatant.

Letting out a deep sigh he said, 'Please don't try and play games with me. I've been around far too long. Believe me, you are not the first member of the chorus to make me an offer in the hope that it will advance their career. Now go before I get really annoyed!' He started to leaf through his papers, ignoring her.

Lily flushed with embarrassment and anger. She stood up. 'If I was Bonny Burton, you wouldn't turn me away.'

He glared at her. 'Bonny Burton wouldn't cheapen herself this way. Now, for goodness' sake, leave me alone to get on with my work.'

She stormed out of the room.

Lighting a cigarette, he ran his fingers through his hair. 'Women!' he muttered angrily. There was always one among the chorus who was trouble one way or another. Well, if Miss Lily didn't pull her socks up he'd get a replacement. He couldn't be doing with all this shenanigans.

* * *

Rob's friend Sammy Kendrick was having a much better time. He and Belle had settled in the dining room of the Dolphin Hotel, and after a succulent lunch and some good wine, they departed to Belle's room.

Here, they both renewed their old relationship. After Sammy slowly removed Belle's clothing and then his own, they climbed into bed. Taking the woman into his arms, Sammy breathed deeply as he felt her bare flesh beside him.

'Darling Belle, how I've missed you,' he whispered as he rained kisses on her and caressed her firm breasts.

She lay back against the sheets and smiled with satisfaction. 'I do like a man who knows his way round my body,' she purred.

He kissed her neck, then buried his head between her breasts before kissing them, raking each nipple gently between his teeth.

'Careful, darling,' she said as she pushed his head lower.

Eventually, they lay entwined — both sated by their love-making — and slept.

* * *

It was Saturday night and the show was going well. Sammy had left Belle in her hotel room and was standing at the back of the stalls in his usual place, watching the show with Rob beside him, looking at the closing number.

Whereas Sammy was enjoying the spectacle, Rob was searching for any faults from his dancers, and he saw Lily make one mistake as she exited. He was not happy. Storming backstage, he knocked on the dressing-room door and walked in. 'You messed up your exit,' he said angrily, pointing at Lily. 'Don't let it happen again!'

As the door slammed behind him, Lily looked mortified and her face was flushed.

Shirley, unable to let the opportunity pass, said, 'Oh dear, you'd better not do that again or His Highness might have to replace you, you know what a perfectionist he is!'

'You mind your own business!' the girl snapped. 'Anyway, I have other plans and they don't include Mr bloody Andrews.'

'Your sugar daddy going to take you away from all this, is he?'

Bonny, sitting beside her, kicked her friend in the shins.

Lily refrained from answering and changed out of her costume. The other girls sniggered at her discomfort.

When Lily had swept out of the room, Bonny said, 'You need a wooden spoon, you stirrer!'

Grinning, Shirley looked at her and said, 'You didn't expect me to let slip such an opportunity to take that bitch down, did you? She's so damned high and mighty! She needs teaching a lesson.'

As they left the theatre, they saw Lily driving off in a taxi with her new man. The girls looked at each other and smiled.

'Wonder what she's offering in return?' Shirley pondered aloud.

Before she could answer, Bonny felt a light touch on her arm. A young man stood there, holding a bunch of flowers. 'Miss Burton, would you please accept these as a token of my admiration for your dancing? I think you're wonderful.'

Bonny was completely taken aback. 'Thank you,' she said.

The young man smiled shyly at her and walked away.

'Well!' said Shirley, 'you have made a conquest and no mistake!'

Looking at the bouquet, Bonny was speechless for a moment. 'I wonder who he is?'

Nudging her, Shirley said, 'I'm sure you will be given the opportunity to find out, because he'll be back.'

'Don't be silly.'

Shirley just smiled. 'You wait and see, he's really smitten with you. It showed in his eyes.'

A she walked home, Bonny could smell the scent of the flowers and smiled to herself. How lovely. Someone in the audience thought she was wonderful! But when she told her parents, they both looked concerned.

'You be careful, my girl,' said Frank, her father. 'This young man is a stranger. Perhaps I should come and meet you myself and bring you home in future.'

'You certainly will not!' Bonny was furious. 'I'll look like a schoolgirl and I'll be the laughing stock of all the others. For goodness' sake, Dad. I'm a grown woman, earning a living, not a child!' And she went into the scullery to find a vase for her flowers.

'Now, Frank,' her mother said quietly, 'Bonny is quite right. She's no longer your little girl so don't treat her like one.'

'I know that, but besides being her father I'm a man and I know how they think.'

Millie raised her eyebrows in surprise. 'Whatever do you mean?'

'You've read about stage-door Johnnies. They see a pretty girl on the stage and think she's easy pickings.'

'But our Bonny's not like that. She's been brought up right, and now you have to let her make her own decisions.'

'Maybe, but I don't have to like it.' He folded his paper. 'I'm off to bed.'

Millie sought out her daughter. 'Your father is only being protective,' she explained. 'You have to give him time to get used to the idea that you are now a grown woman.'

'I know, Mum. But what on earth will he be like if I ever get a job in London?'

Millie couldn't answer because she was wondering how she would react if her daughter left home in the future.

Cutting the apron strings was never easy for any mother, but they all had to face up to it at some time. She just hoped it wouldn't be for a while yet. And with that crumb of comfort, she too went to bed.

CHAPTER FOUR

With Belle Carlisle on the bill at the Palace Theatre, the demand for tickets was fierce, and on opening night the stalls, circle and upper circle were full to capacity. Bonny peered through the curtain, thrilled to see the townspeople scurrying to their seats.

The opening number went well and the girls had plenty of time to change before closing the first half of the show. 'I've never seen Mr Kendrick so nervous,' said Bonny to her friend, who was repairing her stage make-up in the seat beside her.

'That's because Belle is on the bill. According to Jack, the stage doorkeeper, she's a handful. Nothing is ever quite right and she complains constantly. But she brings in the crowds, so poor old Sammy is usually tearing his hair out by the end of the week. Or so I'm told.'

The wardrobe mistress, who was helping Bonny to change, leaned forward and in a quiet confidential tone said, 'No doubt he'll be on hand at her hotel later to calm her down!'

Both girls stopped what they were doing. 'What are you inferring, Nan?' asked Bonny, intrigued by this nugget of information.

'They go back a long way,' they were told. 'They've been lovers off and on for years.' And she moved on to the next girl.

'Dirty old devil!' exclaimed Shirley.

'I'm not that surprised,' Bonny said. 'After all, he does have a wicked twinkle in his eye. I've watched him looking at the chorus line with more than a little interest.'

'He hasn't tried anything with you, has he?'

'No. As far as I know he hasn't with anyone.'

'I wonder that Lily hasn't worked her so-called magic on him. After all, he is the producer.'

'She wouldn't stand an earthly against Belle Carlisle now, would she?' And they both laughed at the very idea.

* * *

Belle stood in the wings waiting for her entrance. Smoothing down her dress, patting her hair, taking deep breaths.

Sammy Kendrick walked on to the stage and made his announcement. 'Ladies and gentlemen, it gives me great pleasure to welcome one of London's best loved stars to our stage. Please give a warm welcome to Miss Belle Carlisle!' He held out his hand towards the wings.

As the music began, Belle, wearing a stunning blue gown studded with sequins, made her entrance to huge applause. She walked slowly and deliberately to the microphone, smiled at the audience and started her opening number: '*Night and day, you are the one . . .*'

There was not a sound to be heard from the audience as she sang. She went through her repertoire faultlessly and left the stage to a standing ovation. She waited in the wings for a few moments, returned to the stage, bowed slightly and eventually signalled to the conductor — and then sang an encore.

The chorus were waiting in both wings to close the show as she took her final bow and swept off the stage.

She pushed past Bonny and Shirley, storming and swearing under her breath about the man on the spotlight.

'Trouble at mill!' Shirley remarked as they tapped their way on to the stage.

When the show was closing and the various artists made their way on to the stage, backed by the chorus, Bonny wondered if Belle would appear. But she came on to the stage all smiles, blowing kisses to her rapt audience.

The smile died as she reached the wings. 'Sammy!' she bellowed, 'I want a word in your office!'

As the girls made their way to their dressing room, they could hear the raised voices of Sammy and Belle in heated argument. 'I want that man fired! He's bloody useless,' screamed Belle.

'I certainly will not fire him; he's worked with me for years.'

'Then at least make sure he knows what he's doing,' she cried. 'His spotlight wasn't fully on me, I had to move over. I don't expect to work with incompetents! Get it sorted out before tomorrow or you won't have a star!' And she left, slamming the door behind her.

Sammy mopped his brow and lit a cigar. He looked up with some relief as Rob Andrews walked in.

'Fiery isn't she?' Rob remarked with a grin.

Pouring himself a drink, Sammy grimaced. 'I'd forgotten how difficult she can be,' he admitted. 'But she brings in the punters so I have to keep her sweet. I'll have a word with Bill and tell him for God's sake make sure she's well lit. I've ordered flowers to be sent to her hotel. She'll cost me a bloody fortune by the end of the week.'

With a wry smile, Rob said, 'But you will have at least some reward for your efforts.'

Sammy's eyes twinkled. 'I have to say the lady is worth every penny, but I'll be a nervous *and* physical wreck by the time she goes.'

'How are the bookings for our musical week going?' Rob asked.

'Very well. I hope you have something special lined up with your girls?'

'You won't be disappointed, I promise. I'll see you tomorrow.'

* * *

There was a huge crowd waiting at the stage door that night. They crowded round Belle as she left with Sammy, asking for autographs, plying her with flowers and chocolates. Flattering her with their admiration. She smiled at them all, signed programmes, handed the bouquets to Sammy before climbing into the car and being driven away.

'Thank God that's over,' she complained.

Sammy, a true professional and businessman, was irritated by her remark. 'Don't forget, Belle, without those people, you would be just another singer!'

'I would never be *just* another anything!' she retorted, stung by his sharp tone.

'Don't come it with me, Belle. Remember I knew you long before you hit the big time, and I've seen bigger stars than you fall from that pedestal when they got too big for their boots. I wouldn't like to see you go the same way.'

She looked at him sideways and saw the set of his jaw and knew he was angry. No one else knew her as well as he did and no one else would ever get away with talking to her that way. But Sammy and she had travelled the road to success together. 'I'm just tired,' she said by way of an excuse.

* * *

On Saturday, as the audience filed in for the last performance, there was a buzz backstage. It was rumoured that a talent scout for a big London producer was in the stalls. Every act was full of nervous tension as they waited their turn to perform. Rob Andrews came into the girls' dressing room before the show to talk to them.

'Tonight I want you to dance as you never have before,' he said. 'Out front is a talent scout and I want him to see you at your best. Look as if you are enjoying yourselves, so smile every moment you're on stage.' And he turned on his heel and walked out.

There was a second of complete silence, then the girls all started talking at once.

'Do you think we're good enough for a London show?'

'What if he likes us?'

'Maybe he's only come to see Belle Carlisle.'

Shirley sat back and saw to her make-up, seemingly untouched by the excitement.

'Aren't you thrilled?' Bonny asked her friend.

Shirley shrugged. 'Not really. These men are usually looking for a solo act, one that's a bit different, not the chorus. There's no one on the bill apart from Belle who would interest him, I wouldn't think. After all, the jugglers are much of a muchness, and the comedian is nothing special — yes, he gets the laughs, but I've seen better.'

Bonny felt deflated. Rob had worked so hard with the dancers and she thought they were good, thanks to the many hours of practice. But Shirley knew far more than she about such things.

* * *

The show went well and the paying public showed their appreciation at the final curtain. As the dancers, now exhausted after the week, took off their make-up in their dressing room, Rob Andrews was talking to the man they had all been wondering about.

Bernie Cohen was a short, tubby man with a balding head, who had been in show business all his adult life. Now in his late forties, his nose for fresh talent had not diminished and tonight he had seen a girl who had interested him. 'I can't believe that this is her first professional job,' he told Rob. The girl lives to dance, it shines in her eyes in her every expression.

And she's a natural. I'm sure that you know all this, otherwise you wouldn't have given her that solo spot.'

Rob smiled slowly. 'Quite right. Mind you, she works her socks off so she deserves to be there, but wait until our musical tribute the week after next if you want to really see her potential. I think you'll be even more surprised.'

Cohen shook Rob's hand. 'I'll look forward to it, but please, no mention of this conversation. I don't want to put any pressure on the girl.'

'My lips are sealed,' promised Rob.

* * *

Unaware that she was of any special interest to anyone, Bonny left the theatre. Belle Carlisle had left sometime before and so the crowd at the stage door had dispersed, apart from one or two eager young men, waiting for their date for the night. As Bonny walked down the steps, the young man who had given her flowers once before stepped forward.

'Miss Burton, good show tonight. I thought your solo dance was great. Congratulations.'

'Why, thank you,' she said.

'Would you allow me to take you out to dinner one evening?' He noted her hesitation. 'I realize you are tired after each performance, so we could make it a Sunday if you would rather. Lunch, if you would prefer?'

Shyly, she studied the young man. She thought he was in his twenties. With his blonde hair and blue eyes, he looked a gentle sort, and she felt she would be safe with him, but tonight she was exhausted and couldn't make up her mind. 'Ask me again sometime and I'll think about it, but not now.' And with a smile at her admirer, she walked away.

The young man stood and watched her, before leaving the theatre in the opposite direction.

Rob Andrews had watched the two of them as he stood at the top of the stairs, smoking a cigarette. He'd overheard the conversation and frowned as he heard the young man's invitation. He'd been relieved to hear Bonny's refusal. If he was to get her to the top of her profession, she'd have little time for personal relationships. He'd learned that himself, the hard way.

* * *

The following week was the hardest any of the dancers had known. Rob had worked on several dance routines for the girls to be performed in the new musicals show, and there were long practice sessions as well as their performances in the theatre. But Bonny was in her element when first he told her that she would be doing a Fred Astaire and Ginger Rogers duet — dancing with him. She looked at him with eyes wide with surprise. 'We are going to be dancing together?' She could hardly believe it.

'Yes, you are Ginger and I'm Fred.'

'But they are gods of the dance!' she exclaimed.

Rob looked at her and laughed. 'What's the matter, Bonny? Don't you think I'm up to it?'

She was overcome with embarrassment. 'Good heavens, no! I was thinking about *my* not being good enough.'

'If I didn't think you were, I wouldn't even think about doing it. You'll be fine, but we have a lot of work to do. I need you to come in an hour earlier than the others every morning, because we can't let Mr Astaire down now, can we?'

'Or Miss Rogers, although I have red hair, so I won't look a bit like her.'

'You'll be wearing a blonde wig,' he said, 'and I'll have to smooth my hair with Brylcreem, but it will be our feet that will be doing the talking, Bonny.' He became animated as he told her about the number. 'I'll be wearing evening dress, as will the chorus, which will be backing us. You will have a long dress, and we all have to work with canes.'

'That could be a bit tricky,' Bonny remarked, trying to visualize it all.

'Practice will make us perfect,' he assured her.

And practice indeed was what he demanded of them all.

* * *

Bonny showed up early for her first rehearsal with Rob. She couldn't help feeling nervous, as she was to dance with him. But he put her at her ease as he showed her the opening set of steps. He then told her to take a break as he showed her what the rest of the number would be like, telling her as he danced what she would be doing.

She was mesmerized by his ability. And soon she was dancing with him, trying to master the use of the cane with some aplomb. But as Rob held her and led her into the steps, she felt as if she was flying and wondered when ever she had been happier.

The girls in the chorus were put through their paces also, until they gasped for breath and a drink of water. But there was a great air of excitement as they all realized that this was going to be something special.

Shirley and Bonny had a duet also. The scene was set in a toy shop and the girls, dressed as toy soldiers, came to life when the clock struck midnight. They worked well together and Rob was pleased with the result.

'Excellent!' he cried at the end of their final rehearsal. 'You've both worked well, the audience will love it!'

They sank to the floor, tired beyond measure.

'Dress rehearsal is on Sunday morning!'

There were several moans from the girls.

'Sorry, but it will be in the morning so you'll have the afternoon and evening to recuperate.' His eyes twinkled. 'Once you are in costume, you won't mind quite so much, and as a treat, I'll buy the coffee and add a few cakes in the break.'

There were cheers all round. Rob had threatened them all about gaining weight and so cakes had been forbidden.

As they strolled home after, Shirley said, 'I'm really looking forward to next week. I have a feeling that it means something special to our lord and master, and I have to say, Bonny love, when you two dance together, it really is something else to watch.'

'In what way?'

'You two together have a great chemistry. It's like watching a love affair in dance.'

'Don't be daft!' Bonny protested, flushing as she chastised her friend. Secretly thinking that being in the arms of Rob Andrews was every young girl's dream.

CHAPTER FIVE

The dress rehearsal went well. The girls, once in costume, seemed more animated. There was a sense that this show was something special and the adrenalin was running high. Some of the dance numbers were a background for a singer, who featured songs made popular by Jessie Mathews and Gertrude Lawrence, taken from West End shows such as *Anything Goes* and *Ever Green.* Others were specialized dances for the chorus alone, but the Fred Astaire and Ginger Rogers number to be featured as the finale was a knock out! The dancers were dressed in top hats and tails, as was Rob Andrews, and Bonny was in a long white evening gown covered with sequins and bugle beads, which glistened under the spotlights.

Sammy Kendrick, sitting in the stalls, became more and more excited as he watched every number, but when Rob and Bonny covered the stage in intricate steps with such precision and flare, he was bewitched by the spectacle. At the end of the dance, he rose to his feet, applauding wildly — knowing he had a hit on his hands.

'Bravo! Bravo!' he cried as he ran up the steps to the stage and threw his arms around Rob. 'That was spectacular!' He held his arms wide as if to embrace the chorus line. 'Well done, girls, you were terrific and the use of the canes . . . Well, what can I say?' He put his arm around Bonny. 'Ginger Rogers couldn't have done it any better. I am holding the show over for a second week.'

Rob looked concerned. 'But what about the acts that have been booked?'

'I'll find them bookings elsewhere, and if I can't they will be compensated. Don't worry, my boy, this show will be a hit, you see. I have to go and make some phone calls.' He rushed off into the wings.

Rob turned to the dancers. 'Well done, all of you. Today you made me very proud, and as I'm sure you heard, the show is being held over, so we mustn't let Mr Kendrick down. Off you go and get a good night's sleep, we open tomorrow.' As they walked off the stage, he caught hold of Bonny. 'You were terrific,' he said.

She looked at him, eyes shining with excitement. 'So were you. I can't wait to do it all over again.'

Back in the dressing room, the buzz of conversation was loud. Everyone was thrilled with the rehearsal and the promise of an extended week. Nan, the wardrobe mistress, helped Bonny out of her gown and hurried away with it to give it a quick press for tomorrow's performance. Shirley sat down beside her friend and started to remove her make-up. 'Well, I have to say, Bonny Burton, you and our Rob were the stars of the show.'

But Bonny was sitting staring into space, reliving every step of the routine and feeling Rob's arms around her, dreaming of doing it again every night for two weeks.

At the same time, Sammy Kendrick was in his office, conducting a campaign of advertising that would catch the public's eye and would have queues for tickets stretching around the block in the coming days.

* * *

The first performance played to an almost full house, which was unusual for a Monday, and backstage the excitement was palpable. Nan, the wardrobe mistress, was berating one of the dancers for dropping cigarette ash on her costume and burning a small hole, some of the girls were out in the hallway, practising twirling their canes for the finale, and a messenger, carrying a large bouquet, knocked on the dressing-room door asking for Miss Burton.

'That's me!' Bonny stood up and took the flowers from him 'Thank you.'

'Well, open the card,' urged Shirley as the girls gathered round.

With trembling fingers, she did so. 'To my very own Ginger Rogers. Rob.'

There was loud ribbing from some of the girls and murmured comments from others. 'What did she have to do to deserve that, I wonder?' queried Lily spitefully.

'I practised until my feet bled!' Bonny retorted.

'If you put as much effort in your rehearsals as you do flirting and buttering up your sugar daddy, you'd be a better dancer!' Shirley added, to the girl's discomfort.

But nothing could spoil Bonny's enthusiasm. She chose to ignore the others. She'd worked hard for her place and Rob had rewarded her.

Shirley was there when Bonny had opened the card. Peering over her friend's shoulder she said, 'He could have put a kiss at the end!'

'For goodness' sake, Shirley, apart from being my partner for one number, you forget he's the boss and I'm just a member of the chorus.'

'Look, girlie, with your talent I don't think you'll stay in the chorus for very long. Rob Andrews has already realized what he has in you, otherwise why would he risk his own reputation? He hasn't danced on stage in a show for some time. He's just been the musical director, putting a performance together — but not this time. This time he's a performer. Think about it.'

But Bonny was content to be Ginger Rogers for two weeks; she didn't want to think further than that. As long as she could dance and be paid, she was happy. This one number was a bonus, but she didn't visualize it being a regular occurrence, so she'd make the most of the two weeks being in the spotlight.

* * *

The following day, the local paper gave them a good spread, filled with compliments about the choreography, the costumes and Southampton's own Astaire and Rogers. Sammy beamed as he read it. He had invited a personal friend to the Saturday evening show, knowing that he wrote a showbiz column for one of the nationals. The journalist owed Sammy a favour and had said he would come down and review the performance for him.

Rob had heard from the talent scout, asking him to save a seat for him on the Saturday night and to keep it quiet. He wondered what would happen if Bonny was offered a part in a London show. It would be a great opportunity, but he would miss her, she was so good. He also wondered how she would cope with life in the metropolis. Here she was sheltered, living at home, whereas being in London was very different. The theatre was a cut-throat business, with so many people after too few jobs. At the moment, Bonny was unspoilt. She lived to dance and had absolutely no idea how good she was. He wouldn't like to see her become hardened, as had so many of the people he knew.

* * *

It was the final performance of the first week. The house was packed and the show was running well and it was time for the finale. Bonny stood in the wings with Rob, waiting for their music to start. First of all, the entire chorus danced on to the stage from either side, canes whirling, to great applause.

Bonny felt Rob's arm around her waist. He gave her a squeeze and whispered in her ear, 'Come on, Ginger. Let's knock 'em dead.' And they moved into the spotlights.

Each night they danced together as one, but tonight there seemed to be a special magic between them as they used the stage seemingly without effort. And when the number finished, the audience rose to their feet in a standing ovation.

Bonny was beside herself with glee. As they stepped forward to take their bow, Rob bowed and then, lifting her hand, he gazed into her eyes as he bent to kiss it. She felt herself flush with delight and surprise.

When eventually the final curtain dropped, he lifted her off her feet, swung her round and said, 'I am so very proud of you, Miss Bonny Burton. You seemed to fly tonight.'

'Wasn't it wonderful?' She beamed at him. 'A standing ovation — imagine! And we have another week to go.'

'We do, so for goodness' sake, rest up. Don't go tearing around. I'll see you on Monday.' He leaned forward and kissed her. 'Well done.'

As Rob walked away, Bonny put her hand to her mouth. How unexpected, but how nice.

Rob went straight to his office before changing as Bernie Cohen, the talent scout, sent a message backstage that he wanted to see him. Whilst he waited he poured himself a scotch and water, sat in the chair behind his desk, sipped the drink and lit a cigarette. After a performance, even when he wasn't dancing himself, it took him a while to unwind, and he was pleased to have this short time to himself.

Ten minutes later there was a knock on his door and Cohen walked in, the aroma from his cigar wafting before him. 'Congratulations, Rob. Great show. It was good to see you dancing once again. I always thought you should have continued to perform.'

'Well, you know how much I wanted to produce my own show, but I must confess, Sammy, it felt great to be up there in front of an audience again.'

Sitting down, Bernie Cohen waited whilst Rob poured him a drink. 'How would you feel about doing it permanently?'

'Whatever do you mean?'

'You and young Bonny sizzle when you dance together. It would be a great partnership. Have you considered that?'

Rob was thoughtful as he looked at the man. 'To be honest I hadn't. Yes, I did consider featuring more specialist numbers in future shows, but that was as far as it went.'

'Look, Rob, I know a West End producer who is looking for something new for a musical he's putting together and I'm sure he would be interested in you and that delightful girl.' At Rob's hesitation he said, 'Think about it. I'll bring him down one evening next week and see what his reaction is.' He rose to his feet. 'I'll be in touch.' He shook hands and said, 'You are a great musical director but you are a great dancer too. Perhaps you could combine the two.'

Rob poured himself another drink. Bernie Cohen had given him something to think about. Until he put together this show, he'd never intended to perform again, but Bonny had inspired him, and the idea of an Astaire–Rogers number wouldn't go away. He'd realized that here was someone who could dance well enough to take the woman's part, and he desperately wanted to dance with her. He hadn't felt like that since he given up performing. He also had to admit it had felt really good. They did make a good duo. It was certain that Bonny would be offered a job with a London show in the near future, now that Cohen had seen her. Her dancing was certainly good enough, but how would she cope? It would be like throwing a tender lamb to the wolves of the theatre world. But — if he were to partner her, at least he could take care of her, see that she was handled properly by an agent . . . and he confessed to himself that the standing ovation they had received tonight had whetted his appetite to be on stage once more.

Then again, how would her parents feel if she was to leave home? From what he could deduce, her parents, although encouraging her, still hadn't quite realized her potential and probably thought she would stay close to home, content to be in the chorus in the local theatre. That could be a problem if Bonny wanted to move on.

Now he felt tired. Removing his bow tie, he decided to get changed, go home, have something to eat and see if anything came of Bernie's ideas. After all, there was another week to go.

* * *

Bernie Cohen wasted no time when he returned to London. He arranged a meeting with Peter Collins, the West End producer.

'I think I have found just what you're looking for to feature in the show you want to produce,' he told the man. 'Let's meet tomorrow for lunch. How about the Savoy Grill at one?' He listened for a moment and then put the receiver back in its cradle. So far so good. If everything worked out as he hoped, his reputation as a scout would be even more enhanced, and that was good for business.

* * *

All the girls in the chorus were delighted with their success, with one exception. Lily Stevens was eaten up with jealousy. She had watched Bonny rehearse with Rob daily and had learned the routine thoroughly, practising it whenever she had the chance, desperately wanting to play the Ginger Rogers role to show Rob Andrews that she was good enough, but she would never get the chance . . . unless for some reason Bonny was unable to do so. There was no understudy for her part, as Rob hadn't envisaged dancing with anyone else. What could she do? There was another week, and then her opportunity would be lost forever.

It was now Wednesday and Lily was desperate. Then fate gave her a helping hand. As the chorus trooped off the stage at the close of the first half, Bonny was behind her. Lily paused to let the girl go by, just as they had to go down three steps to the dressing room. As Bonny walked past, Lily put out a foot and tripped her, sending her hurtling down the steps, landing with a cry of pain at the bottom, clutching her ankle.

Rushing to her side, Lily asked, 'Are you all right?'

The others gathered round, Shirley helping her friend to stand. 'I've hurt my ankle,' Bonny told her as she limped painfully to the dressing room.

'Nan, fetch Mr Andrews,' said Shirley, 'and tell him it's urgent.'

Lily stood back watching, with a sly smile.

Rob came rushing in. 'Whatever is the matter?'

'I fell down the steps and twisted my ankle,' Bonny told him.

'Fetch me some ice in a cloth,' Rob told Nan, 'and please be quick.' He pressed the ankle and Bonny winced.

Shaking his head, Rob said, 'I can't see you dancing any more tonight.'

'Don't be ridiculous,' Bonny snapped, 'I must do the finale!'

Nan came in with the ice pack and held it round her ankle.

'If we bind it up and I take a couple of painkillers, I'll be fine,' Bonny insisted.

Lily frowned. 'But what about the rest of the week? If you dance tonight you'll only make it worse.'

'She has a point,' Rob admitted.

Bonny was determined. 'I'll dance tonight, go to the hospital tomorrow, get them to bind it up, rest it all day, and if I don't dance in the other numbers, I should be all right for the finale.' She saw the worried look on Rob's face. 'I have to. After all the publicity, the audience will expect it. We can't let them down, Rob . . . Please!'

Nan handed him a bandage and looked at him quizzically.

'Right, if you insist, but if by the end of the finale I don't think you can continue for the rest of the week, there will be no argument about it.'

Lily stepped forward. 'I could take her place if that's the case.'

Rob looked at her in surprise. 'You?'

'Yes, I've been practising, I know every step of the routine, I could stand in for Bonny. After all, as she said, you can't let the public down.'

There was a stunned silence in the dressing room.

Rob's eyes narrowed. 'My, Lily, such concern from you is overwhelming.'

She sidled up to him. 'You wouldn't be disappointed, I can promise you.'

'Thank you for your consideration, but that won't be necessary. Should Bonny be unable to dance, I'll do it alone.'

'But how can you?'

'I once saw Astaire do a number where he pretended to have a partner, I'll do the same.'

'But . . .' Lily began.

'There are no buts,' snapped Rob and he knelt down and bound Bonny's ankle. 'The chorus will dance without you in the other numbers, and in the finale I'll take as much weight off you where we dance together, but I can't help you other than that.'

'I'll be fine,' said Bonny, taking two painkillers from Nan and swallowing them down with a glass of water.

'I'll help you change,' Nan said. 'Now, all of you — and you, Mr Andrews — give the girl some room.'

'I'll see you in the wings,' said Rob, and with one last worried glance walked out.

Lily slunk away to get changed, but Shirley, who had been watching her, sidled over. 'It didn't quite work out as you planned, did it?'

'What do you mean?' Lily looked startled.

‘I seem to remember that you came off the stage next to Bonny. What did you do, give her a shove down the steps?’

‘I did not! Ask Bonny. She tripped.’

‘Over what, I wonder?’ She glared at the girl. ‘I wouldn’t put anything past you, you little bitch, but if I find you had anything to do with this incident, I’ll sort you out and that’s a promise.’ And she walked away to get changed.

CHAPTER SIX

Sammy Kendrick bought a copy of the *Daily Telegraph* and read the entertainment column. His friend had kept his promise and had written a glowing report about the show at the Palace, asking why these two talented dancers, Bonny Burton and the well-known musical director Rob Andrews, were not appearing in the West End. Sammy grinned broadly. Great! This was exactly what he'd hoped for.

Peter Collins, the West End producer, also read the report, which only added to his curiosity after dining with Bernie Cohen, who had praised these two dancers highly. Collins held the columnist in high esteem, knowing that his reputation as a theatre critic was well respected. If he didn't like a performance he could be vitriolic, so praise from him was well earned. And so it was with great interest that he waited to accompany Cohen to Southampton for the Thursday evening performance.

* * *

Bonny sat alone in the dressing room whilst the other dancers were on stage. Her ankle throbbed but the painkillers were beginning to kick in, and by the time the finale came round she hoped the throbbing would lessen. Nan had strapped her foot up well and now she was sitting with it up on a chair. Even so, she could see the foot was swollen.

By now she was convinced that Lily had tripped her. After all, there was nothing for her to trip over. The staff backstage were always so careful about keeping the area free and clear to avoid such accidents. Conniving little bitch! She gave a slow smile. But her plan had failed, and Bonny was determined that even if she was in agony, she would dance.

The girls filed back into the dressing room after their number and changed hurriedly for the finale. All the girls — except Lily — asked how she was.

'I'm fine, a bit sore, but really I'm fine.'

Shirley sat next to her and quietly remarked, 'Like hell you are.'

Bonny knew better than to try and fool her friend. 'I *am* going on if it damn well kills me, if only to spite Miss Lily Stevens!'

'I had a quiet word with Rob Andrews just now,' Shirley told her. 'I'm sure she tripped you up, and by the look of thunder on his face I would say she's for the chop at the end of the week.'

* * *

Bonny limped to the wings as the music started for the finale, praying that her ankle would hold up during the routine. Rob came up behind her as the chorus danced on before them.

'Are you all right?'

'I'll be fine, don't you worry about me,' she said, and as their entrance came she smiled broadly as she danced on to the stage.

The dance seemed endless. Rob, true to his word, took most of her weight during the lifts and when they were together, but when Bonny and he danced apart the pain in her ankle brought tears to her eyes, but she blinked them away and smiled throughout. At the end of the number, Rob caught hold of her, taking the weight off her feet.

'Well done you,' he whispered as they took their bow.

Back in the dressing room, Nan had a large basin of ice cubes ready. 'Here, put your foot in that,' she said as she piled the ice around the swollen ankle.

Rob entered the room and looked down. 'I'm taking you home in a taxi,' he said, 'and tomorrow morning I'll collect you and take you to the hospital. I want a doctor to take a look at you.'

'I don't honestly think that's necessary,' Bonny argued.

'You may not think so, but I do. When you're ready to go home, send Nan along and I'll get a car.'

'The master has spoken,' said Shirley dryly. 'Besides, he's right, you should get it seen to.'

'But what if the doctor tells me I can't go on?'

'Then Rob will have to do it alone, as he said he would.'

'After all that publicity! No, I can't let that happen. I'll ask the doctor if I can't have an injection for the pain before I dance. There are two nights and Saturday's matinee to go. After that I can rest my foot at home. After all, I have only the final number to dance. Surely I can manage that?'

'You'll have to wait and see what happens,' Shirley said, but she doubted that any doctor would advise such a thing.

Once in the taxi, Bonny put her idea to Rob. 'If the doctor at the hospital agrees with the injection, we could have a local doctor standing by before each performance, couldn't we?'

Although Rob admired Bonny's determination, he didn't want her to add to the damage. As a dancer, he knew just how important it was to treat any injuries with care, but he also knew that Bernie Cohen was bringing the producer down one evening and Bonny's future would depend on her being seen. It was a dilemma. It would all depend on what transpired at the hospital tomorrow morning.

* * *

Bonny put her case the following morning in the emergency ward. 'I have three evening performances to do only,' she pleaded. 'I can rest my foot all day until Saturday when we have a matinee in the afternoon, and then until the evening performance. Please, Doctor, this is vital.'

'The show must go on, Miss Burton, is that what you're saying?' But his tone was sympathetic.

'There! You do understand.'

'I have tickets myself for tonight's performance,' he said with a smile, 'but, of course, that won't sway my judgement.' He examined her foot carefully. 'You should rest it completely, but I am prepared to go along with your idea . . . as long as you don't put any weight on it in the meantime and you keep the foot elevated. I'll get a nurse to bandage it to give you some support, but you must rest as much as possible, and after the weekend you really need to keep any weight off it altogether.'

'Oh thank you, Doctor. I promise I'll do everything you tell me.'

'I'll see you get a pair of crutches to use in the meantime.'

'Thank you, Doctor,' said Rob. 'Come backstage after the performance if you like.'

The doctor grinned broadly. 'Thanks, I'd like that and so will my wife.'

Rob took Bonny home and was ushered into the living room by Millie, who was anxious to hear the verdict. She made a cup of tea whilst Rob told her what the doctor had said.

'I'll send a car for you tonight,' he told Bonny.

'Don't you worry about her, Mr Andrews,' Millie said. 'I'll make sure she sits on the settee with her feet up until then.'

He drank his tea and then rose to his feet. 'Nice to meet you, Mrs Burton, and thanks for the tea.' Turning to Bonny, he said, 'I'll see you this evening.'

'He seems a nice chap,' said Millie after she'd seen Rob to the door.

'You'll see just what a wonderful dancer he is when you come to the theatre on Saturday.'

'Yes, imagine you dancing with the likes of him! Whatever next, I wonder?' Millie remarked as she walked into the scullery.

* * *

That evening, Bernie Cohen and Peter Collins took their places in the stalls as the auditorium began to fill. Collins was intrigued about the evening before him. He thought about the report he had read about the show. It had been unusual for the man to write about any show other than one in the West End, and his enthusiasm for the Astaire–Rogers number was quite rare.

The lights dimmed and the overture began.

Backstage, Bonny, with the help of Nan, the wardrobe mistress, had dressed and put the final touches to her stage make-up, before sitting with her foot up on a chair — a doctor standing by to give her an injection during the interval.

Having rested her foot all day, the swelling had gone down considerably, but she knew that after her performance it would be swollen once again. *Never mind*, she thought, *as long as this gets me through every performance it doesn't matter*.

The second half was all but over when Rob came to her dressing room to collect her. 'Use your crutches,' he said. 'Nan will hold them in the wings during the dance. How's the foot?'

'Fine. The rest has brought down the swelling and the injection has deadened the pain.'

He smiled slowly and squeezed her hand. 'You are an amazing young woman. Right, here we go,' he said, and they danced on to the stage.

Peter Collins sat upright in his seat and watched carefully.

* * *

At the end of the show, Bernie Cohen sent word to Rob that he wanted to see him and Bonny in Rob's office, so Rob went along to the girl's dressing room and asked Bonny to accompany him. Puzzled, she took hold of her crutches and followed him. Just as they reached the office door they were met by Bernie and his associate, who looked askance at Bonny. 'Miss Burton, whatever is the matter?'

Rob intervened. 'Please let's go inside.' He didn't want anyone to see his visitors.

Once inside, Bernie introduced the man. 'Rob, Bonny, this is Peter Collins, the West End producer.' Looking at Bonny, he said, 'I'm Bernie Cohen, a talent scout, and I asked Mr Collins down here to see the two of you dance.'

'Why the crutches?' asked Collins. 'After seeing you dance just now, I can't believe you need them.'

'I had a fall last night and twisted my ankle,' she explained.

'But you still danced. Wasn't it painful?'

She grimaced. 'Yes it was but a doctor gave me an injection during the interval. I couldn't let Rob and the public down after all the publicity.'

He looked at her with admiration. 'That is the sign of a real trouper, Miss Burton, and are you able to complete the week this way?'

'Yes, then I'll be able to rest up.'

Collins turned his attention to Rob. 'I really must commend you on your choreography; it was first class throughout the evening. Your chorus work was very innovative but the finale was spectacular.'

'Thank you.' Rob looked pleased.

'I am putting together a show to be held at the Adelphi Theatre in the West End in four months' time and I would like the two of you to join the cast.'

Bonny gasped and turned to Rob, who was looking thoughtful. 'I would have to know a lot more about it before I could possibly give you an answer,' he said.

'Of course,' said Peter. 'I would also like to offer you the job as choreographer, but we need to meet up and discuss it in detail. Are you free next week to come to my office in London?'

'Yes, that would be fine.'

The two men arranged a day and time and Collins rose to his feet. He shook Rob's hand and then Bonny's. 'You are a very talented young lady and I would love to have you in my show.' Then the two men left the office.

Bonny, who had been shocked into silence, spoke. 'Am I dreaming?'

With a chuckle, Rob said, 'No, Bonny, we have been offered a place in a West End show. How do you feel about it?'

'Absolutely stunned!'

'Well, I would need to find out what it entails before I was able to even think about accepting, but if everything works out would you be willing to take the job?'

'Are you joking? Of course I'd accept, it's my dream. How could you even doubt it?'

'What about your parents? How would they react to you moving away from Southampton and home?'

'I am a professional dancer, they couldn't possibly imagine I'd be staying put, not if I'm any good.' A frown creased her forehead. 'Do you really think I'm good enough?'

He took her hand in his. 'Do you think I'd have danced with you if I had any doubts? Of course you're good enough! Peter Collins himself told you that you were talented and he should know.'

'Were you aware that he was coming?'

Rob told her about Bernie and how he arranged this meeting. 'Bernie is a brilliant talent scout. He was so impressed that he invited Collins down to see the show.'

Seeing how tired Bonny looked, he insisted they booked a taxi to take her home. 'I'll come in and have a word with your parents, if you like, and pave the way should we decide to accept Peter Collins' offer.'

Bonny thought the idea was sound. In her heart she thought her mother would approve, but she wasn't at all sure about her father. But no one would stop her if Rob decided the move was a good one. And she was right.

Sitting around the table in the living room of the Burton's house, Rob told them what had transpired that evening. Bonny's mother, Millie, was thrilled, but Frank, her husband, was shaken to the core.

'But Bonny is only eighteen!'

'So are many others in the profession,' Rob said quietly. 'I cannot impress upon you enough the great opportunity this is for your daughter. She has an immense talent that should be nurtured. Peter Collins is a renowned producer, one of the finest in the country. He doesn't make these offers unless he thinks he has a star on his hands. When you come to the theatre on Saturday, you will see for yourself why he's done so.'

'You can't stand in her way,' urged Millie. 'After all, this is what Bonny's worked for. What we paid for when you agreed to let her have dancing lessons.'

'Yes, but she was a child, I never thought it would get this far.'

Bonny gazed at her father. 'But it has, Dad. I've never wanted to do anything else but dance. This is my great chance. If you tried to stop me I don't think I could ever forgive you.'

Such was the determination in her voice, Frank knew she meant it.

'There's lots of negotiations to go before I would commit either Bonny or myself to this project, so let's wait and see what transpires,' suggested Rob, wanting to defuse the moment.

'That's a good idea,' said Millie. 'Now I want to bathe Bonny's ankle in cold water before she goes to bed.'

'I'll send a car for you tomorrow, Bonny,' Rob said as he took his leave.

Later, when mother and daughter were alone, Millie looked at Bonny and said, 'Don't you worry about your father, I'll have a good talk to him. You will go to the West End, even if it's over my dead body!'

Bonny hugged her. 'Oh, I do love you.'

'Of course you do, I'm your mother!'

CHAPTER SEVEN

Bonny Burton sat in the train heading for Waterloo Station — and her future. She peered out of the window but the passing scenery didn't register — her mind was in a whirl. So much had happened so quickly during the previous month. There had been meetings between Rob Andrews and Peter Collins, discussing the new musical extravaganza opening at the Adelphi Theatre in which he wanted Bonny and Rob to feature their Fred Astaire–Ginger Rogers routines. Bonny had been a part of these meetings once Rob had clarified the points he thought important to both of them: the terms of their contract, their fees and how much input he would have as musical director.

Once he had settled all this, he and Bonny had spoken to her parents. Millie had talked to her husband Frank earlier and persuaded him that he couldn't stand in the way of his daughter's future. 'Dancing is all she's ever wanted to do, and after seeing her performance with Rob Andrews, you have to admit our Bonny has great talent. You stand in her way, love, you'll lose your daughter. Is that what you want?'

'Of course not!' He frowned. 'She's always been my little girl, that's all, and I'm having a hard time accepting that she's now a young woman.'

Millie put an arm around him. 'I know, I'll miss her too, but after all, she's only in London, not the other side of the world. Just think how proud we'll be on opening night to see our girl on a West End stage.'

Rob Andrews had been able to persuade them that he would look after Bonny and her interests and had told them that he had chosen good theatrical digs for her with a nice family who were used to dealing with folk in the theatre. 'Mr and Mrs Gregg are a middle-aged couple who provide home cooked meals and a clean home. Bonny will be well cared for, I can assure you. They have both been in the theatre in their younger days so understand the needs of a performer. And I'll make sure she's safe and sound.'

Thus reassured, Millie and Frank had given Bonny their blessing, and now she was on her way to London to start rehearsals.

Bonny looked across the train carriage at Rob who was immersed in his work, sorting out dance routines in his head and writing the moves and music down on a pad balanced on his knee. He looked up and smiled at Bonny. 'You all right?'

'I'm sitting here unable to believe what's happening,' she admitted.

He gazed at her with affection. He would enjoy this new challenge, especially as Bonny was part of it. They were like-minded souls, whose world was the theatre. How fortunate he was to have found her, he mused.

'We work well together, Bonny, and you have no idea how happy that makes me. We are going to have so much fun, but once we start rehearsals in the morning, you'll believe it's all happening, you'll be so tired!' And he returned to his work. He was directing all the numbers that they were dancing and had been given carte blanche by Peter Collins.

'I love your style, Rob,' Collins had said. 'I want you to bring that to your part of the show. I've hired excellent dancers for the chorus, who will be thrilled to work with you. I have only one favour to ask.'

'And what's that?'

'One of our backers has a girlfriend and he insists that she is in the chorus. She's not a bad dancer, but nothing special. However, I desperately need his money, so I had to agree, I'm sorry.'

Rob was not pleased. 'What if she can't cut the mustard?'

'Then, old man, you'll have to work with her and make sure she does.'

There was a steeliness in Collins' voice and Rob knew he had no option but to agree.

'Right, let's hope she isn't useless or I'll work her until her feet bleed, then perhaps she won't be quite so keen on the idea!' And the subject was closed.

* * *

On their arrival in London, Rob took Bonny by taxi to her digs. She liked the Greggs at once and was delighted with her bedroom, which was small but filled with light from the window. It was reasonably close to the theatre, and once she was settled, Rob walked her to the Adelphi to look at the theatre and talk to Peter Collins.

He put his arm around her shoulder as they walked, telling her about the city and the shows that were currently being performed in the West End, adding to her excitement.

The show was already in rehearsal when they arrived, and the three of them sat in the stalls and watched the early attempts of the opening numbers. The chorus were being put through their steps by Collins' musical director, who halted the rehearsal to come over and meet Rob.

Dan Mansfield was an up-and-coming young man in the theatre and he greeted Rob with enthusiasm. 'Mr Andrews, it's a great pleasure to meet you. I'm one of your most ardent admirers and I look forward to working with you.' The two shook hands.

'When did you start rehearsing?' Rob asked.

'Only yesterday, so everything and everyone is pretty raw at the moment, but we'll get there.'

'I'm sure you will. Please, don't let me disturb you.'

They watched as he instructed the chorus line in their opening number and suddenly Rob saw a familiar face and guessed which dancer was the girlfriend of one of the backers.

Bonny recognized her at the same time. 'That's Lily Stevens!' she said with surprise.

Rob closed his eyes in despair. He had fired Lily at the end of the show in Southampton for tripping up Bonny and causing her to sprain her ankle. The girl had heartily denied it, of course, and there had been an angry scene as Lily had left Rob's office — and the show. Now, here she was, and Rob was stuck with her — like it or not. The only saving grace was that Lily was good enough for the chorus with a bit of hard work, but in his bones Rob knew she wouldn't be satisfied with that — and that would be his problem. One that he would keep from Bonny. He didn't want anything to interfere with her performance. Besides, it was his concern, not hers.

* * *

The following morning Rob began his rehearsals. The chorus stood before him, waiting eagerly for his instructions, knowing his reputation. He quickly laid out the scene to which they were to perform and showed them the opening steps. Collins was right, they were all very competent dancers, the weakest by far was Lily Stevens. He moved her to the back row, which made her cheeks redden and her eyes flash angrily.

And at the end of rehearsals she stormed up to him. 'In case you are unaware of the situation, my fiancé is a backer of this production, and when I tell him I'm in the back row, he will not be pleased!'

Rob looked coldly at her. 'Don't you try blackmail with me, Lily. You are only here because of your fiancé, as I'm sure you know. I will not ruin my production on a whim. I'm sure your fiancé would not be pleased to see a number spoilt by your incompetence. Think about it, Lily. If I put you in a prominent position then your man will see for himself you are not up to standard and that would be embarrassing for him.' He paused. 'Then, I don't think he'll pursue your ambition with quite so much enthusiasm. After all, he's a canny businessman, he's put his money into this company because he wants a return. I can assure you he won't put you before that, however good you are in bed!' He turned and walked away.

Lily stood fuming, her cheeks flushed. She rushed off the stage, muttering to herself.

Rob was not at all sure how enamoured the backer was with the girl and hoped the man was a shrewd businessman first before being a man in lust or love. If it was the latter, he was in deep trouble.

* * *

The rehearsals were going well and Peter Collins was busy selling his forthcoming show to the people who mattered in the theatre. To this end, he'd arranged a cocktail party at the Savoy Hotel on the coming Sunday evening, which would be good publicity as he'd also organised for the press to attend.

'Go and buy Bonny an evening dress,' he told Rob. 'I want her to look stunning when I introduce the pair of you. You will be in a dinner jacket, of course.'

'Of course,' smiled Rob. 'Who have you invited?'

'Jack Buchanan and Noel Coward, and CB Cochran said he'd try and look in. Apart from several theatre critics — and the backers, of course. We must give them the opportunity to meet the stars; it's a bonus that comes when they give me their money.'

Rob frowned. No doubt Lily would be among the guests, with her sugar daddy, and that could be very awkward.

* * *

Bonny and Rob had a great time shopping for her dress. Away from the rigidity of his role as dance director, she discovered his charm and sense of humour. He also, she discovered, had an innate sense of style.

As she tried on yet another model, chosen by him, curiosity overcame her. 'How do you know so much about a woman's apparel?'

He chuckled wickedly. 'Most of my adult life has been around women. I picked up a few tips.'

'Mm, I bet you did!'

'What are you implying, Bonny?' He raised his eyebrows as he waited for her reply.

'Nothing, but I am seeing another side to you and it's a little disconcerting, if I'm honest.'

He started to laugh. 'I am definitely an unknown quantity, but that's how I like it!'

* * *

On Sunday evening, Bonny stood before a full-length mirror and gazed at her reflection. She was wearing a pale russet evening gown that had been their final choice. It showed the deep auburn tones of her hair to perfection. It was a simple style but the cut and swathe of the bodice fitted perfectly. Beneath it she wore black evening court shoes with a diamanté buckle, and around her shoulders, a pale mink jacket that had been hired for the evening. Round her neck was a diamanté necklace and matching earrings hung from her ears. Her long hair was dressed back from her face and cascaded with ringlets. She looked stunning.

Amy Gregg, her landlady, fussed about the hem of her dress, then stood back. 'There you are, girl. Fit for a king, you are!'

Bonny did a twirl. 'I've never looked like this in my entire life!' she exclaimed.

'Well, dear, if you dance on stage as good as you look tonight, you'll be a sensation.'

'I'm a bit nervous about meeting all these important people,' Bonny confessed.

'We'll soon put a stop to that! You're a dancer, so you stand tall, move gracefully and be yourself. Don't try and make clever remarks, just be normal.' She smiled wryly. 'Take it from me, in the theatre there are too many people who make-believe twenty-four hours of the day. They will appreciate someone who doesn't.'

The front doorbell rang. 'That'll be Mr Andrews for you,' Amy said as she walked to the door. She paused. 'If I was younger I wouldn't mind going out with that young man. He's gorgeous!'

And as Rob entered the front room, Bonny could see what Amy meant. He had the stature and elegance of a dancer, and in a dinner jacket he did indeed look handsome.

He eyed Bonny with admiration. 'You look lovely.' He leaned forward and kissed her. 'Are you ready? The taxi's waiting.'

* * *

There was a small orchestra softly playing songs from the current shows on the stage of the room Peter had booked at the Savoy, and as Rob and Bonny entered he walked over to them. 'My dear Bonny, you look amazing, just as a star should. Here, have a drink.' He took three glasses of champagne from the tray being offered by a waiter. 'Now, come with me and meet Jack.'

'Jack?' queried Bonny.

'Yes, Jack Buchanan. He's starring in a show with Elsie Randolph, who couldn't come this evening.'

Bonny felt her heart race. Jack Buchanan was a major star in the theatre and in films as well. Her mother adored him and now she was about to meet him.

Peter put his hand on the arm of a tall man, immaculately dressed, with dark hair. 'Jack, I want you to meet my up-and-coming stars.'

'I'm delighted,' the man said as he took Bonny's hand.

'My mother absolutely adores you,' she said before she could think.

Mr Buchanan beamed with delight. 'Is she here this evening?'

'No, I'm afraid not.'

'Then you must make sure I have her address before I leave and I'll send her a signed photo.'

'Thank you so much, that would make my mother's day.'

Peter introduced Rob to the star, who said, 'I know you by reputation, Mr Andrews. I will certainly look forward to seeing the show when it opens.'

The evening seemed to speed by. Bonny's head was in a whirl as she was introduced to the upper echelon of the theatre. She had taken Rob's advice and substituted orange juice for champagne after a couple of glasses.

She was more than a little surprised to see Lily Stevens at the party with an older man who was in conversation with Peter Collins at one time. Lily made a point of ignoring Bonny and Rob, which was a great relief to them both.

Rob was called away and excused himself, and Bonny stood alone for a moment.

'Can I get you a drink, young lady?'

She turned and looked up into the piercing blue eyes of a tall man with dark hair who smiled softly at her. He raised his eyebrows in question.

'That's very kind of you, but no thank you. I don't want any more alcohol, and frankly I can't face another orange juice.'

He chuckled. 'I know what you mean. Come with me,' he said, and he took her by the arm over to the bar. 'Two of your special fruit cocktails please, George,' he told the barman.

'Yes, Mr Gilmore, coming up.'

Bonny looked at the stranger with curiosity. 'He seems to know you well,' she remarked.

The man was amused. 'Well, George knows my needs; he's looked after me for quite a time. Giles Gilmore,' he said with a slight bow of the head.

'Bonny Burton,' she replied, copying his bow.

The barman poured two drinks over crushed ice from a cocktail shaker and placed the glasses before them.

'Chin chin,' said Giles.

'Cheers,' Bonny replied and sipped the content of the glass. 'This is lovely!' Turning to the barman she asked, 'What's in it?'

'My secret, I'm afraid, madam.'

She looked at Giles for assistance but he shook his head. 'I have no idea.'

George left them to attend another customer.

Giles Gilmore intrigued Bonny, and she wondered just what he had to do with the theatre. Was he a producer, a critic, an actor? He was certainly good-looking but there was an air about him that was different. This man would never have to pretend, she didn't think. He was too self assured.

At that moment, Rob Andrews walked over. 'Excuse me,' he said to Giles, 'but Bonny, you are needed,' and he led her away.

She looked back over her shoulder. Giles raised his glass at her and smiled.

Peter Collins was on the stage talking about his forthcoming show. 'And now, ladies and gentlemen, allow me to introduce a couple whose names will be on everyone's lips after opening night. Rob Andrews and Bonny Burton.'

To Bonny's acute embarrassment she was led up on to the stage by Rob.

'These two dancers will be the talk of the town. Remember, you heard it here first!' Peter led the applause and the orchestra started to play. 'Please, you two, get on the floor and show them what you're made of!'

As Rob led her on to the dance floor he whispered, 'Just follow me, come on, you've been doing it for months.' And that's what she did. As always, in Rob's arms she was safe. He guided her firmly and managed to put in a few Astaire moves, which Bonny followed faultlessly. At the end of the dance, the applause was enthusiastic.

The band started the next number, and as the other guests joined them on the dance floor, Rob gathered her in his arms, holding her close and carried on dancing.

'Sorry about that, I didn't know we were to perform, but this is a promotional night for the show, we should have expected it from Peter.'

'It's alright, bit of a shock, but tonight has been strange altogether. This is a different world to what I've been used to.'

'You'd better get used to it, Bonny, because everything has changed for you now. You have to make the best of it and not get carried away with the artificiality of it. So much is just glitter, without depth. Keep both feet on the ground and you'll do just fine.'

As they traversed the floor, Bonny relaxed. As he rested his head against hers, she really enjoyed herself until the music stopped.

As they left the floor, Giles Gilmore stood in front of them, and holding out her glass he said, 'Miss Burton, you didn't finish your drink.'

CHAPTER EIGHT

Rob Andrews asked, with a wary look, 'And you are?'

'Giles Gilmore.' He shook Rob's hand. 'I hate to see a good drink go to waste, especially one of George's special cocktails.'

Bonny took it from him. 'It's a fruit cocktail,' she explained. 'Mr Gilmore came to my rescue when I was standing alone. He introduced me to George the barman when I said I didn't want any alcohol.' Turning to Giles she said, 'This is my dancing partner, Rob Andrews.'

'Yes I know, I saw your exhibition just now. You both dance so well together. I can't wait to see the show.'

Rob was now curious about the stranger. 'Are you anything to do with the theatre?'

'Oh yes, quite a lot,' was the enigmatic reply. 'Now you must excuse me. I look forward to our next meeting, Miss Burton.'

'Extraordinary bloke!' Rob remarked as he watched him walk over to another small gathering. 'I wonder who he is?'

'I have no idea,' said Bonny, but she felt that wasn't the last time she would see the handsome gent. There had been a determined look in his eyes whenever he had gazed at her.

* * *

There was a pleasant surprise for Bonny when she walked into rehearsal the following morning. Her friend Shirley Gates was standing chatting to the other members of the chorus.

'Shirley!' The two girls rushed to meet each other, hugging and laughing with glee. 'What are you doing here?' asked Bonny.

'Well, my dear girl, I was summoned by Mr Andrews. When I got the phone call at the Palace I couldn't believe it. He wants me in the show! Bloody marvellous, isn't it? And what's more he wants us to do a number together, like we did in Southampton!'

'That's wonderful. I am *so* pleased to see you. The others are nice but I do feel a bit lonely. After all, most of them have worked together before so I feel a bit of an outsider.'

'Don't you worry, now I'm here, and guess what? Rob has got me fixed up at the same digs as you!' She leaned closer so as not to be overheard. 'What the bloody hell is Lily Stevens doing here? She's outclassed, I would have thought.'

'Well, the gossip is that her fiancé is one of the backers. So Peter Collins had to take Lily if he wanted the money.'

'Must be that old fellow she cottoned on to in Southampton. She is such a crafty bitch. She'd claw her way through a sewer to get what she wants. Does she have a solo spot?'

'No! She's not good enough, you know that.'

'Hmm! Bet she gets one, one way or another.'

'Not if Rob has anything to do with it, I wouldn't think.'

At that moment Rob called the dancers together and rehearsals began. He then ran through a number that featured Shirley and Bonny with the male dancers only. Lily looked on in fury.

It was a lively and tricky number but as the girls were so used to dancing together, it progressed very quickly.

At the end, Shirley turned to Bonny and whispered, 'Blimey! There's some very juicy blokes around, I *am* glad I came!'

Rob called a break for lunch and Shirley wasted little time getting to know the men who had featured in the number.

'You and I are off out this evening,' she told Bonny a little later.

'Really, where?'

'Don't know yet. We've got a date with a couple of the boys.'

'What!'

'Listen, girl, we work bloody hard and when we go into production we'll be too damned tired, so we'll have a bit of fun whilst we can. Right?'

Bonny realized how much she'd missed Shirley. Life had been nothing but hard work until now, and carried away with her friend's enthusiasm she grinned broadly. 'Right!' she agreed.

* * *

Whilst Bonny and Shirley learned the delights of the Metropolis with the chorus boys, Lily Stevens was working on her benefactor and fiancé, Charles Kendal. Now that Shirley had joined the chorus and had been given a number with Bonny, Lily was even more determined to feature in a solo spot.

Snuggling up to Charles in bed, she gently traced her finger across his lips, kissing his ears and moving her naked body close to his.

'Charlie, darling, you do love me, don't you?'

'Of course, you know I do.'

'You want me to be happy, don't you?'

His eyes narrowed. Now what? he wondered. 'I thought being with me was enough to make you happy, Lily.'

'Oh darling, where else would I want to be? You are so good to me and I adore you.'

'Then what's the problem?'

She slipped her hand between his thighs and fondled his genitals. 'It's only that I don't think Rob Andrews appreciates my talent. He's brought a dancer in from Southampton to do a number with Bonny Burton. Now, I can't see why he has to go to that extra expense when I am perfectly capable of doing the number. It seems to me he's wasting money.'

Charles, now aroused, wasn't concentrating on the career of his young bed mate. He pulled her on top of him, but Lily wasn't ready to concede to his wishes just yet.

'You have a lot of money invested in the production and I think you should have a word with him, don't you?'

'I'll come along to rehearsals tomorrow and see him,' he promised.

She slowly lowered herself on to him and kissing him passionately said, 'Thank you, darling. I knew I could rely on you.'

* * *

Rehearsals started early the following morning and it wasn't until Rob called a break that he was aware of the gentleman sitting in the stalls, watching. He recognized him as the man who had been with Lily at Peter's party and he guessed that Lily had been whingeing to him about her position in the chorus. It had to happen sometime, he supposed, but he would wait to be approached.

Charles Kendal watched the rehearsals until lunchtime. He realized the talent of the dance director and was most impressed with the choreography of each production. Not being a fool, he also realized that Lily was not as good a dancer as she perceived herself to be. But he was a man of the world, well versed in handling women. Lily suited him. She was attractive and pliable. Charles was well aware that she was using him to her own ends, but he was doing the same. A permanent woman on his arm, wearing his ring, kept other young women from pestering him. Lily was good in bed and the present situation suited him. He would never marry her, of course — but she didn't know that.

As the company broke for lunch, he approached Rob Andrews. Holding out his hand, he introduced himself. 'Charles Kendal, one of your backers.'

'I'm pleased to meet you, Mr Kendal. What can I do for you?'

With a sly smile, Charles said, 'I'm sure you already have an inkling about that. Why don't you and I go and have a sandwich and a beer, then we can talk?'

Lily smiled with pleasure as she saw the two men leave the theatre. Glancing over towards Shirley and Bonny her mouth tightened. Those two would soon realize she was not to be messed with!

Once in the nearby pub, the two men sat in a quiet corner. Charles came straight to the point. 'Lily wants a solo spot. What do you have to say about that?'

'She isn't nearly good enough.' Rob didn't mince his words. 'You have watched the rehearsal all the morning. You must have seen for yourself that she is just an average dancer.'

'I agree.'

This comment took Rob by surprise. 'Then you must realize that I can't give her a solo spot.'

Charles sipped his beer. 'There is always another way to skin a cat than the obvious one, Mr Andrews. If we can work something out between us, our problem will be solved.'

Rob looked thoughtful. He liked Charles Kendal. Realizing the man was canny, he asked, 'Have you any suggestions?'

'As a matter of fact I have.'

* * *

Giles Gilmore greeted his secretary as he walked into his office in Jermyn Street. 'Good morning, Jennifer, any messages?'

'I've put a list on your desk, Mr Gilmore. Jessie Matthews called and asked that you call her back. There's some problem she wants you to take care of. The rest are not life-threatening.'

'That makes a change,' he laughed.

Giles came from a theatrical background. His father, James, was an agent, his mother, Frances, had been a well-known singer but had given up her career to become a wife and mother. Giles had helped his father before branching out on his own. He started with a small theatre, which he bought, and put on his own shows before selling out at a profit. He then bought properties around London and sold them on, amassing a small fortune, which he ploughed into backing West End shows, which made him a renowned angel in the business. He had a nose for success and every producer with a show to finance hoped for his interest.

Giles moved effortlessly among the glitterati of the theatre and with big businessmen in the City. His financial acumen was recognized by them all. His success had bought him a fine apartment in Sloane Square and a house in Virginia Water. He was unmarried, but was never without a good-looking woman on his arm when the occasion merited one, such as on an opening night.

Whilst working for his father, Giles had had to do business with a wide spectrum of clients, which had sometimes taken him into the seedy world of the City. He had dealt with boxing promoters, for instance. A rough and tough world inhabited by a doubtful mix of people, many of whom were unscrupulous. But Giles, although full of charm, could be as ruthless as the next man. This sometimes had made him a few enemies. Especially when he had come across a betting syndicate who had paid one of his fighters to throw a fight. The fallout had been spectacular. He'd taken the men to court, which meant some of those involved had served time. He had been threatened, and for some time after had employed a bodyguard. Now he had moved on.

It took a lot to excite the business side of Giles Gilmore, but when he'd seen Bonny Burton dance with her partner at Peter Collins' publicity party, he had felt a certain buzz. Here was a truly talented girl. One who, so far, seemed untouched by life in the theatre. He knew without a doubt this girl could become a big star with the right backing.

After he had dealt with Jessie Matthews' problem, he made discreet enquiries. It would seem that Rob Andrews was handling all Bonny's business affairs, so there was no agent involved. Andrews, he felt, was more than a little protective of his young star, for which he didn't blame him one bit, but if the show was a success, Giles wanted to be in a position to take over this charming girl's career. He picked up the telephone and made a call.

* * *

Lily Stevens walked on to the stage at the following morning's rehearsal with great expectations. Charles had assured her he'd had a word with Mr Andrews and they had come to an agreement.

Rob put the dancers through the first two numbers without making any changes and then when it came to the number which involved a statue, centre stage, he made an announcement. 'I've decided to use a dancer instead of a figurine, so Lily, I want you to stand on this plinth and don't move.'

She hurried forward. Rob gave her a box to stand on.

'This, of course, will be taller in the actual production,' he explained. 'Then, at the end, you jump down and dance around it, then exit left. Let me show you what I want.'

Lily was thrilled. At last she had her solo spot. But the dance was very brief and before she knew where she was — she was off stage!

She fumed. 'Is that it?' she asked after the number finished.

Rob raised his eyebrows in surprise. 'I don't understand?'

'I have about three minutes after I get down, then I'm off stage!'

'And?'

'I was given to understand that I was to have a solo spot.'

He gazed steadily at her. 'And that's exactly what you have, Lily. Now, everyone, get into your places for the next number,' he called and walked away.

Shirley was convulsed with laughter. She clung on to Bonny, holding her stomach as she laughed until the tears ran down her face. 'Oh Bonny, did you see the look on her face? She thought she was going to be a star.'

'Now don't be unkind,' Bonny remonstrated. 'She can't help the way she is. I think Rob has been sneaky but really clever. I saw him yesterday with Lily's boyfriend. I suppose they thought this up together. Otherwise how could Rob get away with it?'

'If that's the case, Lily's in for a bit of a shock. She certainly expected much more. I bet she gives the old boy hell tonight.'

* * *

Lily was indeed raging at Charles when she burst into their apartment after rehearsals. She stormed up and down the room, calling Rob every name under the sun. But Charles just sat, smoking his cigar, sipping his drink until eventually she stopped in front of him.

'So what are you going to do about it?'

'Absolutely nothing!'

The girl was stunned. 'What do you mean, nothing?'

'You have your centre stage spot. That's what you asked for and that's what you've got.'

Her eyes flashed with anger. 'For a few moments only. That's not what I was expecting. And frankly, it's not good enough!'

'No, Lily, *you* are not good enough!'

She couldn't believe what she'd heard and was speechless.

'I sat through a morning's rehearsal yesterday. I watched the numbers being performed and I watched you. Lily, darling, you are a lovely girl. You delight me between the sheets, but as a dancer . . .'

The girl was outraged. 'How dare you make that assumption! You haven't seen me at my best, as that bloody Rob Andrews hasn't given me the opportunity to show my talent.'

He cast a cool and icy glance in her direction. 'Your talents, my dear, are purely sexual. There, you are a star, but on two feet . . . there is much to be to be desired.'

Her legs seemed to give way and she sank to her knees on the carpet. 'Charles, how could you say that?'

'Because it's true and Rob Andrews is right. You are only in the chorus because of me. Now, unless you can accept that and stop bleating about how unfair it all is . . .'

His threat wasn't wasted on Lily. She knew that she now had to be clever if she wanted to maintain her comfortable position with Charles and continue to enjoy his lifestyle, and that to do so, she would have to concede. 'Have I been foolish, darling Charles?'

He smiled, knowing he had won.

* * *

The following day, Giles Gilmore sat in the office of Peter Collins. With a determined look in his eye, he spoke. 'Peter, I have a business proposition for you.'

CHAPTER NINE

Rob Andrews was holding a meeting with the set designer, going over the details of the backgrounds to feature in his numbers, when Peter Collins walked in with Giles Gilmore. 'Rob, can I have a word?'

Folding the plans of the sets, Rob nodded to the set designer and then walked over to the two men. 'What can I do for you?'

'You know Giles, I believe?'

'We did meet briefly the other night.'

'Well, Mr Andrews, we'll be seeing a lot more of each other in the future,' said Giles with a smile.

'Really, how so?'

'I have just bought the contracts for you and Miss Burton from Peter. I am now your manager!'

Rob looked astonished and angry. 'You what?' Then, glaring at Collins, he asked, 'You did this without consulting me?'

'Yes, old chap. Giles made me a good offer and I feel he can do more for you in the future than I can, so I wasn't being absolutely selfish, I did have both your interests at heart. Giles is prepared to invest a considerable amount of money in you and Bonny. With his help you will go far.'

'But you've never seen us perform, so on what have you based such a decision?'

'As a matter of fact, I have. I heard that Peter was going to Southampton to watch a show and this made me curious, so I made it my business to find out why. I liked what I saw.'

'So this is a fait accompli and there isn't anything I can do about it, is that what you're saying?'

'I wouldn't put it quite like that,' said Giles, 'but if you insist, yes, that about wraps it up.'

'Then perhaps you would be good enough to enlighten me. After all, I have no idea just what it is that you can do for us and that makes me very nervous.'

Laughing heartily, Giles said, 'Believe me, you will be delighted with my plans. I suggest that you and Miss Burton come to my office after rehearsals and we can discuss the future.' He handed Rob his card. 'Shall we say six o'clock this evening?'

As the two men walked away, Rob read the card. *Giles Gilmore. Impresario. Jermyn Street, London.* Now he was intrigued.

Bonny, unfamiliar with the business side of the theatre, was more than a little confused by the news, however, when Rob sought her out shortly after his conversation with Giles. 'What do you mean, he bought our contracts?'

'He's now our manager and not Peter Collins. Collins has sold us as a package. We have to meet Gilmore this evening to hear his plans for the future.'

'Is this good news, Rob?'

'Time will tell. I'll pick you up in a taxi at a quarter to six. Then we'll see what Mr Gilmore has up his sleeve.'

* * *

As she and Shirley walked to their digs, Bonny told her friend what had transpired.

'Well, imagine that. Who is this man?'

'I've only met him briefly, he said he was something to do with the theatre, but honestly, Shirley, I have no idea.' She gave the matter some thought. 'He does have a certain air about him, you know. He comes across as somebody important with a lot of clout, and there is something about him that is truly fascinating, but I believe he could be quite ruthless. Although he oozes charm, there is a certain steeliness about him too.'

'Is that good?'

'I really don't know, but it will be interesting to find out. All I do know is that Rob is not happy about it.'

* * *

Rob Andrews was fuming about the change of circumstances. With Collins he knew exactly where he was. He had complete control over the choreography of his part of the show and that was just as he liked it. Now, things could change and he wasn't at all sure that would sit well with him — and he had decided if the meeting tonight didn't please him he would fight for the things he wanted. Giles Gilmore would learn that he was no pushover.

* * *

For his part, Giles was more than a little aware of the hostility from Andrews, and if he had been in the man's position he would have felt the same. However, he felt that the ideas he had for a new show would meet with the approval of the talented musical director. If Rob became too difficult, then of course he would deal with that too. Bonny was the star he was most interested in. True, at the moment, it was in a partnership with Andrews, as it would serve to establish her in the public's eye when the present show opened. After that it would be up to him as her manager to decide her future, and he had already made up his mind: she would be a solo artist.

Eventually, Rob Andrews, as her partner, would become redundant!

* * *

In the East End of London, an impresario of another kind was making his plans too. Charlie Gordon, known as Foxy, was a fight promoter and ran a boxing agency and gym. He had several fighters of repute on his books and his successes in the fight world were impressive. He was a tough individual with a colourful past. Not particularly tall, he was thickset and muscular and could lay out a man with a fast right hook and sometimes a knee in the groin when the occasion arose.

He himself had once been a boxer with a good record in the ring. As a young man he'd been involved in bare fist fights held privately and against the law. Such bouts had left their mark on his features. His nose was twisted where it had been broken, and his left ear was well described as a cauliflower. A trainer had eventually taken him in hand, and he'd earned a good living in the ring until he decided he'd had enough and had started his own gym.

Foxy was not adverse to breaking the law but was clever enough — hence his nickname — to cover his tracks, most of the time, but he had been in prison for being part of the betting syndicate that Giles Gilmore had taken to court several years ago. It had taken a very long time for him to re-establish himself and he never forgot the man who had been responsible for his incarceration. He had watched Gilmore's rise to fame and fortune and vowed that one day, however long it took, he would get even with him. He could wait but he was certain that one day he'd find the right moment to teach Gilmore a lesson he wouldn't forget. The man would pay for every year that he had spent in prison. But now, he had a prize fight to organize.

* * *

Rob and Bonny were ushered into Giles's office by his secretary. There was a quiet air of opulence about the room. It was tastefully furnished, with a couple of paintings on the wall; comfortable chairs were placed in front of a heavily carved walnut desk.

'Please sit down,' Giles invited. He noticed that Bonny looked a trifle perturbed but Rob Andrews sat upright and stiff, ready for battle. Giles hid a smile. 'When I saw the two of you dance in Southampton, I was most impressed,' he began. 'I could see great potential being wasted and was delighted when I heard that Peter Collins had taken you both on to his books. You should be performing in the West End as stars, you *deserve* to be in the West End, and with my help, you will become the public's favourite performers.'

'How do you intend to do this?' asked Rob.

'It has been my aim to produce a musical that will make the theatrical world sit up and take notice. I have the finances to do this, and now with the two of you, I have the stars to front it.'

'Just exactly what have you in mind?' Rob was now becoming interested.

For the next two hours, Giles laid his plans before the two of them. The show was to be a musical spectacular with a host of dancers of the highest calibre, with Rob and Bonny the stars.

Rob could see that without a doubt this show, which Giles had masterminded, would be an incredible theatrical event. 'And who do you have in mind as the musical director?'

'Why you, of course, Rob. Why would I want anyone else? You have the talent, you have a fresh approach, I like your ideas and I'm sure together we can put together a brilliant show.' Giles looked at Rob and thought, *I've got him by the short and curlies!*

Bonny had been sitting listening to the discussion with bated breath. This sounded wonderful. It was more that she had ever imagined. Her name would be in lights over a West End theatre. It was every performer's ambition.

Giles turned to her and asked, 'Well, Bonny my dear, let me hear what you think about all this.'

'It all takes my breath away, to be honest. It sounds almost too good to be true.'

Chuckling, Giles said, 'Believe me, it will be a sensation and so will you. I believe you have even more to show the public than we have seen already.' He turned to Rob. 'I want Bonny to have several solo spots in the show, backed by a great chorus line, so bear that in mind, Rob, when you start to choreograph the dances.' He rang for his secretary. 'Champagne, please, I do believe we have something to celebrate.'

Whilst they all drank to the future with Giles, Rob's mind was in a whirl. He was torn between being a performer and being a dance director . . . The fact that Giles wanted Bonny in several solo spots would give him the extra time he needed to put something spectacular together.

Giles watched Rob with interest; he knew what was going through the man's mind. Rob was an exceptional choreographer and Giles understood how much that meant to him. In Rob's mind, that was what he really loved, it was only Bonny's talent that had put him back on the boards. His ambition was the other side of the footlights and this suited Giles plans beautifully.

As they left Gilmore's office, Rob lifted Bonny off her feet and spun her round, before placing her back on the pavement. Then, to her surprise, he kissed her. 'This is going to be great! Gilmore can take us to the pinnacle of our careers. You have no idea just how lucky we are. Come on, I'll buy you dinner to celebrate.'

Over dinner he enthused even more, telling her he had some superb ideas for the show. 'For once I'll have the finances to do just what I want, and with you as the star, I know we will be successful.'

He took her home in a taxi, walking with her to her front door. He gazed into her eyes and said softly, 'Bonny Burton, you will be the toast of the West End if I have my way,' and he leaned forward and kissed her softly.

As she made her way to her bedroom, Bonny's head was in a whirl. So much had happened today. What with the promise of a starring role in a new production and now . . . Rob kissing her, but not like a dancing partner. Oh no, it was much more than that and she didn't know how to handle it.

* * *

The present show was due to open in four months' time, and now this great opportunity beckoned, Bonny was beside herself with excitement and desperate to share the news with her parents, so on Sunday she took the train to Southampton.

Millie and Frank were delighted to see her and plied her with questions about the rehearsals, her life in London — and her mother queried the food she was given in her digs!

'Oh, Mum! Mrs Gregg looks after us very well. As I told you, Shirley has now moved in, so that's great. But I have some really exciting news to tell you!' And she told them all about Giles Gilmore and his plans for her future.

They were both astonished as Bonny told them all the details.

Millie hugged her daughter. 'That's wonderful, isn't it, Frank?' She turned to her husband. 'Imagine! Our Bonny's name in lights!'

Frank Burton looked somewhat apprehensive. 'It's a very big step for one so young.'

Millie was furious. 'There you go again, blowing cold air on everything instead of being a proud father. What on earth is wrong with you?'

'It's not that, love. But Bonny is so young and this will change her life completely. Fame is a two-edged sword. It brings with it a great deal of responsibility.'

'What do you mean, Dad?'

'You will be in the public eye. Your every move will be watched. You carry the responsibility of the show on your shoulders as the lead. Are you ready for all this, Bonny?'

'To be honest I hadn't thought of it in those terms.'

'Well, don't you think you should before you agree to take it on?'

'I have already agreed. But nothing will change who I am inside. Fame won't go to my head, I can assure you. I've had to work too hard to get where I am and I know that there is even more hard work in front of me. Don't you understand, Dad, that this is exactly what I've been training for?'

'Of course I do. It has come earlier than I expected, that's all. I just think it's a great deal to take on at your tender age.'

Bonny knelt beside her father. 'I do understand your concerns, but you must remember, I am no longer your little girl. I am a grown woman, a dancer, a performer. It's all I live for.'

Putting an arm around her, Frank looked at the concern mirrored in her eyes. 'And you are a talented performer, at that. I am so proud of you, Bonny, but I am still your dad and I worry about you and this life you have entered. Listen, I'm just an old fool, who has never done anything exciting in his life . . . except marry your mother, and that was brave of me.' He smiled wryly.

'Frank Burton! How could you say such a thing?' Millie chided.

'Ah well, Millie love, you were and are a formidable woman. Bonny takes after you.'

'Bloody good job too! If she took after you she wouldn't go anywhere that was different. Think about it. We go to the Isle of Wight for a week's holiday every September and to the social club on a Saturday night. How exciting is that?'

'Now then, you two, enough arguing. Let's put on our coats and go for a walk.'

But that night, when he climbed into bed next to his wife, Frank Burton couldn't help but feel that his daughter was stepping into a world full of difficulties and some danger. He hoped that she would prove him wrong.

CHAPTER TEN

Felix Pearson, a chorus boy in the Peter Collins show that was about to open, was working out at the gym owned by Foxy Gordon. The young good-looking boy liked to keep fit, and as his father and Foxy were old mates, Felix was allowed to come and go as he pleased. He was tall, blonde and had a build that was the envy of every man in the building. He was a talented dancer and took care of his body and his looks, which, apart from his talent, were paramount to his career. No one wanted a chorus boy who was unattractive.

He was also, without knowing it, a good source of gossip about the theatre and what was going on in that world to Foxy, who liked to keep abreast of things, especially if it had anything to do with Giles Gilmore, and today Felix had a juicy bit of gossip to pass on.

The promoter wandered over to the boy, who was working on a rowing machine. 'All right, lad?'

'Fine, thanks, I'm just about to finish. Can you get me four tickets for the big fight? Only I'd like to bring some friends to see it.'

'No problem, Felix. So what's been going on, the rehearsals going well?'

'Yes, thanks. You must come and see the show. We have Rob Andrews the musical director dancing with a fabulous girl called Bonny. They're doing an Astaire–Rogers set of numbers that will knock your socks off . . . and Giles Gilmore is so impressed by them, rumour has it he's bought their contract off Peter Collins for a new show he's producing! It should be fantastic. If you come to the Adelphi to see my show when it opens, you'll see them for yourself. They are terrific together.'

Foxy was more than interested. 'Are you bringing them to the fight?'

'I'm bringing Bonny and her friend Shirley, and a mate of mine, Bryan, another chorus boy. They know I train here and when I told them you had a big fight coming up I suggested they might like to see it.'

'You must introduce me to them after,' said Foxy. 'I'd like to meet this new star and I certainly will be at the show. I'll book the tickets today.' He walked away, pondering over this scrap of gossip, curious to know more about Giles Gilmore's plan for a new show. Gilmore was a wealthy man but he surely must need more backers to spread the cost. It took a great deal of money to finance a show in the West End, and knowing Giles was going to produce it himself, it would be a spectacular. Foxy planned to make a few discreet enquiries.

* * *

At Streatham Town Hall, the crowd were taking their seats, ready for the several bouts of boxing that came before the main event: a middleweight title fight. Foxy's fighter, Mickey O'Halleran, the pride of Ireland, was the favourite to beat battling Joe Granger, a southpaw, who had a few good wins under his belt and was the present holder of the title.

Bonny and Shirley were very excited as this was their first visit to such an event. As they settled in their seats, near the front, Bonny was questioning Felix as to what was about to happen.

He explained that the three judges would mark each round, and at the end the man with the most votes would be the winner. The fanfare sounded for the first bout. Two lightweights were about to enter the ring, and the crowd grew restless watching the men walk from the dressing rooms as they were announced over the loudspeaker by a man in the ring dressed in an evening suit. And soon after, the fight began.

Both Shirley and Bonny chose their favourites and cheered him on and groaned when he was eventually knocked to the floor and counted out. After two more bouts, the crowd waited noisily for the main event to start. The fanfare sounded and the boxers walked into the arena.

The Irishman was first to climb into the ring and as he was introduced; he walked to the centre, held up his gloved hand and saluted the crowd. He caught Bonny's gaze and winked at her. She felt her colour rise. He didn't look at all like a fighter. He was tall, well built, but his handsome face was unblemished. Bonny hoped it wouldn't be disfigured during the fisticuffs that were to follow.

His opponent climbed into the ring and Bonny's heart sank. The man looked a bruiser. His nose was slightly twisted and he had a mean look about him. He didn't walk to the centre of the ring when his name was announced; he just looked around at the crowd with an arrogant stare, as if to say, you came to see me because I'm the best. Bonny took an instant dislike to him.

She turned to Felix and said, 'That man looks a killer.'

'Oh, he's tough all right, but Mickey is a great boxer and skilful. My money's on him.'

Bonny prayed he was right. The referee called the men into the centre of the ring and had a few words with them and they returned to their corner. The bell rang for the first round.

By the fifth round, Bonny was a nervous wreck. Granger was a good boxer with a dangerous left fist, but he was cumbersome, whereas O'Halleran was light on his feet and faster. The two men exchanged punches, all of which counted in the marking,

Felix explained, but as the fight progressed, the Irishman was getting the upper hand and tiring his opponent. One lucky blow to the chin, quickly followed by another, sent Granger to the floor, where the referee stood over him and counted. Bonny held her breath. But at the eighth count, the man rose to his feet. Just then the bell rang for the end of the round.

'Damn!' muttered Felix. 'This break will give him time to recover. Look how the seconds are working on him.'

The men in Granger's corner were fanning their man with a towel, giving him some water to swill his mouth out, which he spat into a bucket, and then he sniffed on some smelling salts as the bell rang for the next round.

The following round was furious. Mickey sensed that he had his man on the run and Granger fought hard knowing he was behind in the fight, but with a sudden jab and a hard punch from the Irishman, Granger was again on the canvas . . . and this time he was counted out.

Felix and the girls jumped to their feet, yelling and clapping as were those around them. The verdict was unanimous in the Irishman's favour. A new middleweight champion was announced. There was a ceremony after, where the Irishman was presented with the Lonsdale belt, which was strapped round his bare torso, and then the boxer was carried on the shoulders by the seconds in his corner, which all added to the excitement of the evening.

After the fight, Felix escorted the girls and his friend to the dressing room of the winner, where the promoter was waiting with his man.

Felix introduced his friends, who shook their hands and introduced them to the new champ. Bonny looked carefully at Mickey's face, which was red and swollen across the eyebrows. She covered her mouth with her hand, thinking how awful it was for such a good-looking man to be so marked.

The fighter looked at her and smiled. 'Don't worry, it's nothing serious. The swelling will go down and the bruises fade.'

'Is it worth being hurt this way?' she asked.

'Boxing is what I do best and this comes with the job. And what do you do best, darlin'?'

'I dance for a living.'

'Now tell me, princess, don't your feet hurt and don't you get bruised in the process?'

She had to smile as she confessed she did.

'And does that ever make you think you'd give it all up?'

'Never!'

'There you go! Now tell me, where do you do this dancing?'

She told him and explained that the show was due to open in a few days.

'Then I shall come and watch you, Bonny.'

Foxy Gordon watched this interchange with a slow smile. O'Halleran had the natural charm of the Irish and he could see that this beautiful young girl was flattered. Well, that suited him. If his boy was interested in her, this could work to his advantage. He would encourage it. 'Come along, people,' he said, 'my boy needs a good massage and a shower, so let's leave him alone.'

Mickey smiled at Bonny. 'Good luck, princess. I'll be at your opening night.'

As they left, Shirley dug her friend in the back. 'Hey, the champ likes you and he's so good-looking. You lucky girl!'

'Don't be daft. He was just being nice, that's all.' But as they walked away she secretly hoped he meant what he said.

* * *

At last it was opening night. Peter Collins was strutting around backstage checking that all was in order — his nerves on edge. He hated first nights. It was exciting but a great worry. There were always a few weak spots that needed to be ironed out, but it would be tonight that the theatre critics took their seats and Peter knew that their reviews the following day could quickly close a show — if they panned it. Not that he expected bad reviews — the rehearsals showed him he should have a success in his hands — but you never could be too sure.

Backstage, the atmosphere was electric. First night nerves affected even the most seasoned performer and the noise in the dressing rooms was like being at a zoo. Rob Andrews soon put a stop to it all. He strode from one dressing room to another and laid down the law.

'Enough of this noise! Settle down and focus. Sit and think of your opening number while you put your make-up on, instead of wasting your breath twittering away like a lot of frenzied monkeys! Enough, do you hear!'

It had the desired affect and a sudden calm descended.

The orchestra could be heard tuning their instruments. 'Overture and beginners please,' came a voice over the loudspeakers. And the show opened.

The house was packed, with not a spare seat to be had. Among the audience, Bernie Cohen, Giles Gilmore, the theatre critics, Mickey O'Halleran and Foxy Gordon sat and watched the opening number.

The first half went well and then after the interval the second half that Rob Andrews had choreographed began. The first number, which featured he and Bonny, was greeted with tumultuous applause, while the final number had the audience on their feet. Shouts of, 'Bravo! Encore!' could be heard.

Rob nodded to the conductor, who, holding his baton, led the orchestra in another number. Rob had anticipated the reaction of the audience and he and Bonny had practised an extra routine. In this finale, the whole cast came on the stage to a rousing number, and when Rob and Bonny finally danced down the staircase in the background, once again the audience were on their feet. One of the front of house staff walked on stage and handed Bonny two sumptuous bouquets. Then the final curtain came down.

Rob picked Bonny up in his arms, kissed her and said, 'Well done, Bonny, you were magnificent. The audience loved you.'

Removing her blonde wig, which after so much exertion was making her feel so hot, she grinned at her partner. 'They loved *us,* Rob, not just me.'

Peter Collins and Dan Mansfield, the other musical director, rushed over and shook Rob by the hand.

'Bloody brilliant job!' Dan enthused. We, my friend, have a hit on our hands.'

Rob laughed. 'I do believe you're right. Your half of the programme was great too. Congratulations!'

'Well done, everybody,' Peter cried. 'Now don't forget we have another show tomorrow, so don't go mad tonight.'

Shirley and Bonny flopped into their chairs in the dressing room that they shared. 'I am completely knackered,' said Bonny, 'but you know, I could do it all over again, it was so great out there.'

'Who sent you the flowers?' asked Shirley.

'Oh my gosh, I forgot to look in all the excitement.' She took the card out of the small envelope of one of the bouquets and read it. *Tonight, a star is born. Congratulations. Giles Gilmore.* She passed it over to her friend.

After reading it, Shirley said, 'He's right, you know. After tonight's performance, your name will become very well known. It will be in all the theatrical columns tomorrow, so you'd better start getting used to it, because your life is going to change.'

'How can you be so sure?'

'I've seen it happen before, but not very often.' She nudged Bonny. 'I'll be able to say, oh, yes, I knew her when she was nothing!' And she burst out laughing. 'Now see who sent the other,' she urged, her curiosity unbowed.

Bonny did so. The card read, *Congratulations, princess. When can I take you out to dinner? Mickey.*

Shirley, who read the card over her friend's shoulder, whispered, 'See, I was right, he fancies you. Will you go?'

Bonny looked at her with shining eyes. 'I think I might just do that.'

There was a knock on the door and then it opened. Mickey O'Halleran stood there, looking resplendent in a dinner jacket, his face, apart from a little yellowing over his eyebrows, looking as handsome as when Bonny had first seen him.

'Well, princess, that was indeed a championship performance if ever I saw one. You were magnificent!'

Bonny was thrilled. 'Did you really think so?'

'Sure I did, and so did every member of the audience. How about letting me take you out to celebrate? We'll go to the Savoy, have a meal and some champagne to drink to your success.'

'I'd love to! But I must get changed first.'

'I'll wait by the stage door for you; don't be too long, I know what you women are like.'

Bonny laughed. 'You forget we dancers are used to quick changes, I promise I won't be long.'

* * *

Foxy Gordon walked out of the Adelphi Theatre deep in thought. He had been in the business of training champions all his life and he knew a winner when he saw one. He wanted a part of the action of these new dancers. They could take the West End by storm, and with Giles Gilmore behind them, there was no limit to how far they could rise. Despite the bitterness he felt about the impresario, Foxy acknowledged the man's impeccable eye for a hit. If there was a way of his getting a share of the new show, he too would make a mint of money, which he was never averse to doing, by whatever means. He pulled out a cigar from his jacket pocket and lit it. Puffing on it as he walked — making plans.

CHAPTER ELEVEN

Rob Andrews changed and decided that he would take Bonny out to celebrate, but when he knocked on the dressing-room door, it was Shirley who opened it.

'I thought I'd take Bonny for a meal,' he said and stepped into the room.

'You're too late; she left a quarter of an hour ago.'

'Left for where?'

'The Savoy, I believe.'

'With whom?' he demanded.

'Mickey O'Halleran.'

'The boxer? I didn't know she knew him.'

'Oh, yes, we were introduced to him after we watched his title fight and he came here tonight to see the show.'

Rob looked around, saw his bouquet — and then the other. He picked up the card that came with it, read it and put it down, turned on his heel and left the room, his face like thunder.

'Oh dearie me,' Shirley muttered, 'he didn't like that.'

Rob left the building, barely acknowledging the stage doorkeeper, who wished him goodnight and congratulated him on the show. As he strode away down the street he asked himself why he felt so angry. After all, Bonny was no more to him than a talented dancer and his partner. But nevertheless, he was furious.

* * *

Bonny, however, was having the time of her life. When she entered the Savoy Grill with Mickey O'Halleran, they were greeted warmly by the maitre d', who led them to a table by the window and made a great fuss of the boxer. 'Congratulations, sir, on a magnificent fight the other night,' the man said.

Mickey thanked him and introduced him to Bonny saying, 'This young lady is going to be a big star. We want a bottle of your best champagne to celebrate her opening night, then we'll look at the menu.'

The Irishman was charming company, Bonny discovered. He told her about his family, how he started boxing, his hopes and dreams for the future and how delighted he was that they had met.

She wasn't sure what she had expected from the man. Probably that he might be loud and maybe a little rough round the edges, after all he was in the fight business, but Mickey was gentle, considerate, with a aura of quiet calm about him. When he spoke of his family it was with a great feeling of responsibility. Through his success, he was able to help them financially, making sure that his parents were comfortable, his siblings behaving. A father figure — which she found endearing. And even in so short a time of making his acquaintance, she found she was more than a little attracted to him.

So enamoured was she that she didn't see Giles Gilmore enter the room, accompanied by Peter Collins.

The two men made their way to the bar before being taken to a table. It was then that Peter saw Bonny and Mickey, deep in conversation. As he sat down he pointed them out to Giles. 'Your young star is enjoying herself.'

Giles looked up from the menu and followed Peter's gaze. He frowned momentarily, then excused himself and walked out of the room, returning a short time later.

'Where did you dash off to?' Peter asked.

'I rang the news desk of several papers to make sure when Bonny leaves here with O'Halleran, she's photographed. It should make the morning papers. After all, the publicity will be good for Bonny. I made sure they knew who she was.'

Collins shook his head and smiled. 'You never miss a trick, do you?'

'Listen, old man, I've got a lot of money invested in that girl and this was a perfect opportunity. I wouldn't be where I am today if I missed it.'

Later, when Bonny and Mickey walked out of the Savoy Hotel, they were met by a barrage of flashing bulbs from the myriad of photographers waiting for them.

'This way, champ. Smile, Miss Burton.' Instructions were called out to them.

Mickey, used to the fame, smiled, talked to the reporters and urged Bonny to do the same.

Eventually, when they climbed into a taxi and escaped, Bonny sighed with relief. 'I wasn't ready for that.'

'Listen, darlin', you must learn to take all the publicity you can and always with a smile. Those boys will treat you well if do the same to them. They can make or break you in the press. It's a double-edged sword.' He smiled and took her hand. 'You'd better get used to it, young lady. It will become part of your life very soon. Tonight was just the beginning.'

As the taxi drew up outside her digs, Mickey helped Bonny out of the car, took her to the door and kissed her gently on the lips. 'Goodnight, princess, I will be in touch very soon.'

'Thank you for a lovely evening and the beautiful flowers,' she said, her head in a whirl.

'It is the first of many, Bonny darlin'. Take care and good luck for tomorrow night. I'll be thinking about you.' And he kissed her again.

When she walked into the sitting room, Shirley was waiting for her. 'Come up to my room and tell me all!' she demanded.

After she had heard all about the evening, Shirley said, 'Rob came looking for you just after you left.'

'What did he want?'

'He wanted to take you out to celebrate, but when I told him he was too late, he looked furious.'

'Whatever for?'

'He read the card that came with Mickey O'Halleran's flowers. He didn't like it one bit! I reckon he fancies you!'

'Don't be so daft. He doesn't think about me like that. You should see us rehearse, he can be a devil. I can assure you he doesn't have any sentimental feelings towards me at all. I'm off to bed now, all this excitement has drained me and we have a show tomorrow.'

But once in bed and alone, Bonny thought of the times Rob had kissed her unexpectedly and she began to wonder if her friend was right.

* * *

Foxy Gordon sat in the saloon bar of a pub in a seedy part of the East End of London. The pub, the Four Feathers, was a meeting place for the boxing fraternity and members of the underworld. It was here that many a crime was planned and the result of a dodgy boxing match decided.

Wally Cole, the leader of the Firm, a collection of the toughest villains in London, was in deep conversation with Foxy, an old schoolmate of his. They were talking over old times. 'Do you remember how we sorted that bastard of a school master, Jim Bradbury, who liked to beat young boys before he took them into the toilets?'

With a wide grin, Foxy thought back. 'He was a wicked bugger. I'll never forget young Derek Green. Poor little sod. Remember how we found him, crouched down in a corner of the gym, hiding behind a stack of matting, crying his eyes out?'

Wally nodded. 'What a state he was in. It took some time before he'd tell us what had happened.'

'I remember it very clearly and I remember you told him it would never happen again. And it didn't.'

Putting his head back, Wally roared with laughter. 'I'll never forget the look on old Bradbury's face when we caught him coming out of the bog. Especially when we pushed him back inside the cubical and shoved his head down the lavatory bowl and pulled the chain. He thought he was going to drown.'

'That was nothing to his shriek of pain when you squeezed his nuts.'

Both men chortled at their recollections.

'I wonder if the Head was surprised when he resigned?'

'I wonder what excuse he gave?'

'Whatever it was, it was better than waiting for us to tell his wife what he'd been up to, as you threatened to do.'

Foxy grinned. 'I told her anyway.'

'I never knew that!'

'I didn't see why his resignation should let him off the hook. I took young Derek Green round to see her. I made him tell her what happened. Why do you think she left him?'

'I wasn't aware that she did.'

'Oh yes, that woman has some spirit. She was so shocked and disgusted she threatened that if he ever tried for another teaching job, she'd spill the beans about him, so in the end he lost his wife, his home and his livelihood. Serves the bugger right!'

Wally ordered more drinks. 'If only our troubles could be so easily solved these days, eh?'

Foxy asked, 'You got some sort of problem?'

'Some new young shaver on the block is trying to flex his muscles, that's all. It happens. He'll be sorted by the weekend.'

Foxy knew better than to ask how.

The conversation turned to boxing. 'Your lad O'Halleran put up a good fight in his last bout. I won a bundle on him.' Wally looked pleased with himself. 'Who's he up against next?'

'I've got a couple of irons in the fire, but as yet nothing has been decided.'

‘Ah well, he’ll be the favourite to win whoever he meets. No money to be made there — unless, of course, he should lose.’ Wally stared hard at the promoter.

‘Knock it off,’ said Foxy. ‘I went down for the last fight that was thrown. I’m legit these days. I’ve got a world contender on my hands and nothing will get in the way of that!’

‘If you change your mind, let me know,’ said the villain as he got up from the table.

Foxy lit a cigarette and drew deeply on it. The hackles at the back of his neck were bristling. Wally Cole never made an idle suggestion. Gordon knew that he’d be back in the future, sometime, to persuade him to his way of thinking. It made his blood run cold at the thought. Cole was not a man to be crossed, but Foxy had great plans for his fighter and no one was going to screw that up.

CHAPTER TWELVE

On his way to rehearsal, Rob Andrews called into the newsagent to buy his morning paper, as was his habit. He was more than surprised to see pictures of Bonny and Mickey O'Halleran on the front pages of several editions, alongside the national news. He bought copies of three different papers.

Giles Gilmore sat at his desk with all the nationals featuring his new star laid out before him. He sat reading them with a self satisfied smile.

Foxy Gordon also smiled as he read the articles featuring his champion with the up-and-coming young dancing star. This was working out just as he had hoped.

But by far the most excited by the news was Shirley. She spotted the photographs walking along with Bonny on their way to the theatre. 'Bloody hell, Bonny, look! You're on the front pages of the daily papers!' And she rushed inside the newsagent's, emerging minutes later with several in her arms. The girls stopped to read what the headlines said:

IRISH CHAMPION ON THE TOWN WITH MAJOR NEW DANCING STAR.

Shirley continued to read. '"*Mickey O'Halleran was seen leaving the Savoy Grill with Bonny Burton, the new star of the latest*

West End musical, Let's Dance. He says she will be the next sensation in the West End theatre." Blimey!'

Overcome with embarrassment, Bonny said, 'Well, he's Irish. You know what they're like. They all have the gift of the gab. Come on or we'll be late for rehearsal and then Rob Andrews will be angry with us.'

* * *

Rob was in a foul mood. He put the chorus through stringent rehearsals, tightening up their routines, and then called Bonny up on stage to go through a couple of numbers with her and the full assembly.

He was relentless in his execution of the steps, berating Bonny constantly — until she suddenly stormed off the stage.

There was a deadly silence and then Rob went rushing after her, yelling at the top of his voice. 'How dare you walk out of one of my rehearsals without my permission?'

Bonny turned on him. 'And how dare you speak to me like that in front of everyone, making me look an idiot when there is nothing wrong with my dancing?' She walked into her dressing room, slamming the door in his face.

He burst in. 'Just because your picture is in every newspaper with that Irish mauler doesn't make you a star yet. You still have a *very* long way to go!'

Eyes blazing, Bonny looked scornfully at him. 'That's what this is all about, isn't it? There's nothing wrong with my dancing, oh no, it's because I was seen out with Mickey O'Halleran. Well, Mr mighty Andrews, what I do in my own time has nothing at all to do with you!'

'It has everything to do with me. You're my partner; we are starring in this show. We have to be very careful of our public image.'

She bristled with indignation. 'My being with Mickey, who I might say is a perfect gentleman, will do absolutely nothing harmful to my image, as you call it. For your information, he knows how to treat the press, they love him. And they were very nice to me, treated me with respect, which is more than I can say about my musical director and dancing partner.'

Rob realized he had gone too far but he was still angry. 'Well, are you coming back to rehearse or not? We still have work to do.'

'As long as you are reasonable — but be *very* careful.' Bonny swept past him and along the corridor to the stage.

The cast, waiting with breathless anticipation, wondered what was going to happen next, but Rob continued, still being a hard taskmaster but without nagging Bonny.

As they left the theatre, Shirley tucked her arm through her friend's and asked, 'What was all that about back there then? We were all flabbergasted when you stormed off.'

'Bloody Rob Andrews! What it really boils down to is that he was furious about me being out with Mickey. As if it's any of his business . . . and I told him so.'

Shirley was triumphant. 'There! Didn't I tell you? He fancies you.'

Bonny, still a bit fraught, was in no mood to hear this. 'Don't you dare start that again, Shirley, or you and I will certainly fall out!'

* * *

The show was doing well, playing to packed houses, and Peter Collins had been approached about doing a special charity show on a Sunday. He was very enthusiastic about this, as it would be attended by many of the stars of the West End, and VIPs too, which would be great publicity. It was to be a red carpet affair and all the national press would certainly be in attendance.

The cast of *Let's Dance* were thrilled by the prospect. Jack Buchanan had booked seats for a party of friends, Noel Coward was said to be coming as well, and Peter had arranged for an after-show party to be held at the Cafe Royal in Regent Street.

It was a reasonably balmy September evening on the night of the charity show. The red carpet was laid, waiting for the guests to arrive, spotlights were erected, the press were out in full force, and backstage the air of excitement was tangible.

Cars started to arrive. One of the first contained Jack Buchanan, who stepped out of the vehicle, resplendent in evening dress, accompanied by Elsie Randolph, in a glamorous gown, with a fur cape around her shoulders and wearing sparkling jewellery.

The press went wild. 'This way, Jack. Smile, Miss Randolph.'

Ralph Reader of the *Gang Show* joined the stars on the carpet, as did Noel Coward, who smiled and waved to the crowd. But the biggest cheer was for Mickey O'Halleran, accompanied by Foxy Gordon, the fight promoter.

'Going to watch your girlfriend dance, champ?' called a cheeky reporter.

The boxer grinned broadly. 'Sure, where else would I be? She was born to dance. The girl's a sensation, mark my words.'

'Are we going to see a wedding in the near future, Mickey?' called another.

O'Halleran just pointed to the reporter. 'Now then, don't be naughty!' And he walked towards the entrance, signing autographs for his fans as he did so.

Giles Gilmore and Bernie Cohen, the talent scout, arrived together. Giles spent time with the press, giving them good copy for their morning columns, telling them about the new show he would be producing, starring Bonny Burton. He made no mention of Rob Andrews.

At the final curtain, the applause was thunderous. Bouquets were carried on to the stage for Bonny — so many that a stagehand came on to help carry them off.

As she walked back to her dressing room, Bonny was in a state of euphoria. The show had been a great success and the routines with Rob had gone really well. Now she had to get changed for the party. Before she could do so, there was a knock on her door. When she opened it, she was astonished to see Jack Buchanan standing there.

'Hello, Bonny. We meet again.'

'Mr Buchanan,' was all she could manage to say.

'I just wanted you to know how much I enjoyed your dancing, and later at the party I may not have the opportunity. You have a great future ahead of you, my dear. Enjoy it, and who knows? Maybe we can dance together on stage one day.' He took her hand and kissed it, smiled and walked away.

Bonny was flabbergasted. One of the biggest stars in the West End wanted to dance with her! As she made to close the door, Mickey O'Halleran appeared. He picked her up in his strong arms and swung her round. 'Well, darlin', you wowed the audience out there tonight and I'm going to escort you to the party before some other man comes to claim you.' And he kissed her. 'Bonny, I'm so proud of you. You were a sensation.'

She was by now completely flustered but thrilled by his praise. 'Do you really think so?'

'I know so. Now go and get changed, I'll wait out here for you.'

Her heart aflutter with all the excitement, Bonny closed the door. Giles Gilmore had sent her to a high-class store to buy a dress for the occasion. He had told her, 'You must look the star you are. Tonight you will be the centre of attention and I want you looking fabulous, as a star should be.'

She took down the dress. It was the softest green, which complimented her auburn hair and green eyes. The style looked simple, but the cut of the material meant it fitted her like a glove. And Giles had hired a necklace and matching earrings of emerald and diamonds for the night, which highlighted the whole ensemble. She brushed her hair, wearing it loose, which only accentuated her youth and good looks. Draping a matching stole over her shoulders, she emerged from the dressing room.

Mickey let out a long low whistle. 'Princess, you look good enough to eat. Let's go.'

As they walked along the corridor, Rob Andrews emerged from his dressing room. 'Bonny, I was just coming to collect you.'

'Sorry, sport, but Bonny already has an escort,' Mickey said and, taking her arm, walked on.

* * *

That night, the Cafe Royal was the venue for the best impromptu performance of the year. Noel Coward sat at the piano and entertained the guests with some of his witty songs, Jack Buchanan sang with the orchestra, Jessie Mathews also sang, and when the dancing began, Jack Buchanan asked Bonny to dance. 'Just in case we never have the opportunity to do this together on the stage,' he said.

Bonny stood up and took his arm. 'My mother will never believe this,' she said.

Jack laughed. 'Dear Bonny, don't ever change. This business can ruin people, I've seen it happen. You are a complete delight; I wouldn't like to see that happen to you.'

'If you do see that happening, give me a quick kick in the shins, will you?' she teased.

'I promise. How is your mother? Did she get the photograph I sent to her?'

'Yes, thank you, she did. It is in a special frame by her bed. I'm surprised that you remembered,' she said in astonishment.

'Really? Don't ever neglect your fans, my dear, or believe me they will soon forget you.'

At the end of the extraordinary evening, Mickey escorted Bonny home. As they drove in the taxi, he took her hand in his. 'You are very special to me, princess. I hope that we will be seeing a lot of each other in the future.'

'I'd like that,' she told him.

'Perhaps next Sunday we can spend a quiet day together. Are you free?'

With a look of disappointment she said, 'I have promised to go to see my parents in Southampton.'

'How about I come with you?'

Her eyes lit up. 'Really? My dad would love that, he's a great fight enthusiast,' she told him.

'Right. I'll be in touch.' And he kissed her, at first gently and then with a mounting passion that took her breath away.

'Goodnight, princess,' he said and climbed back into the taxi.

* * *

Foxy Gordon was feeling very pleased with himself as he journeyed home. He had managed to invest a chunk of money in Giles Gilmore's new production. He'd used a nom de plume in which to do so. Giles would be completely unaware that the man he sent to prison was now a major shareholder in his new venture.

CHAPTER THIRTEEN

Bonny and Mickey took the train to Southampton on the following Sunday morning. Bonny had written to her mother warning her of the visit and that she was bringing a friend to lunch, without saying who it was. She had planned to take her parents out to eat, but Mickey had said he was looking forward to some home cooking, so she had shelved the idea.

'I start training next week,' Mickey told her, 'so this will be my last chance to eat a family meal.'

'Have you another fight lined up then?'

'Nothing's finalized, but nevertheless, I have to be prepared. I intend to hang on to my title for as long as possible.'

'My dad is going to be so surprised when I walk in with you. He listens to all the big fights on the wireless.'

'Maybe I can take him to his local for a beer before lunch and then we can have a chat about boxing. Do you think he'd like that?'

'Are you kidding? To walk into his local with you would be the biggest thrill of his life!'

Laughing, Mickey said, 'Then that's what we'll do.'

They took a taxi from the station and when they arrived at Bonny's home, she let herself in calling out as she did so.

'Mum, Dad, we're here!'

Frank Burton walked out of the living room to greet his daughter. 'Bonny!' he said. Then he saw who she was with. 'Bloody hell!' he exclaimed.

Mickey held out his hand and shook Frank's. 'Hello, Mr Burton. I'm delighted to meet you.'

Frank was speechless.

'Close your mouth, Dad, or you'll catch a fly in it,' Bonny teased.

'Millie! Millie!' Frank called. 'Look who our Bonny has brought with her.'

Eventually the excitement died down, introductions were made and both Mickey and Bonny were delighted when they saw that Millie had framed one of the pictures from the newspaper, showing them both together, coming out of the Savoy.

'Sure, that was a great night.' Mickey told them. 'You have a very talented daughter, I'm certain you know that.'

'Indeed we do,' Millie assured him. 'We are going up to London soon to see the show for ourselves.'

'You haven't been yet?' Mickey was surprised. 'We can't have that. You must come as my guests. I'll book tickets, then after we'll go out for a meal and celebrate together! How will that be?'

Bonny's parents looked thrilled, and so it was arranged. But Frank Burton's day was made when Mickey suggested that whilst the two ladies prepared the lunch and caught up on each other's news, he and Frank should go to the local and down a couple of beers.

When they were alone, Millie looked speculatively at her daughter. 'The young Irishman is a nice chap, isn't he? Is this serious between you?'

'Mum! We've only just met . . . but I do like him. He's kind and gentle, not at all what you would expect from a man in his position. After all, boxing is such a rough, tough sport. It can be quite brutal. I know; I've been to one and seen for myself.'

'And what does your dance partner think about it?'

Bonny's tone sharpened. 'This has nothing at all to do with him. Rob Andrews and I have a purely business arrangement and that's all.'

Millie decided to leave it there, but she wondered at the sudden hostility in Bonny's voice and came to the conclusion that Rob Andrews was not at all happy about the arrangement.

* * *

The day was soon over. Frank had arrived back from his local with Mickey, walking like a man who was ten-foot tall.

'You should have seen the look on the people in the pub when I walked in with the champ!' he crowed. 'They couldn't have been more surprised if I had walked in with the King George V himself.'

Mickey winked at Bonny. 'Nice crowd,' he said.

'Mickey bought everyone a drink,' Frank told them.

'I need the fans,' the Irishman joked.

On the way home on the train, Mickey put his arm round Bonny. 'That was such a lovely day, princess; thanks for letting me share it with you. I miss my family, so it was nice to be with yours.'

'Thank you, Mickey, my dad will dine out on that day for years to come and Mum is thrilled to think you sat at her table and ate her food. You gave them both a great deal of pleasure.'

He tipped up her chin and softly kissed her. 'And you give me a great deal of pleasure. I'm going to be tied up for a bit with my training, as we have a camp in Buckinghamshire, but I'll contact you as often as I can. I don't want you to forget about me.'

She gazed into his eyes and caressed his face. 'I certainly won't do that, I promise.'

'I'll be back, anyway, to take your parents to the theatre, just keep those stage-door Johnnies away. Tell them you have a big Irishman as a boyfriend, who'll punch their lights out if they bother you!'

And when eventually Bonny's parents joined Mickey as his guests, for a visit to the theatre as was planned, the papers were full of the event, complete with pictures of Mickey, his arm around Bonny and her parents, beaming happily beside them, with many a suggestion that love was in the air for the two young people, which didn't please Giles or Rob — but delighted Foxy Gordon.

Giles frowned when he saw the pictures. This was not the kind of publicity he wanted for his blossoming star. He had great plans for Bonny Burton and there was no room in them for a boyfriend. He needed her to be totally focused on a career. There was a lot of work to do after this show finished its run and her time would be fully occupied with rehearsals. The champ would have to take a back seat, or fade away altogether — if he had his way.

As for Rob Andrews, he was surprised by the feeling of jealousy and possessiveness that overcame him as he gazed at the pictures. He had discovered Bonny. He was the one who had set her on the road to success and now this good-looking boxer was moving in on her. If she truly wanted to be a star, she would have to dump Mickey O'Halleran!

* * *

In an old barn in a farmyard, outside of London, young Charlie Black, one of Foxy Gordon's up-and-coming boxers, was watching a dog fight avidly. He had his last money riding on the outcome and his luck had deserted him tonight. The two bull terriers in the man-made ring were tearing at each other, teeth barred, blood spilling out as one dog eventually caught the other by the throat. The shrieks of pain from the injured animal only fired the enthusiasm and bloodlust of those watching, and they called out to their favoured dog. Not one of them had any sympathy for the animals involved. Least of all the bookmaker, in whose hand was a fist full of notes from the bets that had been laid.

Charlie watched as the fight ended and the dead animal was removed. He was livid and tore his ticket into shreds, heeling the pieces into the ground.

Wally Cole walked up to him. 'Not lucky tonight then, young Charlie?'

The boy shook his head. 'How's my credit, Wally? Can you give me a bit more?'

The man smiled and patted his shoulder. 'It's always good with me. I'll tell the bookmaker to give you some leeway.' And he walked away.

Charlie was aware that he was doing wrong. Foxy knew about his weakness for gambling and had been adamant that to be part of his team of fighters, he had to be clean, and Charlie had given his word, but the lure of an illegal dog fight had been too much of a temptation.

This was on top of the poker school, also run by Wally Cole, every Tuesday in the back room of a pub in the East End of London. Charlie owed a huge amount of money there too. He was not a good poker player, making wild bets on poor hands and getting trounced by experienced players.

A week later, when Charlie once again came to play cards, Wally made his move. 'Come into my office, lad, I need to have a word.'

Once there, Wally sat at his desk and told the boy to sit opposite him. 'Now, Charlie boy, you are into me for a lot of money — and it can't go on.'

Charlie's heart sank. 'I know, Wally, but I'll pay you back, I promise.'

'They all say that. I don't think you know just how much you are in to me for.'

The lad had no idea. 'How much?'

Wally referred to the accounts book before him. 'Two hundred quid for the dog fights, and five here at the poker school. That's seven hundred nicker in all. Now, how on earth are you going to cover that amount?'

Charlie's heart was racing. He had no way of paying what he owed. He knew that, so did Wally Cole, and Charlie also knew what happened to those who tried to welsh on the criminal. He felt sick!

'Now, I can see you're worried about this, but there is a way out.' The gang leader smiled, but his eyes were ice cold.

'There is?' stammered Charlie.

'You've got a fight lined up in two weeks' time, haven't you?'

Charlie nodded.

'Is the fighter any real competition?'

Shaking his head, the young boxer said, 'No way. The fight shouldn't last more than a few rounds.'

'Wrong!' snapped Wally. 'You will make sure it lasts a good time, and then in round six — you hit the canvas.'

'I can't do that, Foxy would kill me!'

'If you don't . . . *I'll* kill you.' The tone was deadly and Charlie knew that this was no joke.

The gangster continued: 'You will make it look good to allay any suspicions, but you will throw the fight and then we wipe your slate clean. You will have paid your debt.'

Charlie staggered out of the pub, his mind reeling after agreeing to Wally Cole's plan. He had no choice, he knew that, but what effect would this have on his future? He would *have* no future if Foxy found out. As it was, it would be difficult to fool the promoter. Despite the gambling, Charlie had trained well, and he knew that his opponent had little chance against him. Although in the past, the man had been a good fighter, he was now over the hill in boxing terms, but good enough to give Charlie experience in the ring.

* * *

The fight took place on a Sunday night and the venue was packed. All of Foxy's members were there to watch and cheer their man on, including Mickey O'Halleran and Bonny

Burton. There was a big crowd waiting in anticipation, although the result was almost a certainty, but young Charlie Black was a fighter to watch for the future and had a lot of money riding on him, despite the odds being poor. For the punters, he was a sure bet.

In the dressing room, Charlie Black sat as Foxy gave him his instructions whilst massaging his shoulders, and one of the seconds put on the boy's gloves.

'What's the matter with you, Charlie?' asked Foxy, pressing his fingers into the boy's flesh. 'You are so tense. For goodness' sake, relax! After all, this man is no real threat if you remember what I taught you. You should walk it tonight. But let it go a few rounds before you finish it — give the crowd a bit of a show.'

Charlie felt his heart sink, knowing what he had to do.

He made his entrance, shadow-boxing, giving the crowd what it wanted, and climbed into the ring and stood in his corner. As he waited, his second put the gum shield in his mouth, and Charlie looked out at the audience and saw Wally Cole sitting in the front row. The gangster just stared at him, his face expressionless, and Charlie felt his blood run cold.

Further along the front row, Mickey O'Halleran was telling Bonny about the prowess of the young boxer. 'He's a great hope for British boxing,' he told her.

'Is he going to be hurt?' Bonny asked nervously.

'No, he's too good and his opponent is really at the end of his career. Don't worry, princess, there'll be no blood spilt tonight,' he said, and he held her hand to reassure her.

The referee called the two men together in the middle of the ring and spoke to them, and then they returned to their respective corners. The bell rang for the first round.

The older boxer came out strongly, trying to show that he wasn't the loser they all thought he was and Charlie let him get in a couple of blows to the body before retaliating, but pulling his punches. If he put the man down he'd be in a hell of a mess.

Foxy, watching from Charlie's corner, wasn't concerned at this point — after all, young Charlie was just following orders — but when it came to the end of round four, he stepped into the ring, gave Charlie a swig of water and said, 'Right, lad, take him out in this round.'

Out of the corner of his eye, Charlie saw Wally's eyes narrow as he looked at him and the man, maybe anticipating what Foxy was saying, slowly, shook his head and unobtrusively held up the five fingers of one hand and a single digit of the other. Six in all.

The bell went for round five.

Charlie Black danced around the ring throwing punches, but still allowing the other man to land a few to the chin, which he rode, so as not to be hurt. He kept his eyes focused on his opponent, gauging the oncoming blows, but at the end of the round when he went back to his corner, Foxy was absolutely livid.

'What bloody game are you playing at, lad? You could have taken him out at any time in that round.'

'Sorry, boss, I thought I'd give the punters one more round. I'll do it after the bell, I promise.'

Picking up the slop bucket and towels, Foxy climbed out of the ring. 'I should bloody well think so!'

Mickey O'Halleran was suddenly quiet as he watched the sixth round. There was something going on with young Charlie Black tonight and it didn't make sense. As the bell rang and the boxers faced each other, Mickey saw Wally Cole sit up straight in his ringside seat and saw the grim expression on his face.

As the round progressed, Mickey's frown deepened. Charlie had so many chances to floor his opponent but he ignored them all. It didn't make any sense.

Charlie, carefully watching the other man, saw that he was about to take a wild swing at him and deliberately walked into the flying fist. He staggered and the other fighter had the experience to follow this up with several more blows to the head.

Slowly Charlie Black sank to the canvas and was counted out.

The crowd was aghast. Mickey quickly looked across at Wally Cole and noted the smile of satisfaction on his face as he rose, left his seat and walked out of the hall.

CHAPTER FOURTEEN

There was pandemonium in Charlie Black's dressing room. Foxy Gordon was reading the riot act to his young boxer. 'What the bloody hell were you playing at out there? You could have taken that has-been at any time, yet you walked into a right hook that a blind man could see was coming!'

'I just lost concentration for a minute,' Charlie murmured as his gloves were being removed.

'Lost concentration! You lost your bloody marbles, that's what you lost!'

Mickey and Bonny entered the room and heard the caustic comments. When Foxy saw Mickey he continued his tirade. 'Did you see what happened out there?'

'I did,' Mickey said quietly, looking at Charlie, who refused to meet his gaze.

'Then perhaps *you* can explain it to me, because I'm damned if I know.'

'Come on, Foxy, give the lad a break. These things happen sometimes.'

'Not after my training, they don't! What a bloody waste of my time.' He stormed out of the room, slamming the door shut behind him.

'Get dressed,' Mickey told Charlie Black. 'You and I are going to have a serious talk. I'll wait for you.' Turning to Bonny he said, 'I'm sorry about this, princess. I was going to take you out to dinner but do you mind if we go somewhere quiet with this young man instead?'

'No, of course not.' Bonny wasn't at all sure what was going on but she realized that something significant was amiss.

There was a small crowd waiting outside when Mickey, Charlie and Bonny left the building, and to Bonny's consternation there was an outcry and a lot of booing. The feeling of hostility was frightening, and as the crowd began to jostle them, Mickey tightened his hold on her as they made their way to a waiting car and climbed in, followed by Charlie Black.

To Bonny's great relief, the irate mob parted as the driver moved slowly forward, but one or two angry men banged on the windows as they passed. Flash bulbs went off as several reporters held up their cameras to capture the scene.

'Sorry about this, princess,' said Mickey as they drove away. 'This kind of publicity isn't good for you.'

It was the last thing on her mind and she said so.

Mickey told the driver to take them to a hotel he knew of. 'At least there we will have some privacy,' he said. 'The press have all the pictures they need for their editions.' He looked across at Charlie Black, but he said nothing, his gaze downcast. His shoulders hunched.

Mickey settled them in a quiet corner of the residents' lounge and ordered some drinks. Then he looked at Charlie. 'Right. Talk to me. Tell me what's going on.'

'Nothing's going on,' the young boxer stammered.

Mickey didn't raise his voice but he was insistent. 'Don't lie to me, Charlie. I saw the look on Wally Cole's face when you hit the canvas. He's behind all this, isn't he?'

The young man went white. 'I don't know what you mean.'

'For God's sake, Charlie I'm trying to help you here, and how can I do so when you won't level with me?' He paused.

'Have you been gambling again? Is that what all this is about? Are you into that bastard for a lot of money? Because nothing else makes any sense.'

Charlie Black crumbled. Fighting back the tears he said, 'I owed him seven hundred pounds and he said if I threw the fight it would clear my debt.' He looked at Mickey, his eyes full of fear. 'He said he'd kill me if I didn't!'

'Jaysus!' Mickey put his hand to his head. 'Why in the blazes didn't you come to me and tell me what was going down?'

'I was too scared to tell anyone. What's going to happen to me now, Mickey?'

Bonny watched the interchange, horrified by what she heard.

'I don't know, my son. You have betrayed Foxy, the one man who took you in, who gave you a chance. Even if he knew the truth, how could he ever trust you again?'

'I've been such a fool, but I was so scared. I didn't have a choice.'

'The hell you did! You made that choice when you started gambling again.' Mickey was furious. 'Not only that, you've tarnished the sport of boxing. You heard the crowd. They realized you threw the fight. You lose their trust; you'll never get it back. You had a great career ahead of you and you threw it all away tonight!'

Bonny leaned forward. 'Can't you do anything?' she asked Mickey.

'I'm not sure that I can.' Looking at Charlie he said, 'You realize I'll have to tell Foxy.' As Charlie started to protest, Mickey said, 'You owe him the truth, at least. What he'll do about it I don't know, but he has to be told. If Wally got to you, maybe he will want to make another financial killing with another fighter, and we certainly can't have that.'

Eventually, Mickey ordered a taxi to take the boy home and another for himself and Bonny. In the back of the vehicle he put his arm around her and apologized for getting her involved with tonight's proceedings. 'I'm worried about the publicity, darlin', you saw the crowd. The press will have a field day tomorrow and your picture will be in all the papers for the wrong reasons. I wouldn't have had this happen to you for all the world.'

She caught hold of his hand. 'I'm more worried about young Charlie Black. He said that man, Wally something, threatened to kill him. Was he being serious?'

'I'm afraid so. Wally Cole is a dangerous man. I don't know how he's kept out of prison. Had Charlie not carried out his orders, then he'd have been found floating in the Thames . . . unless he'd had the sense to tell Foxy about it. That was his only way out, but I guess the kid was more scared of Wally than of his manager.'

* * *

The following day, the pictures of the two boxers and Bonny leaving the venue, surrounded by an angry mob, was front-page news. When Giles Gilmore saw it he was livid! What the bloody hell was the girl thinking of? All publicity was supposed to be good publicity, but this, with the accompanying story with suspicions of fight rigging, was not what his star should be involved with. He would have to do something to counteract the fallout. But first he would have to talk to Bonny herself and find out exactly what this was all about and how she got entangled. He drove to the theatre.

Bonny was sitting in Rob's office, listening to his fury when he'd read the papers. He flung one down in front of her. 'Look at it! My God, how could you get yourself involved in such a mess?'

'It wasn't my fault,' she protested. 'Mickey was only trying to help one of his friends who was in trouble!'

'Mickey O'Halleran again! Well, it seems to me the sooner you stop seeing him the better.'

'How dare you tell me how to run my life!'

'I dare because what happens to you reflects on the show and on me as your dance partner. You need the public's support if you are to become a star. They won't tolerate you if there is a whiff of scandal around you.'

At that moment, Giles Gilmore strode into the room. 'Rob's absolutely right!' he snapped. 'We have to do something to counteract this.' He paced up and down.

* * *

In the gym, Mickey and Charlie were ensconced with Foxy Gordon in his office, where Mickey was explaining to the trainer what had happened the previous night and why.

Foxy glared at the culprit. 'How could you let me down like this? You gave me your word that your gambling days were behind you.'

'I'm really sorry, Foxy. What will happen to me now?'

'You'll have to appear in front of the boxing commission. They will have to look into these accusations. You are finished in the fight game, son. There's nothing I can do, and frankly, I could never trust you again.'

'I can't tell them about Wally Cole. I'll be a dead man if I do.'

With a shrug, the trainer said coldly, 'That will be your choice. As for me, I wash my hands of you. You had the chance to really make something of yourself, and you threw it all away, now you will pay the price. Collect your stuff from the locker room.'

When the boy had left them alone, Foxy swore. 'That bloody Wally Cole! I'm going to have a few words with him. I will not have him mucking about with my fighters. This is my livelihood and theirs. I'll make sure the bugger keeps clear in future or I'll shop him myself.'

'You have no proof,' Mickey said.

'Charlie Black is my proof. I'll persuade him to tell the truth.'

'He'll be too scared.'

'We'll see about that. Once he realizes his career is finished, maybe he'll see he has to pay Wally back. The kid loves boxing. It was his life until he started gambling. I'm sure he'll come good at the right time.'

Mickey was doubtful and said so.

But the following morning, the body of Charlie Black was fished out of the Thames, and the proof Foxy needed died with him.

CHAPTER FIFTEEN

The death of the young boxer made the front pages again. There was to be an autopsy, of course, but the general consensus of opinion was that Charlie Black had taken his own life. Mickey O'Halleran and Foxy Gordon thought otherwise, but their hands were tied without proof.

'Poor little sod,' said the champ. 'He didn't stand an earthly, did he?'

'Now you listen to me, Mickey. He had the best chance in the world. He had the makings of a world-class boxer; it was his gambling that ruined it all and that was down to him!'

'I can't believe you are so heartless. Don't you have any pity at all for him?'

'No! To get anywhere in this game you have to be ruthless. I've no time for losers.'

'Well, I will be at his funeral when the time comes. Gambling is a sickness, Foxy, and he just wasn't strong enough to fight it.'

'You'd be better off getting back to your training than wasting time worrying about Charlie,' snapped the trainer.

'You don't have to worry about me, but I do worry about you, Foxy. A man without compassion is a sad person.' And Mickey rose from his seat and left the room.

* * *

Bonny read the news of Charlie Black's demise with a heavy heart. She had felt a great deal of sympathy for him, listening to him and Mickey talk. The fact that he said he feared for his life made her wonder if his death was indeed suicide, as was rumoured, or something far more sinister, and she realized she had inadvertently become involved with dangerous people.

Giles Gilmore called a press conference to explain that his star had just happened to be at Charlie Black's last fight, purely by chance, and had nothing to do with the young fighter whose death was such a sad loss to boxing.

He parried questions about her being seen with Mickey O'Halleran so often, and was there an engagement in the offing?

'Certainly not! Miss Burton is far too busy to be seriously involved with anyone, now and in the future!' He then called an end to any more questions.

After, he had a talk with Bonny and told her that hopefully he'd stemmed any fall from grace for her from the public, but no way was she to contemplate going to the funeral of the young boxer, as the press would be out in force. 'I do not want to see further pictures of you that involve you in any way with this whole mess. Do you understand?'

'Yes, totally, but don't you feel sorry for the young man?'

'He's not my business but you are. His career is over, yours is just starting, you'd be wise to remember that!'

* * *

As Giles predicted, the funeral was covered in all the newspapers. The coroner had brought in a verdict of accidental death, which had allowed the Black family to bury their young son. True to his word, Mickey O'Halleran was at the funeral, as was Foxy Gordon as the boy's manager. The two of them hardly spoke. Both gave separate interviews after the funeral, saying the boy had been a rising star with great potential, and how sad they were at the loss to boxing, and expressing their condolences to the family.

After the funeral, Foxy Gordon made a visit to the Four Feathers pub in the East End of London, where he knew he'd find Wally Cole.

He walked up to the bar and ordered a large brandy. Glancing around he saw Wally seated with a couple of his hard men, and picking up his glass, he walked over to the gang leader.

Wally gazed at the promoter. 'Hello, Foxy. How are you?'

Foxy returned his gaze and coldly remarked, 'I was surprised not to see you at young Black's funeral this morning.'

Cole's eyes narrowed. 'Why would I be there? I didn't know the boy.'

Foxy sat beside the man. 'Now, we both know that to be a lie. He was a regular at your poker school and your dog fights. He was into you for a bundle.'

The villain just raised his eyebrows but didn't comment.

'But, of course, he settled his debt when he hit the canvas in the sixth round, didn't he?'

'Did he?'

Foxy felt his anger rising. He knew he had to tread carefully, but he was here to make a point and make it he would. 'Don't arse about with me, Wally. You had that lad over a barrel. He was too terrified of you to come to me and tell me what was happening — until it was too late. How convenient that he went into the Thames!'

'Convenient for whom?' asked Cole with a smirk. 'Certainly not for him. Such a waste of talent, don't you think?'

Foxy could hardly contain himself. He wanted to swipe the smile off the man's face, but he knew to do so at this moment would be hazardous. But he too had come up the hard way and was no slouch.

He glared at Cole. 'You just keep away from any of my boys in the future or I'll have you, I give you my word! You will forever be looking over your shoulder — wondering when.'

Knowing Foxy as well as he did — after all, they had grown up together — Wally Cole knew that this was no idle threat. But he couldn't be seen to be backing down by his men. 'How's the champ's training going?'

Foxy rose to his feet. 'Just remember what I said.' He downed his drink, put the glass on the table and walked out of the bar. He then made his way to his gym, changed into a loose pair of trousers and a singlet and worked through his anger with a punchbag.

* * *

Mickey and Bonny didn't meet again for some time, as he was in training and she was appearing in the closing weeks of the show, which was still being performed to packed houses.

The atmosphere between Bonny and Rob had been somewhat cool for a few days after the scandal, but as time wore on, their love of the dance and the theatre brought them closer together once again, and they relished the performance and the adoration of their audience, who gave them a standing ovation each night as the final curtain fell.

The photographs in the papers were now of the two of them, appearing at various prestigious venues. Always together and smiling. All arranged, of course, by Giles Gilmore, but thoroughly enjoyed by Rob.

The press had a field day. *Has the champ lost his lady?* printed one paper. And others headlined in a similar vein.

When once Bonny protested, fed up with the public speculation about her love life, and said she'd rather have an early night and go to bed, Giles snapped at her. 'Once you are established, you can. At the moment I'm building you for stardom. Keeping you in the public's eye. It's necessary!'

Rob was happy because O'Halleran was out of the picture. What he didn't know was that flowers arrived for Bonny at regular intervals, and letters, telling her what he was doing and how much he was longing to see her again.

* * *

It was the final performance and the theatre was packed. It had the feeling of a gala night, and the men dressed in evening clothes, the ladies in their finery and jewellery. Adrenalin was flowing back stage and the atmosphere was electric.

Bonny's dressing room was filled with flowers from various admirers. Rob had sent some with a card thanking her for her hard work, saying how he was looking forward to working with her again. Mickey had sent a bouquet and said he would be in the audience, and a magnificent basket of wonderful blooms arrived from Jack Buchanan, saying he wished her a happy future.

Shirley walked in and looked around the room at the floral display. 'Bloody hell, Bonny. It's like a funeral parlour in here! When you open the door the scent of all this nearly knocks you off your feet!' She walked over to her friend and gave her a hug. 'You are already on that staircase to stardom . . . Didn't I tell you you'd make it, way back in Southampton at the Palace Theatre?'

With a happy smile Bonny looked at her friend, her eyes glittering with excitement. 'That seems so long ago, doesn't it? Oh, Shirley, haven't we done well?'

'Yes, love, we have. And — I have some great news. Rob has told me he'll want me for the new show that Giles Gilmore is producing. He's doing the choreography for it, apparently.'

'That's wonderful. Oh, Shirley, what would I do without you!'

Shirley was reading the card that Mickey had sent. 'It seems to me you are doing well on your own. Is this serious?'

‘I really don’t know. Mickey is such a lovely man. I could do worse.’

With a frown Shirley looked at her friend. ‘If you are really going to get to the top of your game, you won’t have much time for Mickey O’Halleran, I’m thinking. Rob Andrews will make sure of that.’

The ‘overture and beginners’ call came through and stopped any further conversation.

* * *

There were so many curtain calls at the end of the show that Bonny wondered if the cast would ever leave the stage, but eventually the curtain fell finally and the cast gathered as Peter Collins came on stage, thanked them all for their hard work and invited them to an end-of-show party at the Cafe Royal.

When Bonny returned to her dressing room it was to find Mickey O’Halleran waiting for her. He took her into his arms and kissed her. ‘Oh I’ve missed you, princess. You were terrific tonight, I was so proud of my girl. I’ve been invited to the party, so I’ll wait for you and we can go together.’

At that moment there was a knock on the door.

‘Come in,’ called Bonny, still held in Mickey’s embrace.

Rob Andrews walked in. The smile on his face changed as he saw the two of them. ‘Hello, O’Halleran. I didn’t know you were here.’

‘I’ve come to take my girl to the party,’ Mickey declared in such a tone as to defy an argument from Rob.

‘I see. Well done tonight,’ Rob said to Bonny. ‘You were superb. We have two weeks free and then we start rehearsals for the new show, so I would advise you to get as much rest as you can.’

As Rob left the room, the boxer smiled to himself. ‘That man thinks he owns you. Don’t let him run your life, darlin’, or he won’t let you breathe.’

'Rob only has a professional interest in me,' Bonny protested.

'That's what you think. Come on, get changed and we'll go and celebrate.'

* * *

The party was a huge success. The cast, now free, let their hair down and enjoyed the food, the drinks and the dancing. In a corner, Rob and Giles Gilmore were in deep conversation about the new show. 'I've been working on some new dance routines for Bonny and me,' Rob told Gilmore.

Giles looked at him and said, 'I want you to be more concerned with routines for Bonny alone. This is my opportunity to make her the star she should be.' At the look of consternation on Rob's face he added, 'We will have only one or two numbers of you together, as you will have enough work on your hands as it is as the dance director.'

As Rob made to protest, Giles interrupted. 'This is going to be a mammoth production and you can't wear two hats. I need your expertise and originality. Don't disappoint me. I'll see you in my office on Monday morning to discuss it.'

Giles walked away to greet one of his backers. He knew that, with his grandiose ideas, the new production was going to be very expensive to finance. He needed to keep all of his angels sweet because he knew he would have to find more money to stage the new show.

* * *

Knowing Giles and his ambitions, and after seeing the show that had just closed, Foxy Gordon knew that Giles would go all out to better it . . . and that would cost. He had already planned to buy more shares in the company, which would suit his plan admirably. It was going to work out just as he hoped. Revenge was going to be very sweet.

CHAPTER SIXTEEN

Bonny packed her bag and caught the train to Southampton. She was looking forward to spending time with her parents during her two-week break. She was really tired and welcomed the fact that she didn't have to perform, although she did exercises every morning to keep supple.

She and Millie went shopping together in the town and Bonny treated her mother to lunch, giving her a chance to tell her how excited she was about the new show. 'According to Giles, I'm going to have several big production numbers.'

Millie looked surprised. 'What about your Astaire dances with Rob Andrews?'

'Giles says there are to be just a couple of those, as he wants Rob to concentrate on choreographing the show. As dance director he'll be very busy.'

'Won't he mind?'

Laughing, Bonny said, 'I wouldn't think so. He loves his work, and until we danced in the last production, he hadn't danced on stage in quite a while.'

Millie looked thoughtful. 'I thought he looked as if he loved performing and I'm surprised he doesn't want to continue. Anyway, how's Mickey, have you heard from him?'

Bonny felt her cheeks flush. 'Yes, he writes all the time and sends me flowers, but, of course, he has to be really fit for his next fight. Defending his title means a great deal to him.'

* * *

Mickey O'Halleran was now back from the training camp and working out in Foxy Gordon's gym. He'd trained hard and was in great condition. His sparring partner was giving him a good work out in the ring when Foxy called a halt. 'That's enough for today! Take a shower and then get a good massage. I don't want you overdoing it at this stage. You've three weeks to go and Jake Forbes, your next opponent, is looking good. You need to be in tip-top condition to face him, he certainly is no pushover.'

Mickey was well aware of this fact. He knew he'd have his work cut out to beat this man, who was as hungry for his title as Mickey was to keep it. It had been billed as the fight of the year and would be a good money-earner for them all.

Foxy himself knew that it would be even more of a money earner if Mickey remained champion, and he needed the cash to invest further in Giles Gilmore's show.

* * *

For his part, Giles, soon realized, as he pored over the plans for the scenery and costumes for the spectacular numbers Rob had choreographed, that he would have to go to his backers for even more money. He had no qualms about this. He was convinced that he had the West End show of the year, and when it opened, his fellow investors would make a small fortune. But he was equally convinced that if he tried to cut back in any way, he could ruin the whole production, and he was not about to do that. If he couldn't persuade the investors, he was prepared to sell his own properties. He sat down in his office and dictated letters to his secretary to be sent to those involved.

* * *

Foxy Gordon tore open the envelope that had dropped on his mat that morning, having read the address of the sender stamped on the back, and grinned broadly as he read the contents.

So Gilmore was asking for more money. Splendid! He lit a cigar and thought about the dilemma that faced him if he was to achieve his goal. All the cash he could raise was already invested in the project; he would need to see his bank manager to raise more. Fortunately for him, the man was a great fight enthusiast and Foxy didn't think there would be a problem. After all, he had Mickey O'Halleran as collateral!

He walked back into the gym just as Wally Cole wandered in with one of his henchman. The men hadn't met since Foxy had faced the villain over Charlie Black's death and the fight promoter was not pleased to see him. 'Out of your territory, aren't you?'

Cole just smiled. 'I was in the area and thought I'd look in and see how the champ was doing now it's so close to the big fight.'

'He's doing just fine.'

'Glad to hear it, because I'll be putting my money on him and I wouldn't be happy to see it go down the pan.'

'You don't have to worry; my boy will win, so your money is safe.'

'Always looking for a good investment, Foxy. You know me. In fact I'm thinking of branching out. I hear that Giles Gilmore is looking for more money to finance his new show.' He smiled softly, 'I thought I might get involved.'

This was not what Foxy wanted to hear, but in no way was he going to let this man know he was financially involved himself. He started to laugh. 'You don't look out of place seated near a boxing ring, but really, Wally, dressed up to the nines in the audience at a theatre — you'd be out of place. A bit too classy for the likes of you. Not your thing at all, I would have thought.'

Cole's eyes flashed angrily. 'If I owned a brothel, it wouldn't mean I'd have sex with any of the brasses, but I *would* collect the takings!' And he stalked out of the gym.

The promoter frowned. He needed to get to see his bank manager quickly. No way was Wally Cole going to take a share in Gilmore's production. That was not part of his plan at all.

When he eventually left the bank, Gordon was in a cold sweat. Although the bank manager was a fight fan, he was first a businessman and Foxy had had to put up his gym — his livelihood — as collateral for the loan he required. As he was told, there was never a guarantee of a winner in the fight game, but bricks and mortar were always solid. But at least he would have the cash to buy more shares in Giles Gilmore's production. He would be the largest stockholder, apart from Giles himself, and that was just where he wanted to be.

* * *

Rehearsals began. Rob had been inspired, it would seem. *Broadway Melody* was to be a sumptuous affair, with incredible scenery depicting all the famous parts of New York, familiar to the general public: Broadway, Times Square, with all its neon lights, the Statue of Liberty, and the Empire State Building, were among them. Street scenes in Harlem, Tin Pan Alley with a jazz band, and the famous St Patrick's Day Parade would be other production numbers, with the full cast on stage.

The man in charge of building the scenery had made the city come to life, and Bonny, looking at the drawings and partially built flaps and backdrop, was astonished at the skill of the team. It was like stepping into another world. But the rehearsals were exhausting.

'One — two — three — four — five — six — seven — eight!' called Rob, keeping the dancers in time as they filled the stage, twirling and whirling to the music.

'No! No! For God's sake, can't you keep in time?' Rob stopped the music and leapt up on the stage. Standing with his back to the dancers he signalled for the music to begin. 'Follow me,' he called and started to dance.

With all eyes on the dance director, the dancers sweated and worked until they ached as they followed his new routine.

At the end he called, 'Take a break and then we'll go through it all again.'

Shirley and Bonny sank to the floor. 'Bloody hell!' exclaimed Shirley. 'By the time this show is finished there won't be anything left of any of us. I've lost so much weight already!'

Bonny stretched her aching back, reaching down to hold her toes and then slowly sitting up. 'Well, I've aged ten years, I swear. When I get back to the digs this evening I'll sit in a hot bath and then fall into bed.'

'We must eat first,' Shirley insisted, 'even if we are too tired. If we don't, we won't have the strength for tomorrow.'

As Bonny and Shirley rested, Giles was in his office, poring over the bills heaped on his desk. Even with the added money from his backers, it was going to be tight, meeting all the costs. It wasn't that he hadn't been in this position before. Every show seemed to cost more money than was first budgeted for but this was an enormous investment. His biggest by far. If it wasn't a success, he was ruined and his career would be over in the theatre. He ran his hands through his hair in desperation. Apart from the costs of the scenery and costumes, there were the wages of the cast and those working behind the scenes to be covered, and he was robbing Peter to pay Paul, keeping what money he had in circulation. He was a past master at this but it caused him many a sleepless night.

He had one saving grace and that was Bonny Burton. In her he knew he had a star. Rob Andrews's choreography had been inspired throughout, but in the numbers featuring Bonny, Rob had been particularly clever, showing her versatility. Some had featured her tap dancing; others were show numbers, with modern dance; and some with him in their Astaire production, yet another style. Oh yes, she would be his key to success, if he could only make the money go round until opening night. Then, please God, he would make a fortune.

* * *

When Bonny staggered out of her dressing room at the end of the day, she saw Mickey walking down the corridor towards her. With a cry of delight, she ran towards him and threw herself into his arms.

Lifting her off the ground, he held her tight and kissed her. 'Hello, princess. I can't tell you how much I've missed you.'

'Oh, Mickey darling, I'm so pleased to see you.' Tears of happiness welled in her eyes.

'Hey, what's this all about?' he asked with a worried frown. 'Are you all right?'

She smiled up at him. 'Of course I am. I'm just so tired.'

He walked her out of the theatre his arm around her shoulders. 'I know what you need,' he said as he called a taxi. 'I'm taking you to a hotel. You need a Turkish bath and a massage. It'll take all your aches and pains away. Then we'll have something to eat and I'll take you home.'

Later in the dining room of the hotel, the two of them exchanged their news. As he held her hand, Bonny felt almost renewed. Her body was relaxed after the massage and now, having eaten, all she wanted to do was sleep, but she didn't want to have to leave this lovely man. When she told him how she felt, he just smiled.

'That can be arranged, darlin'.' He booked them into a room after having a quiet word with the manager, who promised Mickey his complete discretion as he handed over the room key.

Once inside the bedroom, Bonny got undressed without embarrassment — somehow it seemed the most natural thing to do — and climbed into bed. As Mickey walked towards her, she marvelled at his toned frame, his broad powerful shoulders, his muscular arms, which held her so gently as he climbed into bed beside her.

He gathered her to him, kissed her softly and said, 'Now go to sleep.'

Seeing the look of surprise on her face, Mickey smiled softly. 'There will be plenty of time for love, darlin', but now you need to rest.' He felt her body relax and saw her eyes close and then he watched the rise and fall of her breasts as she breathed. He knew he would love this girl for the rest of his life.

Three hours later, Bonny stirred. She could feel the warmth of Mickey's body, which seemed to be like another skin as he matched the curve of her body from behind. His arms around her. She stretched and he woke.

He nuzzled the back of her neck. 'Feel better?'

'I feel wonderful.' She turned within his hold and kissed him.

Their love-making was slow and gentle as Mickey stroked and caressed her without haste, feeling her passion mounting as his fingers explored her supple body. Kissing her neck, her breasts, telling her how much he loved her and wanted her.

Bonny's head was swimming with all the strange and new sensations she was feeling. Her body seemed to have a mind of its own as it responded to the touch of the man beside her. As he climbed on top of her she automatically spread her legs as if she knew what she was doing and had done it all before.

'Relax, darling,' Mickey told her. 'I want you to enjoy this as much as I will.'

And she did.

After, as they lay in each other's arms, bodies entwined, Bonny let out a deep sigh of contentment. 'I never knew it would be like that.'

Mickey looked concerned. 'What on earth did you expect?'

She laughed as she saw the worried look on his face. 'I don't know, but it was lovely. When can we do it again?'

He burst out laughing. 'Are you trying to kill me? I have to keep fit for the big fight.'

'You seemed pretty fit to me,' she said with a chuckle.

'You, young lady, have the makings of a hussy!'

'Oh, I do hope so, it sounds so naughty.' And she snuggled down into his embrace.

CHAPTER SEVENTEEN

Wally Cole was furious! He'd tried to buy into Giles Gilmore's new production without success and had learned, through nefarious means, that Foxy Gordon had quite an investment in the show. The boxing promoter's barb about Wally being out of his class in the theatre still rankled. Who the hell was he to talk down to him in such a manner — and to threaten him in front of his men, as he'd done a while ago?

From all accounts, the new show was going to be spectacular and a sure-fire hit, making its backers a great deal of money, and Wally dearly wanted to be in on it. Unfortunately for him, it wasn't possible. This angered him even more and he wondered how he could spoil Foxy's chances of cashing in. Not only was this eating away at the mind of the criminal, but also the fact that Mickey O'Halleran, Gordon's blue eyed champion, was courting Bonny Burton, the new star of the show, giving Foxy another insight to the theatrical connection.

For his part, Foxy Gordon was delighted with his investment, and especially as now, well into rehearsals, those angels with a vested interest had been invited along to the theatre to watch the first dress rehearsal, no doubt in the hopes of impressing them in case more money was needed. Foxy had decided it was time to show Gilmore his hand and go along, clutching his written invitation in the name of his nom de plume, James Harcourt. A poncey sounding name, which Foxy had thought would appeal to Giles. He couldn't wait to see the look on the impresario's face when he discovered the true identity of his biggest backer.

* * *

The morning rehearsals were over and Rob gathered the full cast on to the stage of the Adelphi Theatre. 'This afternoon we are going to run through the entire show from beginning to end, in costume, as if this was a performance,' he told them. 'In the audience will be the angels who have put their money into the show. Without them we would not be here, so make sure they leave the theatre feeling that their money has been well spent. If they don't feel that way, we could be in serious trouble, so take a lunch break and come back and give me the show that will break all box-office records!'

The cast dispersed with a lot of nervous chatter and excitement. They all knew that they had the means to make history in the musical theatre and the adrenalin was potent.

Bonny entered her dressing room and patted the golden star on the door. She still couldn't believe that it meant her, despite the fact that her name was below it. She sat in her chair in front of the mirror, which was surrounded by bright lights, and stared at her reflection. Her father's words echoed inside her head. He had talked about the responsibility of carrying the show on her shoulders and had wondered if she was ready for such responsibility. She asked herself the same question. She didn't really know. All she did know was that she was exactly where she wanted to be, doing exactly what she wanted to do.

The production was innovative and exciting. Rob Andrews had choreographed spectacular numbers; the scenery was breathtaking and the other dancers were of the highest calibre. And she, Bonny Burton, from Southampton, was the star. The only question that gave her anything like a feeling of disquiet was, how much would this change her life?

She had discussed this with Mickey, who was used to the limelight. He had tried to dispel her fears and advise her.

'You have to get used to the idea that your life will become of public interest. The papers will always be looking for a story, so you will have to make sure you are never seen without looking spic and span. No popping to the shops in an old shabby outfit or they'll fill the papers with photos. Whatever you do, don't volunteer any information about your private life. Try and keep that to yourself.'

'They keep asking me about us and our relationship as it is,' she told him.

He just laughed. 'I know, darlin', they do the same to me. I just tell them it's none of their business. We will have to be very careful in the future where we spend our time together. Mind you, when the show opens that will be limited.'

She looked disappointed. 'Oh, Mickey, I don't think I can bear that.'

'We neither of us have a choice, princess. We are both in the entertainment business; do you want to give that up?'

'Of course not!'

'And neither do I, so we have to play by the rules. It comes with the territory.'

Bonny pondered over this conversation and knew that he spoke the truth. Her thoughts were disturbed by a knock on the door. 'Come in,' she called.

Shirley popped her head round the door. 'Want some company?' She held out two cups of coffee.

'Oh God, Shirley, am I pleased to see you, and a cup of coffee is just what I need. I'm getting more nervous by the minute, sitting here alone.'

Shirley was just the right kind of diversion, and they spent time going over the dance routines, the gossip of the theatre and relaxing together before the rehearsal.

* * *

The angels and a few invited guests were ushered into the theatre at the allotted time and took their seats. Foxy threw a cursory glance at the others, but took a seat away from them. He wanted to sit alone, without any distraction, during the show.

The orchestra were tuning their instruments, and although the theatre was all but empty, there was an air of excitement and expectation among the few seated in the stalls. The lights dimmed and the overture began.

At the back of the stalls, Giles Gilmore slipped into a seat, his heart beating as the curtains opened. His hands were sweating with the concern that coursed through his body. It was always the same at this stage. Had he made a mistake? Would the show live up to his expectations? Would he still have a career in the theatre? He lit a cigarette and prayed, but as the curtain rose and the scenery showed Times Square with all its lights, the sounds of the cars, and the hustle and bustle depicted by Rob's great choreography, he began to relax.

Foxy Gordon was elated. This show was going to be an enormous hit! Each number showing New York City and all its glory and downsides was an amazing conception.

There was a specialty number featuring Bonny, showing the back streets, the tenements, the poor side of the great city. It told the tale of unrequited love — Bonny and one of the boys dancing out the tale as a tenor sang about it, whilst sitting on one of the fire hydrants in a street filled with litter. It was touching, romantic and poignant.

By contrast, the next scene was in a night club on Broadway with a jazz band, well-heeled patrons and some great tap-dancing by the full chorus, which was full of razzle dazzle — led by Bonny.

Rob Andrews had slipped into the seat next to Giles just after the opening. He could do no more at this stage except watch for any weakness that he could rectify before opening night. His nerves were at breaking point as he sat and watched, making notes as he did so, before changing for his own contribution with Bonny.

Backstage was a bustle of activity as the performers changed in readiness for the next number, all hoping and praying that nothing would go wrong.

In between the numbers that the dancers performed, giving them time to change, came the quieter moments. A Negro baritone, seen walking alone along the dockside, singing a ballad about his working life, dressed as a labourer. Another of a waitress, working in a diner, longing to be on the stage. It showed all manner of life, and hopes and dreams of those living in the city. It was truly a story to be told, from beginning to end.

There was just one number with Rob and Bonny doing their Astaire–Rogers dance, and Giles thought it was more than enough. He wanted this to be a showcase for Bonny Burton alone, and my God, hadn't she shown him today that she had been made of the star quality he had visualized! She was really something special.

The final curtain fell and the backers sitting in the stalls rose to their feet and applauded. None louder than Foxy Gordon. As the curtain was lifted, Giles Gilmore walked down the aisle to address the cast who waited with bated breath to hear his observations.

'Well, ladies and gentlemen, thank you for a wonderful show.' He beamed at them all. 'Apart from one or two minor things, which Rob and I will discuss later, I thought this was exceptional for the first dress rehearsal. Well done! Now go and get some rest.' He turned to face his backers and invited them to follow him to his office to drink champagne, to toast what he considered was going to be a huge hit.

Foxy held back and was the last person to enter the room. Giles was pouring champagne into glasses and handing them out. As he looked up to give out the last one he met the gaze of Foxy Gordon. He smiled, but his eyes narrowed. 'Mr Gordon, I had no idea you'd be here.'

With a slow smile, Foxy said, 'I'm James Harcourt, one of your major backers.' He saw Gilmore pale.

'Indeed you are.' The impresario maintained his composure. 'But why the nom de plume? Did you think that was necessary?'

'Oh come on, Giles, don't play games with me. You know damned well you would never have accepted my money, had you known my true identity.'

The gloves were now indeed off. 'You're quite right, of course. I would have wondered at your motivation and I'm sure you do have one.'

Foxy glared at him. 'Five years is my motivation, Giles. The time I spent in prison when you took me and the others to court. I'm going to ruin you, Gilmore, one way or another. They call it revenge!' Gordon drank his champagne and walked out of the room.

Giles was visibly shaken, but before he could move, the other smaller investors crowded round him to talk about the show.

* * *

Foxy Gordon walked to the nearest bar and ordered a large scotch on the rocks. He sat quietly and contemplated the meeting, which had given him great satisfaction. The shocked expression on Gilmore's face had been a sight to behold. But now the promoter was in a dilemma. The show would be a tremendous hit, of that there was no doubt, and he was in a position to make a lot of money, especially if it ran for any length of time, so he didn't want to do anything to spoil that. He would have to think of some other way to get at the impresario. He needed time to think. He was a patient man; after all, he'd already waited some years. As long as he achieved his goal eventually, what did time matter? Meantime, Giles Gilmore could sweat it out.

* * *

That was exactly what Giles was doing, when eventually he was alone. He was livid! Imagine that bloody Gordon owned forty per cent of his new production! That was far too much power in the wrong hands. The threat from the man to ruin him played on his mind. How would he go about doing that? He really was worried. He knew the promoter too well; it had not been an idle threat. Just when he was about to reach the pinnacle of his theatrical career — it was in jeopardy and in the hands of an unscrupulous man . . .

CHAPTER EIGHTEEN

It was a week before opening night and the cast had been given a much needed day of rest on the Sunday. Bonny would have liked to have seen her parents but she was so tired. Mickey had suggested they book into their secret hotel, stay in their room all day, away from everyone — and do nothing. Meals could be sent up and this would give Bonny the chance to recharge her batteries, ready for the last week of rehearsals.

'You can't burn out now, darlin', you need every bit of strength to sustain you at this point. I *know* about peaking too soon.'

She snuggled into him. 'What would I do without you, darling Mickey?'

'You'll never have to find that out, princess, because I intend to be around for the rest of your life.'

She gazed into his eyes. 'What do you mean?'

'You and I are meant for each other, you must know that? Sometime in the future I'm going to marry you, care for you and love you — until death us do part.'

'Oh, Mickey, I would really like that.'

'I'm so glad you agree,' he said and reached into his pocket, taking out a small box. He removed a diamond ring with three large stones set in platinum and slipped it on her finger. 'I guess that makes it official,' he said as he kissed her.

As he released her, Bonny held out her hand and looked at the ring, glistening in the sunlight. 'The reporters will spot this in a second,' she said. 'It's beautiful; they can hardly miss it, can they?'

'I had thought about that,' he said. 'I suggest that we keep this to ourselves for a while. You need all the publicity to be about your performance in the show, not about us, so I suggest you only wear it in private.' He kissed her gently. 'We will know when we can make it public knowledge. But today we can have our own private celebration.'

He booked a room and they drove to the hotel, Mickey parking his car at the back, out of sight, away from prying eyes — as he thought.

Observing every movement that the couple made were two of Wally Cole's heavies. He was well aware of their secret rendezvous, having kept tabs on both of them for the past weeks. The criminal was now obsessed with a way to ruin Foxy Gordon's chance of cashing in on his investment. How he was going to do this, he hadn't yet decided, but he knew that Foxy's main assets — the man and the show — were with these two people and he needed to know their every move.

Unaware that they were being watched, Mickey and Bonny enjoyed a light lunch together in their room, went to bed and made love, before sleeping all the afternoon, entwined in each other's arms. In the evening, they talked about their future and made plans.

'We need to live in London or nearby,' Mickey insisted, 'then you'll be near enough to the theatres for your future shows.'

'You seem pretty sure I'll have such a future,' Bonny said with a note of uncertainty in her voice.

He gathered her into his arms and chuckled. 'You are an amazing woman, you know. You are the only one who has any doubts. One of the most endearing things about you, princess, is that you have no idea just how talented you are. I love that.'

'And what about you, Mickey? How much longer do you have a career in the ring? I hate to see you get hurt when you face an opponent. How much longer can you keep taking such punishment?'

He grinned at her. 'You worried that I may lose my good looks, darlin'?'

'Don't be silly! It's the constant blows to the head that worry me the most.'

'Listen, Bonny, I'm a good boxer and know how to ride such things, and as long as I'm fit, I'll keep defending my title. However, I'm not a fool. I'm well aware that any boxer has a limited time at the top, and one day someone will be better than me — that's when I'll quit.' He saw her worried frown. 'I've taken care of my winnings, I've enough for a nice home and to finance some sort of business when the time comes. Don't you worry, we'll be fine.'

* * *

Rob Andrews, unaware of how serious the relationship between his star and Mickey O'Halleran had become, was watching Bonny rehearse a spectacular finale dance routine with the male members of the chorus. The backdrop was of one of the New York piers with a liner in dock. The men were dressed as ship's stewards, helping the longshoremen load the last of the luggage onboard. Bonny was dressed as one of the passengers, who had arrived late.

The dance was very tricky and physical, with Bonny dancing among and on various types of luggage and being lifted by different male dancers as she traversed the length of the dock to the gangway.

Passengers were lining the rails of the ship, streamers were floating in the air with the aid of a wind machine and there was a roar from the funnel indicating that it was almost time to sail. Eventually, the number ended with Bonny dancing up the gangway on to the deck, climbing on to the rail as the gangway was retrieved, ropes let go and the ship starting to sail as the curtain fell. She did it faultlessly and Rob was delighted. It had been a difficult number to pull together with all the mechanics involved to move the depicted liner just a few feet, and he knew that with the tremendous scenery, which brought the whole thing to life, it was a show-stopper.

He ran up the steps at the side of the stage as the curtains reopened. 'Well done, everybody, that was great! Take a lunch break and be back in an hour. Bonny, can I have a word?'

She walked over to him. 'What is it?' she asked with a look of concern.

'Come with me, we can have lunch together in my office.'

She followed him and saw that he had arranged sandwiches and fruit for the two of them, which was all laid out on his desk.

'Sit down, Bonny, and tuck in. After all the work you've done this morning, you must be famished.'

'I'm actually starving,' she admitted as she helped herself.

He gazed fondly at her. What an amazing transition it had been for this girl, from the chorus in a Southampton theatre, to this starring role in a West End musical. How proud he was of her achievements. They were very alike in many ways, he mused. Both of their lives were driven by their love of the dance and the theatre. What a strong team they were, both being on the same wavelength.

Looking up, Bonny caught sight of his expression. 'What?' she asked.

'I was just thinking how far you had come from when I first auditioned you. It's been a pleasure to watch you grow.'

'I owe a lot to you, Rob, I'll never forget that.'

'How about the two of us going out to dinner tonight to celebrate and drink to the success of *Broadway Melody*?' he suggested.

How could she refuse? She felt obliged. After all, without Rob she wouldn't be here today. 'Thank you, I'd like that.'

During their dinner, in a small but exclusive restaurant, the two of them discussed the show and the various numbers, the production, the dancers, both full of enthusiasm for their shared craft.

'You really are a talented choreographer,' she told him. 'Every number on that stage is inspired. I don't know where you get your ideas from.'

He smiled benignly at her. 'You being the lead was inspirational. We make a great team, you and I.'

There was something in his voice that suddenly made Bonny aware that perhaps this wasn't just a dinner with a colleague and she answered carefully. 'That's very nice of you to say so, Rob, but your reputation was made before you ever met me.'

He leaned forward and took her hand. 'This is true, but you are special, Bonny. With you as my lead I can go beyond what I've done before, knowing that you are capable of delivering. You are a choreographer's dream. I've never met a woman before who thinks along the same lines as I do, who understands what is required without bleating about the hard work involved. We have a great future together.'

She slowly withdrew her hand from his grasp. 'I just thought that getting on with the job, was being professional, that's all. You know, as Mickey says, it comes with the territory.'

The name of the boxer, brought into their conversation, seemed to act like ice down Rob Andrews's back and his expression changed, his voice became harsh. 'He can't possibly understand our world.'

'Don't be silly, Rob, of course he does. After all, Mickey is in the entertainment business too.'

'Then he will understand that when the show opens, you'll have very little time to see him — if at all!'

The atmosphere between them had changed. Bonny was now immediately defensive. 'As long as I perform on the stage and do my job, my private life is just that! Private! I will see Mickey O'Halleran whenever I choose and it has not a damn thing to do with you.' She rose from her seat. 'Thank you for a lovely meal, but now I must go. I'll see you tomorrow in the theatre.'

'Wait, I'll see you home,' he started to say, but Bonny was already heading for the door, and after he'd paid the bill and rushed to the exit — she'd gone.

'Damn!' he swore to himself. That wasn't exactly what he'd had in mind for the evening. Pulling up the collar of his coat, he strode off into the night.

Sitting in the back of a taxi, Bonny's mind was in turmoil. Despite the fact that her friend Shirley had always maintained that Rob had more than a professional interest in her, Bonny had never for one moment believed her — until this evening — and it was an unwelcome situation. She admired Rob Andrews and recognized his amazing talent. She felt privileged to be part of the show he'd put together and loved dancing with him as her partner. Both here, and back in Southampton, there had been a special feeling of closeness between them. For her it was purely professional, but obviously not for him. Was this going to be a problem? She sincerely hoped not because their association would continue throughout the run of the production. Any animosity between them could have an adverse affect, if it grew. She would have to make sure that it didn't.

* * *

Bonny's problem was minor in comparison with the one that was now facing Wally Cole. There was a new criminal gang, led by a young man with big ambitions, trying to muscle in on Wally's territory. He remembered mentioning this to Foxy Gordon in friendlier times. Wally had thought he'd taken care of the problem by removing a couple of the gang, but Gerry Pike, twenty-nine, son of an old lag, was out to prove himself better than his father. With the arrogance of youth and cunning of a criminal, he'd pulled off a couple of audacious bank robberies on Wally's patch, which infuriated the gang leader, and he needed a plan to rid himself of this unwelcome intruder. He summoned his men.

'I want to know the name of every man in this organization. I want to know everything about them. Where they live, who their parents are, if they have siblings and who they are sleeping with. There must be a weak link among them somewhere. Find him! We can use this person to our advantage.' He turned to his head man. 'You watch young Gerry. He must have an Achilles heel and I want you to find it. I want to know who he sees, where he goes, even where he takes a piss, because I'm not going to let some snotty nosed newcomer take over my patch. Understand?'

There was angry muttering from the others. After all, they all lived the high life through their criminal activities. Fear of the Firm was to all their advantage, and any sign of weakness would lose them any respect from the underworld.

Apart from all this, Wally had a plan. He had discovered that Giles Gilmore paid his cast and crew every Friday night, after drawing a large amount of money from the bank, which he carried to the theatre in a large briefcase. He planned to rob him of this money and lay the blame at Gerry Pike's door, thereby killing two birds with one stone. His old ally Foxy Gordon would not be pleased because it would be a great loss to the finances of the production, and Wally had discovered that Gilmore was having to be very careful with every penny to bring the production to the stage. Wally had recently managed to place a man working in the theatre as an engineer, who was in a good position, if required, to cause problems with the many mechanical devices used in the different scenes. In particular, the scene where the liner seemed to begin to sail away. A clever piece of stage management, but very complicated to accomplish.

He sat back in his chair and lit a cigarette. He'd been around far too long to let a young shaver put him out of business. Gerry Pike was not the first one to have tried and he wouldn't be the last. But Wally certainly wasn't ready to retire. Why should he? He was doing well. He had his illegal gambling meetings, which moved from house to house so as not to be caught. He was in the protection racket, which brought in a good turnover, apart from everything else. He was sitting pretty. He smiled to himself. He would love to see Foxy's face after he'd lifted the wages from Giles Gilmore. That, he would pay money for. He started laughing.

CHAPTER NINETEEN

Gerry Pike was sitting in the corner of the Red Lion, his local pub in the East End docks, feeling very pleased with himself. He'd pulled off two heists in Wally Cole's patch and the money was stashed away in a secret hideaway. It had been a good haul and he had already laid plans to launder the money. Yes, he was sitting pretty at the moment. He was no fool, he knew that Wally would be out for his blood, but he was young and full of ideas. Cole had been around too long, lording it over the underworld. It was time for a change.

When he'd visited his father in Pentonville prison and told him of his plans, his father, Bill, had had a fit! 'You young fool! If you take on Wally Cole, you will have signed your own death warrant,' the old man had warned.

But Gerry had brushed the warning aside. 'He's getting too old in the tooth,' he brashly proclaimed. 'It's time for a change. I've got some good men behind me, all ready for the fight. You see, Dad, I'm going to be king of the jungle.'

'Better men than you have tried and failed,' Bill snapped.

This angered his son. 'I can never win with you, can I? All my life, whatever I do, you knock down in flames. Well, just you wait and see, I'm going to be bigger than you everywhere. Look at you! A failure — serving time. Well, I'm not going down the same road. I'll never end up behind bars like you have.'

His father looked coldly at him. 'You couldn't have said a truer word, boy. You'll end up at the bottom of the Thames tied to a cement block.'

Gerry rose from his chair so quickly it crashed to the ground. The warders on duty looked quickly to see what had caused the noise, but young Gerry was striding out of the visiting room, cheeks flushed with anger.

He'd show the old man! One day his father would have to eat his words and he would sit back and enjoy the moment. But for the now he would lie low, knowing that Wally Cole would no doubt be planning some kind of retribution.

* * *

It came very quickly. Giles Gilmore walked to his car from the bank, carrying the money for the wages for his staff. He drove to the stage door and parked the vehicle. Leaning into the car he picked up his briefcase. Before he knew what was happening, two masked men grabbed him, knocking him to the ground, taking the case with the money from his grasp.

'Here, Gerry, take this,' said one and they both ran to a waiting car and drove off.

The stunned impresario got to his feet, unable to believe what had happened. He rushed into the stage door and rang the police. 'This is Giles Gilmore at the Adelphi Theatre, I've just been robbed!' he reported. 'Two men jumped me and took a bag containing the week's wages.'

The stage doorkeeper looked at him with a shocked expression, seeing the lump beginning to form on the other's face. 'Are you all right, Mr Gilmore?'

'No, I'm not! You heard what happened. I'll be in the office when the police come,' he said and walked off.

Word quickly spread and Rob rushed to Giles's office. Giles was sitting at his desk holding an ice pack to his face.

'I've just heard. Is it right that they got away with the wages for the staff?'

'Every penny! They caught me totally unawares. Bastards!' He looked at Rob. 'We can ill afford the loss. Money is really tight right now.'

At that moment two detectives arrived to question him. Giles told them what had happened and about one calling out the name Gerry.

The two men looked at one another. 'Gerry Pike?' said one.

'That's a bit careless, isn't it?' remarked the other.

'A little too contrived for my liking,' said his associate. Turning to Gilmore he asked, 'Did you always go alone to the bank to collect the wages, sir?'

'Yes, always,'

'Not very bright of you, if you don't mind my saying.'

Giles let out a deep sigh. 'So it would seem. Hindsight is not always useful, but in future I'll make sure I have someone with me.'

'Just how much money are we talking about?'

When Giles told them, one let out a whistle of surprise. They made notes of all the details in their notebooks and left the building, promising to look into it right away.

Turning to Rob Andrews, who had waited, Giles said, 'I'll have to go back to the bank and draw more money. Will you come with me?'

'Of course. Just let me talk to the cast and then I'll be back.'

* * *

Wally Cole grinned broadly when his two men delivered the wages they had snatched. 'How did it go?' he asked.

'Piece of cake, guv. The bloke didn't know what hit him.'

'Did you use Gerry's name like I told you?'

They smiled. 'Oh yes, and loud enough for the geezer to hear. Should prove interesting.'

'Well, that will give young Gerry Pike something to think about, because the Old Bill will be all over him for a while. That will clip his wings, that's for sure.'

* * *

Pike was indeed surprised when two detectives called at his home. He led them into the front room when they said they wanted to question him either there or at the station. At first he was puzzled as to their reason for calling, but he soon realized, when they told him about the robbery, that Cole had been quick to make his move.

'I know nothing about this,' he protested.

'Where were you at eleven o'clock this morning, Mr Pike?'

'I was here at home.'

'Can anyone verify that?'

'No, I was alone. I haven't been outside the door.'

'What about your neighbours?' one of the men asked. 'Would they have seen you?'

Gerry frowned, knowing that the people on both sides would be at work. He shook his head. 'They leave early in the morning.'

'Mind if we have a look round?' he was asked.

'Do you have a search warrant?'

'Do we need one? After all, if you've nothing to hide . . .'

The inference was plain enough and Gerry, knowing there was nothing in the house that was illegal, decided not to be difficult. 'Help yourself,' he said and lit a cigarette. Picking up yesterday's paper, he sat down.

The two detectives searched the house but nothing untoward was found and so they left. As he closed the door behind them, Gerry Pike wondered why they had called on him. The detectives must have had a reason and he surmised that Wally Cole was behind all of this and in some way had implicated him. Well, now the game was on and he would have to really watch his back.

* * *

Later that day, after rehearsals, Felix the chorus boy went to Foxy Gordon's gym for a massage and told the fight promoter what had happened earlier to Giles. 'Two men knocked him down and ran off with the wages.'

Foxy frowned. 'Didn't you get paid then?'

'Oh yes. Mr Gilmore had to draw more money from the bank. He didn't look too happy, I can tell you.'

'I bet he didn't,' said Foxy, surmising that a lot of money would be involved. 'Do the police have any idea as to who might have done this?'

'I did overhear one of the detectives talk about a Gerry Pike. Do you know him?'

The local underworld had been gossiping about the bank robberies, and word was out that it was down to this young bloke who was trying to muscle in on Cole's territory. Every small-time criminal was watching the situation with interest, wondering if Wally was about to be toppled from his high position. Some praying that it was so. Others, who were old hands, praying that this wouldn't end in gang warfare. That was never good for anyone in their game; it brought too much interest in their activities from the local police force.

* * *

All this intrigue was lost on the cast and crew of the show that was about to open. The final dress rehearsal was over, opening night was twenty-four hours away and everybody's nerves were on edge. A great deal of money had been invested in *Broadway Melody* and its success would make or break everyone that was involved.

Giles was a bundle of nerves in case anything major went wrong, Rob was praying that his choreography would live up to his expectations and that the scenery was secure, and backstage the engineers were busy checking all the mechanics that were needed to make things move as scheduled.

Bonny Burton, though excited, was well aware that this could make or break her. If she didn't deliver, the show could flop.

Mickey O'Halleran was on hand to give her confidence. 'Look, darlin', even before a fight I still get screwed up inside. The adrenalin starts pumping and I wonder if I can beat the other bloke, but I try and make it work for me. I know I'm good at my job, you know you are good at yours. Use all this to your advantage. You go out on that stage and do what you do best. The adrenalin will give you extra energy. You love your work, as I do. Enjoy every moment.'

He held her close and kissed her. 'You, princess, have star quality. I know it, Rob Andrews knows it and so does Giles Gilmore. After the opening night, the British public will know it too!'

She hugged him. 'Oh, Mickey, thank goodness you're around.'

'I'll always be around, you know that. Now come outside, there's something I think you should see.'

Outside the front of the theatre in bright lights was the name of the show. *Broadway Melody. Starring Bonny Burton.* 'There, take a look. This is just what you've been working for and you deserve it.'

Bonny was speechless. She'd always entered the theatre at the stage-door entrance and hadn't seen the front of the theatre. Had never even thought about looking. Now she gazed at the words with shining eyes. 'My parents are going to be so proud when they see that,' she said.

'Of course they will, and you will be a hit. I'll have to send a bodyguard to keep all the stage-door Johnnies away from my girl.'

She flung her arms about him. 'You never need worry about them,' she told him. 'You are the only man for me and you know it!'

'Come on,' he said, 'we'll go for a quiet drink and then I'll take you home, you need a good rest before tomorrow. I'll be in the stalls to watch you perform. I'll be the proudest man in Britain . . . apart from maybe your dad!'

* * *

Opening night was Gala Night and the public and VIPs arrived in full evening dress. The pavement was thronged with people; cars and taxis queued in line to drop off their fares. There was a buzz of excitement in the air. Stars from screen and radio arrived. The critics took their seats, wondering if their copy in the papers the following morning would sing the praises of the new production or be a damning report.

Inside the theatre, the cast were in their dressing rooms preparing for the big night. The stagehands and lighting crew were working like mad for the moment when the curtain went up. The orchestra tuned their instruments. The lights dimmed, silence fell in the auditorium, the overture began . . . and finally the curtain rose.

There was a gasp from the audience when they saw the exquisite scenery depicting Broadway and Times Square with its hustle and bustle as the cast danced on to the stage to the music of George M. Cohan's 'Give My Regards To Broadway'. The stage was a whirl as the dancers covered the area and then Bonny Burton appeared. It was as if she had wings on her feet as she danced across the stage. The audience were mesmerized by the young woman and the applause at the end was thunderous.

Giles Gilmore and Rob Andrews, standing at the back of the stalls, let out a sigh of relief, and when the following numbers before the interval were received as rapturously, Giles shook Rob vigorously by the hand. 'By George, I do believe we have a hit on our hands. Thank God for that!'

Rob was equally excited. 'Come along,' he said, 'let's go to the bar and mix with the crowd. If we eavesdrop on them we'll be able to hear what they say.' And the two men took off.

In the bar the patrons were fulsome in their praise:

'Great show!'

'Love the dancers and the scenery, have you ever seen anything quite like it?'

'That girl Bonny Burton is amazing!'

These were only a few of the remarks, and the two men were thrilled.

The second half began equally as well. The Astaire–Rogers number went fantastically and by now there was an air of excitement at the front and back of the stage. This was an exceptional production, one that would make box-office history, was the opinion of the critics, who were duly impressed about what they were seeing. All of them taken with the energy and talent of the new leading lady, whose dancing had left them breathless with her energy, personality and talent. This girl was a star!

Mickey O'Halleran had slipped backstage during the interval to see Bonny. He'd hugged her and said, 'You were sensational, princess. I am so proud of you, I could burst!'

She'd been in her element. 'Oh, Mickey, the audience is wonderful; they really seem to like the show.'

'You should be in the stalls with me,' he'd told her. He'd kissed her forehead. 'They love you, darlin', and why wouldn't they. You danced your socks off.' He'd left her soon after so she could get ready for the second half of the show.

When the final number opened, the audience was thrilled with the scene of the ocean liner waiting to sail, and when eventually Bonny had danced among the luggage, made her way on board, and the ship began to move as the curtain fell, the whole of the audience rose to their feet, clapping wildly.

Bonny lost count of the numerous curtain calls at the end of the show and the number of bouquets that were presented to her. Flushed with excitement, she finally made her way to her dressing room and collapsed on to the settee. Exhilarated yet exhausted.

Rob Andrews tapped on Bonny's door and burst in. He lifted her off the settee and twirled her round in his arms, then kissed her soundly. 'Thank you, Bonny, you were stupendous!' he cried. He was smiling and his eyes glistened with excitement. 'You danced like a woman possessed.' And he kissed her again just as Mickey O'Halleran walked into the room.

He stopped for just a moment then jovially said, 'Take your hands off my girl, Andrews, or I'll have take you apart.'

Bonny rushed over to Mickey and clung to him. 'Wasn't it great? Didn't everybody do well?'

Holding her he said, 'They did, princess, and they loved you too . . . but not as much as I do, of course,' and he gave a hard stare at the dance director as he spoke.

Rob walked towards the door. 'Well done, Bonny. I always knew you were star material.' He looked at Mickey. 'Giles has booked a table at the Cafe Royal for us so we can celebrate and wait for the early editions of the papers. Will you join us?'

'Thanks, Rob. Giles has already invited me, and of course I'll be there with Bonny. I want to see her face when she reads her reviews. Let me see you out,' he said pointedly and opened the door.

CHAPTER TWENTY

At the Cafe Royal, Giles, Mickey, Bonny, her parents and her friend Shirley, with Rob Andrews, drank champagne and ate whilst they waited for the early editions. Both Millie and Frank Burton were overwhelmed by the evening. To see their daughter's name in lights had been such a thrill but the high standard of the production and Bonny's skill as a dancer had taken their breath away. They found it hard to believe this was their little girl, grown up and starring in a musical. It was almost beyond their comprehension.

Frank took Bonny's hand in his. 'I am so proud of you,' he said.

Knowing her father's concern for her when she moved to London and his scepticism, Bonny knew that such a comment was praise indeed. 'Thanks, Dad, that means everything to me.'

Various diners in the restaurant, who had seen the show, came over to the table and congratulated Bonny on her performance. She blushed with embarrassment at their praise and thanked them.

Putting an arm around her, Mickey grinned broadly. 'There you are, princess, you're a star and this is just the beginning.'

Her eyes bright with excitement, she laughed. 'I'm not sure I'm ready for that.'

'You won't have a choice. After tonight's performance you will be established in musical theatre, you wait and see.'

He was proved correct when the papers arrived. The critics were ecstatic with their comments. *A NEW STAR TAKES THE STAGE* was one headline. *BEST MUSICAL OF THE YEAR*, wrote another. *BONNY BURTON TAKES THE STAGE BY STORM*, wrote a third.

Giles ordered more champagne.

Shirley rose from her chair and rushed over to Bonny and hugged her. 'I'm so happy for you, Bonny love. You're really on your way now and I'm delighted to be a part of it all!'

'Oh, Shirley, who would ever have thought it, when you remember how we first met and how it all began!'

There was great jubilation that evening, and the other diners joined in the celebrations. The atmosphere at the Cafe Royal that night was charged with excitement until Giles eventually called a halt. 'Come along everybody,' he said. 'My star needs her rest otherwise she won't be fit to dance tomorrow night.' He hugged her. 'Well done, Bonny, I knew you had the potential when I first saw you and you didn't disappoint me. You are going to be the biggest name in musical theatre for many a year.'

She didn't know what to say. All she had ever wanted to do was dance. She had never ever dreamed of stardom. Her greatest ambition had been to be in a West End production. Beyond that had never occurred to her, and deep down she found being a star somewhat daunting.

Mickey sensed her discomfort, and he arranged for a taxi to take her parents to their hotel and another for him and Bonny.

They slipped into their hotel by the back way. 'After the papers today, we are going to have to knock this on the head,' he told her as they snuggled together between the sheets.

'What do you mean?' she asked.

'Because the reporters will be watching you, princess. One whiff of scandal and it will make headlines. You must appear whiter that white, which means we can't book in here again.'

'Oh, Mickey, that will be terrible.'

'I know, darlin', but in time we will be able to announce our engagement, then things will be different. Anyway, I have a fight coming up soon, so I'll be tied up for a while.'

She clung to him. 'I need you now more than ever.'

'I'll be around and if I can't be I'll call you. Now come on, get some sleep. You look exhausted and I'm not surprised, it's been quite a night.'

Bonny's eyes were heavy by now and she was soon in a deep sleep, curled up in the arms of the man she loved.

* * *

Foxy Gordon had been among the first night audience and had been thrilled at the success of the show, knowing that his financial interest would pay high dividends as a major shareholder. It made his position that much stronger. No way was he going to kill the goose that laid the golden egg, but there would come a time in the future when his position would give him a voice that would have to be heard. He could make life very difficult for Giles Gilmore. He would just pick his moment.

Wally Cole had not been at the theatre, but, of course, he read the glowing reports in the morning papers and was more than a little miffed that he'd been unable to buy shares in the production and Foxy Gordon had. But his time had been otherwise engaged with Gerry Pike recently.

Various members of his mob had been doing their job very thoroughly, collecting information about each gang member behind Gerry Pike and Pike himself. The young blood had collected a strong bunch of villains, some of whom had worked for his father before him. Hardened criminals, out to help their boss move up the ladder and usurp Cole if they could. However, whilst hunting for a weak link in the organization, one of the men had found somebody to suit their purpose.

Jackie Williams, a young thug who had been a mate of Gerry's since their schooldays, was a cocky kid, full of his own importance, who tried to lord it over the other members due to his long history with Gerry. The older men would put him down at every opportunity. Their lack of respect for him only fuelled his anger as he strived to prove himself. His one saving grace was his love for his younger brother, Barry. Fourteen-year-old Barry, retarded with the mental age of a five year old, idolized Jackie. He was his hero.

Barry's love was the only true love that Jackie had ever known. His parents were both drunkards and as young children both Jackie and Barry had been unmercifully beaten regularly in the father's drunken rages until one day, when he was old enough, Jackie had retaliated and turned on his father, putting him in hospital. Then when, shortly after, he became a member of Pike's gang and had a little money behind him, Jackie moved his brother into a shabby flat to live with him.

The boy had been so grateful to his brother that, when they moved in, he had thrown his arms around Jackie and hugged him. 'Oh, Jackie, thanks a million. We can now be happy on our own.' He suddenly looked scared and glanced at the front door. 'Dad won't come here, will he? He won't beat me any more, will he? He hurts me real bad.'

The complete innocence of the youngster touched Jackie deeply. 'No, Barry, you're safe now. We need never see the old bugger again.'

Barry beamed. 'The old bugger!' he kept repeating and laughing as he walked around the flat, exploring every room. 'You'll take care of me, won't you, Jackie? You won't let anything bad happen to me, will you, Jackie?'

'I promise, nothing bad will ever happen to you ever again. I give you my word. Look—' he led him to a small box room with a single bed in it — 'this is now your own room. I'll sleep in the one next door.'

The boy sat on the bed and patted the cover. 'Mine, all mine,' he kept saying quietly to himself. 'No old bugger 'cause Jackie's going to take care of me.' He looked up at his brother and grinned broadly. 'I'm hungry!'

The two of them settled down to what to them seemed like paradise. Barry was able to dress and feed himself and keep his room tidy, which he did almost to distraction. Forever tidying the bed, dusting the chest of drawers and wandering from room to room with absolute delight. He would walk to the nearby park and play on the swings. Go to the corner shop with a list and money that Jackie would give him from time to time to do the shopping. Then he would spend the day reading comics and listening to the wireless. He loved music and would dance around the room as it played.

His schooldays were now behind him. They had been torturous times for the boy, who had been teased unmercifully until Jackie turned up at the playground and threatened the boys concerned. But it was with great relief to both of them when it was time for Barry to leave.

When, during the following days, Barry saw publicity photos in the newspaper from the show *Broadway Melody* he pestered his brother to take him to see it. The only tickets that were available were in the gods, so Jackie booked them.

Barry was ecstatic about going to the Adelphi Theatre, and the morning of the performance he bought a small bunch of flowers to take with him to give to Miss Bonny Burton whose picture was also in the paper.

Once he sat in the theatre, Barry was enthralled. He bounced about in his seat to the music as he watched the dancers perform, and when the show was over, he dragged his brother to the stage door to wait for the star to appear. Clutching his now somewhat battered flowers.

When she emerged, Bonny was surrounded by fans. She signed autographs, smiled and chatted to the people, until a small fist pushed a bunch of flowers into her hand. She looked up and saw young Barry. 'Thank you,' she said, smiling at him, 'these are lovely.'

The youngster blushed, but with bright shining eyes he said, 'You are beautiful. I saw you dance, it was great. I can dance,' he stated proudly. 'I play the wireless and dance around the room all on my own.'

Bonny immediately recognized the boy's weakness and was deeply touched. 'What's your name?'

'Barry. This is my big brother Jackie.' He pulled Jackie forward by his coat. 'He takes care of me, making sure nothing bad happens to me. He brought me here tonight to see the show.'

Seeing the embarrassment on the older lad's face, Bonny tried to put him at ease. 'I hope you enjoyed the show, Jackie?'

He looked relieved. 'Yes, thanks, miss. Mind you, we couldn't see too clearly. We were up in the gods, and everything looks smaller up there.'

Bonny frowned and then she looked at the innocent face of Barry, beaming at her. 'Well, we must do something about that. If you are free on Saturday of next week, I'll have two tickets waiting at the box office for you in the stalls. You'll be able to see so much better there.'

Barry clapped his hands with glee and jumped up and down. 'Say we can come, Jackie, say we can come!'

Ruffling the boy's hair, his brother chuckled. 'Of course we can, and thank you, Miss Burton, that's very kind of you.'

Bonny sniffed the flowers. As she did so, some of the petals fell. The boy looked crestfallen. 'It's all right, Barry, I'll put them in water, they'll soon perk up again. I'll see you again,' she said and climbed into the waiting taxi. She waved as it drove away.

All of this was reported to Wally Cole.

* * *

It was the final performance of the second week and the box-office bookings were pouring in. Giles was greatly relieved. His financial situation would now ease and the worry of meeting his bills lessened. He just prayed for a long run.

Bonny now realized what being a star entailed. She was followed by photographers wherever she went and had been booked by Giles to give interviews to various magazines and on the wireless. This took up all her spare time, and she would return to the flat that she now shared with Shirley completely exhausted. Her picture was seen everywhere and when she went into a store in the West End she was immediately recognized and people would gather round her until she managed to escape. Shopping became a nightmare. However, she remembered Mickey's advice about dealing with the press and used the same approach with her many fans. She was always charming to them and they loved her for it.

After the Saturday evening performance, she left the theatre by the stage door, longing for the peace and quiet of the Sunday before her. She could sleep in and rest up, slip out the back door of the flat with Shirley, scarves over their heads, sunglasses on and walk in one of the parks. Hopefully unrecognized.

As was usual, fans awaited her departure and among them she saw young Barry. Hair slicked down, waiting impatiently, hopping from one foot to another.

Eventually the others left.

'Hello Barry, did you enjoy the show tonight?'

'I did, it was great to be able to see everything.' He smiled shyly. 'You were very good, Miss Burton. The stage looked very big. Do you ever get lost?'

She laughed. 'No, Barry, I have to know exactly where I'm going.'

'What about all those big buildings? How do they move them?'

She realized he meant the scenery. 'Look, come with me.' She looked at Jackie and said, 'I'd like to take him on stage where he can see everything. Is that all right with you?'

'That would be marvellous. Are you sure you can spare the time?'

Putting an arm around Barry's shoulders, she smiled and said, 'For my biggest fan, of course I can.'

Barry was enthralled by everything he saw. To see the enthusiasm and curiosity in the young boy's face, and his complete innocence of life, moved Bonny, and she took him to her dressing room, showed him all the theatrical make-up, the various wigs she wore, and signed a photograph of herself and gave it to him.

He was so excited he didn't know what to say. But Jackie did. 'I can't thank you enough for what you've done for my brother.'

'It was my pleasure.' She walked to the door. 'We'd better go or we'll be locked in.'

As they made their way outside, Barry talked to her non-stop. And when she was ready to get into her taxi, he flung his arms around her. 'Thanks, Miss Bonny. I'll pin your picture to my wall in my bedroom. I've got a room all to myself. No old bugger now!'

She looked at his brother with raised eyebrows.

'It's a long story,' he said and, after shaking her hand, he took his brother home.

CHAPTER TWENTY-ONE

Wally Cole was determined to find where young Gerry Pike had hidden the money from the bank robberies. After all, these banks were on his patch, so to his mind any proceeds from such a raid were rightfully his. So far none of his men had been able to trace the loot and so he had to put his plan into action . . .

* * *

Young Barry Williams bought some sweets at the local grocery shop and made his way to the playground in the park. He headed for the swings and, settling on one, he pushed himself off the ground with his feet, humming one of the songs from *Broadway Melody*, sucking on a sweet as he did so. As he swung to and fro, he was unaware of two men entering the playground.

One of them sat on the swing beside him.

Barry broke into song. '*Give my regards to Broadway*,' he sang. The man beside him joined in. The two swung backwards and forwards until they reached the end of the melody.

The young boy beamed at the stranger. 'I've been to the theatre and seen Miss Bonny dance. She gave me a picture,' he said proudly.

'I've been to the theatre too,' said the man. 'I enjoyed it so much I'm going again this afternoon to the matinee.'

'What's a matinee?' asked Barry.

'It's a show in the afternoon for people who can't go at night.'

'Me and my brother went at night. It was dark, but Jackie took care of me.'

'Would you like to come with me and see the show and Miss Bonny again? I have a spare ticket. I'll take care of you, just like Jackie.'

The boy was delighted. Then he frowned. 'Not in the gods, you can't see very well there. We went again and sat in the stalls. It's better there.'

'I've got seats in the front row!'

This was too much for the boy. He was overcome with excitement. 'You mean no one sitting in front of us?'

'No one! The only thing in front of us is the stage.' He got off the swing. 'If you want to come we have to go now or we'll be too late.'

Barry jumped down. 'I'll wave to Miss Bonny. She's my friend. She said I was her biggest fan.'

'Then she'll be really pleased to see you,' said the stranger. He held out his hand. 'Come along, I've got a car, we can be there in a few minutes.'

The boy went with him.

* * *

It was dark when Jackie Williams put his key into his front door. The house was in darkness and he frowned as he entered the hallway. 'Barry!' he called. There was no reply. With a sinking feeling in the pit of his stomach, he went from room to room, calling his brother's name. Realizing the house was empty, he ran to the corner shop and asked the owner if Barry was there.

'No, Jackie. He came in earlier this afternoon and bought some sweets. He said he was off to the swings. I've not seen him since.'

Jackie ran to the park, but when he got to the playground it was empty. Beneath the swing were a few sweet wrappers — but nothing else. The young man began to panic. Lighting a cigarette to calm himself, he tried to think where his brother might have gone. Knowing how enamoured he was with Bonny Burton, he wondered if the boy had made his way to the theatre. It was highly unlikely, he thought, but he couldn't think of anything else.

Running back to his car, Jackie drove to the Adelphi Theatre and entered the stage door. 'I want to see Miss Burton,' he demanded.

'Yes, son, you and all of London.' The stage doorkeeper was dismissive. After all, his job was to protect his stars.

Jackie became agitated. 'Listen to me, you old fool, my brother's gone missing and he's besotted with Miss Burton. Please . . . at least ask her if she's seen him.'

The man saw the desperation in Jackie's eyes, and getting up from his seat he said, 'Wait here.'

Knocking on Bonny's dressing-room door, the man passed on the message. Bonny looked worried. 'Where is this young man?' When she was told, she hastily made her way there.

'Jackie, what's this I hear about Barry?'

'He's not at home, miss, he went to the swings in the park, but after that I don't know. I'm worried to death; this isn't like him at all. He's always home before dark.'

'Then you must report this to the police. If he comes here I'll ask the stage doorkeeper to tell me immediately. Write down your address and leave it with him. I promise if I see him I'll let you know.'

'Thanks, miss, I'll do that.'

'Try not to worry, Jackie. I'm sure he's all right. You know what young boys are like, they lose track of time.'

'But Barry doesn't like being out in the dark unless I'm there.'

'You'll let me know what happens, won't you?'

'Yes, Miss Burton, I will and thanks.'

* * *

Young Barry Williams was very confused as he was led into a room and told to sit down. This wasn't the Adelphi. He was supposed to be seeing Miss Burton dance and this wasn't the theatre, he knew that. He wasn't silly!

Turning to the man who had taken him from the park, he looked accusingly at him. 'You told me a fib! You said we were going to see Miss Burton dance.'

'Shut your face!' the man snapped.

The threatening tone of voice made Barry cringe with fright. It reminded him of other days. Days when he'd been terrified. Days when he'd been hurt. He looked round the room, scared that the old bugger would walk in, and when the door opened suddenly he hid his head in his hands, waiting for the first blow.

'Hello, Barry.'

The boy peeped out from behind his fingers to see who had spoken.

Wally Cole stood looking down at him, a smile on his face. 'Would you like a cup of tea and some biscuits?'

Suspiciously, he answered, 'I want to go to the theatre like I was promised.'

'Yes, sorry about that, but we had to change our plans.' He placed a mug of tea and a packet of chocolate biscuits in front of the boy. 'Here you are, tuck in.'

'I want Jackie!'

Cole remained cool. 'You'll see your brother soon. He's going to help us and then you can both go home.'

Barry's eyes narrowed as he looked at the man. He wasn't angry at him like the other one. Then he saw the biscuits and slowly reaching forward, he took one. He glared at the first man as he ate. 'I don't like you!'

Cole laughed. 'Don't you take any notice of him, son. He's a miserable old git!'

'He shouted at me. I don't like no one shouting at me. The old bugger did that, then he'd hit me.'

'No one's going to hit you, Barry, I promise. I'm going to call Jackie now. He'll be here soon. You finish your tea.' He then walked out of the room, leaving the boy munching on his biscuit and glaring at the other man.

* * *

Jackie Williams left the police station in an agitated state. What was wrong with these coppers, didn't they realize how serious the situation was? The sergeant on the desk had taken down all the particulars about Barry, but had said the boy would probably turn up, though if he was still missing in the morning, Jackie was to return to the station and inform them. Nothing Jackie could say would change the man's mind.

'Listen, lad, boys wander off playing and forget the time. I'm sure you did the same when you were your brother's age. He'll come wandering back and wonder why there was such a fuss. I've seen it happen time and time again.'

Just as he was about to put his key into the front door, a car pulled up. The driver wound down his window. 'Want to see your brother, Jackie?'

The youth recognized one of Wally Cole's men and his heart sank. This was not good news. Whatever would they want with his brother? They must have a reason but it wouldn't be a good one. 'Where is Barry? What have you done with him?'

'He's fine. Last time I saw him he was tucking into some chocolate biscuits and a cup of tea. Jump in; I'll take you to him.'

Jackie stood hesitating for a moment.

The driver's tone became immediately threatening. 'Don't piss me off, lad. You don't want nothing bad to happen to that boy, do you? After all, he's not the brightest kid on the block, is he?'

Jackie climbed into the car. 'If you've hurt him, I'll . . .'

The man laughed. 'Don't threaten me, son. Older and better men have tried and failed. I could chew you up and spit you out before you knew what happened!' And, putting the car into gear, he drove away.

At an old warehouse in the East End docks, the vehicle drew to a halt and Jackie was led inside to a small room, empty apart from a table with a chair either side. Wally Cole was sitting waiting with two of his men.

'Sit down,' he told the young man.

'Where's my brother?' Jackie demanded.

'He's fine. You tell me what I want I know and you can both go home.'

Jackie Williams racked his brains but he couldn't imagine just what it was that he knew that was of any interest to the gang leader.

'Where has Gerry Pike hidden the money he took from the two banks he knocked over?'

So that was it, thought Jackie, and he was filled with apprehension because he had no idea. If he couldn't give them the information they wanted, what would happen to him and Barry then? He would have to tell the truth; this wasn't something he could blag because it would soon be discovered that he'd lied and then they would be in even deeper trouble.

'Well?' demanded Cole.

'I don't know, guv, honestly.'

'I thought you were good mates with Gerry, having been to school with him.'

'Well, yes, we were mates at school but now he's my boss and he keeps such things close to his chest. He doesn't broadcast that kind of information, it would be asking for trouble.'

'Then who would he tell?'

'Jimmy Knight, his right-hand man, must know, but no one else I wouldn't think.'

'Then you, my boy, will have to find out, won't you?'

'How the hell am I going to do that?'

Wally Cole's eyes narrowed. 'If you don't want no harm to come to your little brother, you'll find a way.'

Jackie pleaded with the man. 'Please, Mr Cole, let Barry go. He won't understand what's going on; he's a bit simple, you see. Being in a strange place will upset him, especially if I'm not around.'

'Then you'd best find out what I want to know, quickly. Until you do, the boy stays with me. Understand?'

'I've already reported him missing to the police,' Jackie told Cole.

'Then in the morning you go back and tell them he's come home. Now don't give me any grief, lad. Just do as you're told — and soon. I'm not a patient man!'

'Can I see Barry before I go?'

Wally thought for a moment. 'Fine, but you make sure he keeps calm whilst you're away. I don't want no trouble with him.'

'Yes, yes I will.' Jackie was anxious to see his brother. Hopefully he would be able to convince him to behave. Otherwise who knew what would happen. He was well aware of Wally Cole's reputation as a hard man. There would be no compassion in him for his brother's mental state. None at all.

Jackie was taken to a room nearby. As he opened the door he saw Barry sitting at a table, munching on a biscuit. There was a man standing around smoking a cigarette looking decidedly bored.

Barry looked up and saw his brother. First he smiled, then he looked angry. 'The man said he was taking me to see Miss Bonny dance. He told me a fib! You take me, Jackie.'

His brother crossed the room and knelt beside him. 'Look, Barry, I can't take you now, I've got to do a job for Mr Cole, the man who gave you the tea and biscuits.'

'They were nice, chocolate ones. I've eaten them nearly all.'

'I'll bring you some different ones. Now you be good until I get back.'

Barry's expression changed. 'I don't want to stay here.' He looked at the other man in the room. 'He shouted at me, just like the old bugger used to. I don't like him. I'll come with you and help you.'

The boy tried to stand but Jackie held his shoulder to stop him. 'The way to help me is to stay here and be a good boy. If you do that, we'll soon go home, I promise.'

Barry leaned closer to his brother and whispered. 'I don't want that man to shout at me again.'

Jackie whispered back. 'Don't you worry. I'll make sure he doesn't. OK?'

'OK. You look after me like you always do.'

'I've got to go now. Remember, be good, don't cause no aggravation. I'll be back as soon as I can.' He ruffled the boy's hair, then walked over to the man standing guard.

'I don't want to hear you've shouted at my brother when I get back, because if I find out that you did, Mr Cole won't get the information he wants and he won't be pleased. Understand?'

The thug just looked at him and didn't answer. Knowing there was no use arguing, Jackie left the room, hoping his threat would be enough to keep the man quiet. But he was shaking inside. How the hell was he going to find where Gerry had stashed the money from the robbery? How long would Wally Cole wait, and how long before young Barry became so scared he would cause trouble? Hands thrust deep into his pockets, he walked away, trying to think of a plan.

CHAPTER TWENTY-TWO

As Bonny prepared for the evening performance, she was relieved to receive a message that young Barry Williams was safe. His brother had called the box office and asked them to tell her the good news. She told Mickey all about it when he called to take her home after the show.

'You say his brother is Jackie Williams?'

She saw his frown. 'Yes, that's right. Why?'

'Jackie Williams is part of Gerry Pike's gang. They're a load of villains; you don't want any part of them, darlin'.'

'But young Barry isn't a member of any gang, for heaven's sake! He's just an innocent boy whose brain hasn't fully developed.'

'That may be, princess, but Jackie is and he *isn't* innocent. Just be careful is all.'

* * *

Whilst Bonny was performing that night, Jackie Williams was giving his own performance, trying to ingratiate himself with his old schoolmate and boss, Gerry Pike. He started reminiscing about their days at school, how close they were as kids.

'And here I am now, working for you, helping you to make a name for yourself.'

Gerry looked sceptically at him. 'I made my name all by myself. I don't remember *anyone* helping me.'

With a quick laugh, Jackie corrected himself. 'Of course you did, you know what I mean. You really are something now. You'll be bigger than your father ever was.'

Jackie had found Gerry's Achilles heel.' 'Do you honestly think so?'

'No doubt about it. Don't get me wrong, your old man was as hard as they come and I respected him as did everyone, but you, Gerry, you've got class!'

The young thug thrust out his chest with pride. 'Bloody right I have. Look at these threads.' He smoothed the material of his tailor-made suit. 'Bespoke! Dad bought his off the peg at Burtons. Fifty shilling tailors! No class, dressed like everybody else, but not me, I've got style.'

'Once you've laundered the bank money, you'll be able to go to London to Savile Row; you know, where the toffs go. After all, money will be no object then, will it? You could have your shoes handmade too.'

Gerry looked at him and smiled. 'Now that — the shoes, I mean — I'd never thought of.' He put his arm around Jackie. 'You're a good mate; I'll have a suit made for you too.'

'Blimey! Thanks Gerry. I hope the cash is in a safe place. It would be a pity if it was lifted, then neither of us would get any new threads.'

'Don't you worry about that; it's as safe as the Bank of England.' Gerry grinned broadly. 'Mind you, that's not so safe is it, otherwise how could I have robbed it?' He doubled up with laughter.

Jackie joined in the laughter. 'I expect you've got some-one standing guard over it so it'll be quite safe.'

'No need,' boasted Gerry. 'It's placed in a clever position that no one would think of looking. You know what they say about the most obvious being the safest. I've got a key and so has Jimmy Knight. We don't need an armed guard. This is enough.' He showed Jackie a key on a chain attached to his trouser belt. 'It never leaves me, and Jimmy's never leaves him.' He patted Jackie's shoulder. 'Don't you worry; your new suit is safe.'

As Gerry walked away, Jackie wracked his brains as to where the money could be hidden. Obviously Gerry had been clever about it, and knowing him as he did, Jackie realized that his friend would have been inspired to choose a hiding place that was different, to fool everyone. He had a devious and clever brain, which had kept both of them out of trouble in their schooldays. He would have to try and get inside the mind of Gerry Pike to solve this problem. In the meantime, poor Barry would be fretting without him.

* * *

Barry was indeed getting restless, fidgeting in his chair until the man guarding him snapped at him. 'For Christ's sake, will you keep still!'

'I want to go to the lavatory, now! Jackie gets cross if I pee my trousers.' The boy held his crotch. 'I want to go badly!'

'Oh, for goodness' sake.' The man grabbed him by the shoulder and led him out of the room along the corridor and, opening a door, pushed him into a room with a toilet. 'There, and hurry up.' Closing the door he muttered angrily to himself, 'I'm a bloody nursemaid now!'

Barry looked around to see if there was any way of escape but there was only a skylight. He relieved himself, tucked himself in and opened the door slowly, but his keeper was ready for him and led him away by the scruff of the neck, but Barry had spied a door at the end of the passage way. If only he could run away. But he was then pushed back into the room he'd occupied since Jackie left him.

'I want my brother!' he cried.

'For goodness' sake shut up or I'll clout you one.'

Barry kicked out at him and caught the man in the shins.

With a cry of pain, the stranger turned on the boy and hit him round the head. 'You behave yourself or I'll beat the living daylights out of you.'

Barry curled up in a ball, holding his head, his ears ringing from the force of the blow. 'I'll tell Jackie about you!' he said, then hid his head again, waiting for the next blow, but the man sat down, cursing to himself.

* * *

When Bonny woke the following morning, she found herself thinking about young Barry, wondering what had happened to him and how he'd got lost. The boy had endeared himself to her with his innocence and childlike behaviour, and having taken note of the address that his brother had left at the stage door, she decided to go and see for herself that young Barry was none the worse for his escapade.

Jackie Williams was shocked to see Bonny Burton on his doorstep. He looked dishevelled, having had little sleep trying to sort out where Gerry could have hidden the money, which would enable him to release his young brother.

'Hello, Jackie! Are you all right?' she asked anxiously.

'Oh, yes, yes, Miss Burton. I didn't sleep very well last night, that's all.'

'I thought I'd come and see Barry and make sure he was all right. Can I come in?'

Jackie couldn't think of an excuse quickly enough to keep her out, so stepped back. 'Yes, of course.' He led her into the kitchen.

Bonny saw the remains of a meal on the table and quickly noted it was for one person only. The house was quiet and knowing that Barry was a noisy boy, Bonny wondered where he was. So she asked.

'He's gone to the shop for some food and a comic,' Jackie said quickly.

But the young man didn't look at her as he answered and he appeared nervous and uncomfortable. Bonny sensed that something was seriously wrong. 'He's still missing isn't he?'

Jackie looked at her in surprise. 'What makes you say that?'

'You're hiding something from me, I can tell. What is it, Jackie? Maybe I can help.'

Her kindness was the young man's undoing. 'You can't, Miss Bonny. No one can help me. It's something I have to sort out myself.' He blinked away tears as he spoke.

'Where is Barry?'

'He's staying with some folks I know but I'll soon get him back.'

'What do you mean, *get him back*? You make it sound as if he's a prisoner!'

Jackie burst into tears.

Eventually the whole sorry story came out. It was such a relief for Jackie Williams to be able to share this enormous burden with someone. 'I promised to take care of him and he'll be scared on his own with strangers.'

'You must go to the police and tell them what you told me.'

He went pale. 'I can't do that! Gerry will kill me. If he doesn't, then Wally Cole's men will get me and they would certainly kill my brother. Don't you see?'

'Oh, Jackie, what can we do?'

'I have to discover Gerry's hiding place. That's the only way out.'

'Have you any idea at all where to look?'

He shook his head. 'He said it was the most obvious place that no one would imagine looking, that's all I have to go on.'

'Where is Barry being kept?'

He described the place to her. 'But it's well guarded. It's not like anywhere that I could creep in and get to him without being discovered.' He began to fidget. 'Look, Miss Bonny, I have to get on with my search, so I'm sorry but I must ask you to leave.'

She reluctantly rose to her feet. 'Please let me know what happens, won't you?'

He nodded as he walked her to the door.

As Bonny walked away she racked her brains as to what she could do. The only person who she could turn to was Mickey. Hailing a taxi, she made for Foxy Gordon's gym.

* * *

Mickey O'Halleran was just climbing out of the ring after a workout with his sparring partner when he saw Bonny enter. He saw her anxious expression and, removing his headgear, he hurried over to her. 'Whatever is the matter, darlin'?'

She quickly told him what had transpired.

His frown deepened with every sentence. 'No way can you get involved with this!' he declared. 'These men are dangerous.'

'How can I stand by and let Barry remain a prisoner? That poor boy will be demented!'

He firmly led her to a nearby bench and put his arm around her. 'Now you listen to me, Bonny. This is out of your hands! For goodness' sake, we are talking bank robbery, gang warfare and maybe murder! You try and interfere and your life could be in danger, and no way can I let that happen.'

Foxy wandered over after seeing the worried expressions on the face's of the two of them. 'Something wrong, Mickey?' His boxer was due to take part in a major bout and he didn't want anything to upset his concentration.

Mickey's frustration boiled over. 'Will you talk to Bonny and make her realize she could be in danger!' He then explained the whole situation to his trainer.

Foxy was intrigued by the tale. So the rumours were right. It *was* Gerry Pike who had pulled the bank jobs — and he was trying to take over Wally's territory. It was a pleasing scenario, he thought. 'So Jackie has no idea where to look for the money, you say.'

Bonny shook her head and repeated what Jackie had told her about the hiding place.

Foxy looked thoughtful. 'Somewhere obvious, you say. Clever little bugger, that Gerry Pike. But Mickey's right, Bonny my dear. No way can you be involved. It's far too dangerous.'

'But what about Barry? We can't leave him there!'

'No, you're right. Jackie's a cocky little bleeder, but he does look after his brother and neither of them have had it easy. You leave this with me, love. But you must promise me that you won't try and get involved, because if you do, you'll be putting your head in a noose. Then my champ here will want to come to your rescue, fight or no fight, and I can't have that. Understand?'

'Yes, I understand.'

'Good.' He turned to Mickey. 'You get a shower and take this young lady away, buy her a coffee somewhere, calm her down.' Then he walked to his office to mull over what he'd heard.

CHAPTER TWENTY-THREE

Giles Gilmore sat at his desk, reading the financial statement before him. The show was booked up for months in advance. The success of *Broadway Melody* was more than he'd hoped for. He was secure and financially he would make a killing, but there was one more ambition of his to be filled. He wanted to put a show on Broadway in New York. That truly would be the pinnacle to his career . . . and he now had a production he felt he could take to America. It would take time to organize — and money. With the show promising a long run, he had the time, but there would be a lot of hurdles to cross first. His backers would have to be approached, of course. He frowned. That meant he would have to consult Foxy Gordon in particular. After all, the man owned forty per cent of the stock. It was not something he contemplated with any great pleasure.

His involvement in Giles Gilmore's production was the furthest thing from Gordon's mind at the moment. He was far more interested as to where Gerry Pike had stashed the money from the bank robberies. He sat quietly in his office in the gym, writing down every detail that he knew of the young hoodlum, trying to gauge his hiding place. A place that was different. One that no one would consider looking in. Young

Pike must feel secure about it if there was no guard on the cash.

He made a list. His home? No, that would be unwise. Where did the young thug go to for fun? He liked clubs, but it wouldn't be there. His office, maybe, where he ran a business under the guise of house clearance and the sale of second-hand furniture. His showroom beneath, perhaps? There would be all sorts of stuff displayed that could be suitable, but wouldn't that be obvious to the police if they were to search? They surely would open every drawer, every chest? He scratched his head. What else was important to Gerry? The only other thing was his love of clothes. He went to a tailor in Whitechapel; Foxy knew that because Gerry used to boast about how good the cutter was. Perhaps he would go along and get measured up for a suit. He could do with a new one and it would be a good opportunity to question the tailor. Maybe he could give Foxy a lead during their conversation. It was worth a try.

* * *

Jackie Williams was in a state. He still had not a clue as to where Gerry had hidden the money. He had searched everywhere. Even Gerry's home, when he'd been asked to take some chairs that Gerry had bought to the house and put them in the sitting room.

Although he'd searched every room thoroughly, opening drawers, trunks and cupboards, he'd found nothing. He'd even stood in each room to look for something that was so normal, it could escape attention. But he had failed. He was getting frantic, knowing that Barry would be fretting and that when he did, he became difficult. That worried him the most. He knew how to handle the boy, but Wally or his men would just get angry and maybe hurt him. He decided to go back to Wally Cole and plead for Barry's release. But when he got there, he discovered that Barry had managed to escape and was missing.

Wally Cole was furious! He'd sent out for some crayons and a colouring book to appease the lad, who was becoming restless and cantankerous. It had settled him, and in the ensuing peace, the man guarding him had fallen asleep. Barry had crept out of the room and was away before anyone realized.

Cole stormed at Jackie when he arrived, 'My men will find that little bleeder, I promise you and he'll pay for all the trouble he's caused me!'

'Please, Mr Cole, leave him alone. You don't need him. I promise I'll find the money; you don't need to hold my brother. I give you my word.'

Cole looked at Jackie with disdain. 'That's supposed to make me feel secure, is it? Don't be ridiculous. I'll make *you* a promise. You find the money and I won't top your brother when we find him.'

Jackie was horrified. 'You can't kill him, he's innocent. He's never done anyone any harm in his life!'

'Well, son, it's up to you. You'd better be on your way, you're wasting time here.'

Jackie fled the building.

* * *

Bonny walked wearily to her dressing room after the final curtain that night. She hadn't slept well worrying about Barry Williams. Had Foxy Gordon done anything about his release, she wondered. It bothered her that he was in the hands of some criminal gang. She decided to send out for some fish and chips, which she could eat in her dressing room, then she could go home and go straight to bed. Picking up the phone in her room, she rang the doorman and asked him to send someone to the fish and chip shop for her as she'd sent her dresser home. She was suffering with a cold, and Bonny had assured her she could manage once she was dressed for the final number.

As she slipped out of her costume and reached for a coat hanger, she let out a scream as the dress rail moved on its wheels.

A head peered out from between the gowns. 'It's only me, Miss Bonny.'

'Barry! What on earth are you doing here?'

The young lad climbed his way out from behind. 'I ran away! The man went to sleep, so I crept out of the room as quiet as a mouse. Then I went to the door and it opened and I was on the street. I ran all the way. You'll look after me, won't you?' He looked worried. 'I don't like those men. They shouted at me and one of them hit me, just like the old bugger used to.'

She gathered him to her. 'Oh dear, Barry, I am sorry, and of course I'll take care of you. Are you hungry?'

'Starving. Got any sweets or biscuits?'

She shook her head. 'No, but I have some fish and chips coming soon.'

He beamed at her. 'Do they have salt and vinegar on them?'

'No, I'm afraid not.'

His face fell just for a moment, then he smiled. 'Never mind, we can pretend they do.'

There was a knock on the door and Bonny looked at Barry. Putting her finger to her lips, she pulled him out of sight, grabbed a handful of change off the dressing table and opened the door, which she carefully locked after the messenger delivered his goods.

Taking a little of the food herself, she gave the rest to Barry, still in the newspaper it was wrapped in. 'We'll have to eat with our fingers,' she said.

The boy tucked into the food and said, 'They always taste better eaten with your fingers anyway.'

As she watched him, Bonny's mind was in turmoil. What was she to do with the boy? She could take him back to her flat for the night and let him sleep there, but what about tomorrow when she was working? If he'd escaped from the villains and she let his brother know he was safe, would they follow him to find the boy?

She rang Mickey O'Halleran and told him what had happened.

'Jaysus Christ, Bonny!' he exclaimed over the phone. 'You stay put; I'm coming to the theatre. Don't tell anyone he's there.'

But before he arrived there was a knock on the door.

Bonny froze. 'Who is it?'

'It's me, Shirley, are you ready to go home?'

Bonny let her in, then quickly locked the door.

Shirley looked puzzled. 'What the hell are you doing that for?' Then she saw Barry. 'Hello, who are you?'

Bonny quickly filled her friend in with all the details. 'We will have to hide him for tonight,' she told her. 'After that, I don't know. Mickey is on his way over.'

'Bloody hell, girl, you do get yourself mixed up with some strange people.' She nodded over towards Barry and in a near whisper asked, 'Would they really knock him off?'

'I'm afraid so. I just don't know what to do for the best.'

At that moment Mickey knocked on the door and called her name. Once inside he questioned Barry as to what had happened to him from the time he was picked up.

Barry had overheard enough conversation between the men to pass on, which made the situation clear to the boxer. 'So it's all about money, as always! People will do anything for greed.'

'I want my brother,' Barry said.

Sitting beside the lad, Mickey tried to make him understand that Jackie might be in danger if he came to see him at the moment. That tonight he'd stay with Bonny, and tomorrow Mickey would take him to safety.

'Where?' asked Bonny.

'It's best you don't know. Foxy and I will keep him safe, don't you worry. But we have to sneak him out of here and there may be a couple of photographers outside.'

'They won't be interested in me,' Shirley ventured. Then with a grin she turned to Barry. 'How would you like to dress up as one of the lady dancers? We could play a game. What do you say? We could put a dress on you and a wig.'

The boy's face lit up. 'I'd like that. Will you give me a lady's name too?'

'Why not, what would you like to be called?'

'Queenie, after my auntie.'

'Right then, you come with me. I'll see you both back at the flat.' Unlocking the door, she peered out to see if the coast was clear, and grabbing Barry by the hand, she left the dressing room.

'I am so sorry, Mickey, to get you involved but I didn't know what to do.' Bonny was distraught. 'I can't let anything happen to that boy, whoever his brother might be.'

Pulling her into his arms, Mickey tried to reassure her. 'Your problems are mine, darlin', and it's my place to look after you, like Jackie does for his brother. Now come along, let's get going.'

Outside a couple of photographers waited. They raised their cameras, took a couple of pictures and then left.

Bonny shook her head. 'Don't they ever get fed up taking our pictures?'

'I told you, princess, it goes with the job. They have to earn a living too.' He hailed a taxi and they made their way home.

Shirley had already made a cup of tea and a sandwich for Barry and herself when Bonny and Mickey arrived.

'This boy has a bottomless pit for a stomach!' Shirley laughed. 'He told me he'd already had fish and chips.'

'He's a growing lad,' Mickey told her. 'But now I must go and see Foxy. I'll be back early tomorrow morning.' Leaning forward he kissed Bonny. 'Get a good night's sleep, sweetheart.'

* * *

Foxy, who lived above the gym, was surprised to hear the front doorbell so late at night. Picking up a crowbar, he went to the door. 'Who's there?'

'It's me, Mickey. Let me in.'

Over a glass of beer, Mickey explained why he'd called. 'The lad escaped, so now we need to hide him. I can't have Bonny mixed up in this after tonight.'

'I'll put him up here. Wally Cole would never suspect that I have anything to do with this. He'll be as safe as houses.'

'But what happens if Jackie can't find the money?'

'I have no idea, but I'm off to Gerry's tailor tomorrow. Maybe he can throw some light on the subject. At least I'll find out a bit more about him. You know men chat away whilst they are being measured. I might strike lucky.'

* * *

The shop was typical of all tailors' shops. Pattern books lay about; rolls of cloth were sorted into colours. A table was being used by the cutter, who followed the chalk marks on the material he was cutting, and sitting cross-legged on a bench was a man sewing on buttons by hand, whilst two others were working at treadle machines. Working at speed, as they fed the pieces of garment through, to be stitched.

Foxy looked through the materials on offer, choosing a black and white dogstooth check, to the agreement of the tailor.

'Good choice, sir. It will suit you very well.' Then he questioned Foxy as to how he liked his suits styled.

'Well, I'll leave it to you,' he said. 'I have always admired the suits you have made for Gerry Pike.'

'Ah, young Mr Pike. A very stylish young man, if I may say so. Exquisite taste. Let me show you a couple of patterns that he particularly likes.'

As he was being measured, Foxy looked around the room. There were a few tailors' dummies with garments draped on them that were in the process of being made. Foxy noticed that the dummies had names marked on pieces of paper.

'Are those for each of your customers?' he enquired.

'Just for a selected few of our regulars.' He pointed to a bare one in the corner. 'That's Mr Pikes'. He had it made to his measurements. I have to say it is far superior to the others, but the measurements are very accurate . . . as long as he doesn't gain or lose weight!' The man chuckled.

When the tailor had finished taking his measurements, Foxy walked over to the dummy and studied it closely. 'What do you mean, he had it made?' he asked.

The tailor smiled. 'Mr Pike took the measurements and had it made up himself. He said he didn't want us to use it for anyone else. He does like to be exclusive, does our Mr Pike. It's much more solid than the others. Beautifully made, I must say. Probably cost a pretty penny.'

A slow smile spread across Foxy's face. 'Clever little bleeder!' he muttered softly.

CHAPTER TWENTY-FOUR

Foxy Gordon drove back to the gym with a satisfied grin. Quite by chance, he thought he'd found where Gerry Pike had stashed the money from the robberies. How very neat. He hadn't been able to turn the tailor's dummy upside down, but he felt sure that at the base, which had been broad, he would find a keyhole. He had tried to lift it but it weighed a ton, as opposed to the others which were much lighter. Now what was he to do with the information? No way would he touch it. He was running a legit business these days, and the last thing he wanted was to lose this status — not with a world-class boxer in his stable. But he didn't want Wally Cole to have it either.

* * *

The police received an anonymous call later that day that caused much excitement. The Detective Inspector in charge of the bank robberies' case called a meeting immediately.

'With regard to the bank robberies, we have received information about the stolen money.' He then told his men about the phone call. 'It would seem that the villain responsible was, as we thought, young Gerry Pike. If our informant is correct, the money is hidden in a tailor's dummy in Whitechapel. We, of course, will have to examine said dummy, and then if our informant's guess is correct, we'll have to wait for it to be collected. There is word going around that the cash is due to be laundered soon, so if we're lucky we won't have too long to wait.'

Plans were then put in place for the tailor's shop to be visited by two detectives, and if the information was solid, a rota would be set up so the shop would be watched twenty-four hours a day.

* * *

Young Barry Williams was having the time of his life! He'd spent the night sleeping at Miss Bonny's flat with her and her friend Shirley, and now, after a hearty breakfast, he was to go out with Mickey O'Halleran to another place. If only Jackie was here too, he thought.

Mickey slipped the lad out of the flat the back way and into a waiting car, before making for the gym.

'Am I going to learn to box?' asked Barry excitedly.

'Would you like to?'

He turned his head on one side to consider the offer. 'I'm not sure . . . You get hurt sometimes if you box, don't you?'

Mickey pursed his lips. 'I'm afraid so, my son. It's part of the game.'

Barry shook his head vigorously. 'Then I don't want to. I don't like to be hurt.'

Putting a comforting arm on the boy's shoulder, Mickey said, 'That's fine and I don't blame you one bit. What do you like?'

'I like comics! And sweets.'

'Then that's what you'll have if you are a good boy and do as you are told. OK?'

'OK.'

Once Barry was settled at the gym and seemed content, Foxy and Mickey sat down together.

'I really feel we should let Jackie know his brother's safe,' Mickey suggested.

'No, we'll wait a while, it won't be for long,' Foxy insisted. Then he told Mickey about his call to the police. 'Gerry is about to move the money; I heard about it this morning. The police are just waiting for him to do so, then Jackie will be fine, and Barry too. Just be patient, it'll soon be over.'

With a frown Mickey asked, 'What happens if Wally Cole finds out he lost the stash because of you?'

With a shrug Foxy grinned. 'How will he find out? The call was anonymous!'

* * *

Wally Cole now knew where Barry Williams was being hidden! The two men watching Bonny and Mickey had been unaware of his presence in Bonny's dressing room, as the lad had slipped in there before she had arrived and therefore the theatre had not been under surveillance, and neither had they recognized Barry leaving the theatre dressed as a woman, when Shirley had taken him home. But they had seen Mickey enter Bonny's flat, and the man watching the back entrance had seen the boxer take the boy to a waiting car and had then followed him to Foxy's gym.

All this had been reported to their boss, who was livid that Foxy had become involved. 'That bastard is interfering with my business!' he shouted. 'I'll make him pay dearly for that.' He was already frustrated, as Jackie had been unable to find the hiding place where the ill-gotten gains were being hidden.

'What do you want to do about the boy, guv?' asked one man.

'Leave him where he is. Jackie is obviously oblivious to the fact that he's safe, so he'll keep digging.' But the situation was unsatisfactory. Cole was aware that the money would have to be laundered — and soon. But where the hell was it?

The villain didn't have to wait long for his problem to be solved, as a few days later Gerry went to the tailor's for a fitting, with his right-hand man in tow, and left carrying the tailor's dummy. As he tried to load it into the back of his car, the waiting police pounced, taking it and both men to the local police station for questioning.

The detectives working on the case gathered round with great excitement as the key was removed from the belt Gerry was wearing, inserted in the lock under the base of the dummy . . . and opened. Neatly packed inside were thousands of pounds in bank notes, each stack wearing a paper band with the stamp of the bank on it.

Detective Inspector Phillips smiled at Gerry Pike. 'You're nicked, mate!' And then he read him his rights.

* * *

Wally Cole went berserk when he heard the news. 'That crafty little bugger! Whoever would have thought to look around a tailor's shop for the loot?' But he had the consolation that Gerry and his associate would go down for the robbery, thus removing the young blade from causing him any more trouble for quite a while. But he wondered just how the police had known of the money's whereabouts. Who had discovered the secret? He pondered over this for a long time and then decided to pay a call on Foxy Gordon. He had a niggling suspicion that the fight promoter was behind it in some way. Call it a gut reaction . . .

* * *

Foxy Gordon was like a cat with two tails, he was so delighted with the outcome of his anonymous call to the police. Gerry Pike would be behind bars, there would be no gang war between the two factions, and Cole hadn't been able to get his hands on the money. Terrific! He looked at his watch and then made his way downstairs to the gym. He was more than a little surprised to see Wally Cole himself and a couple of his henchmen walk in. With a scowl he asked, 'What are you doing here?'

Cole studied him closely. 'I wondered if you had been to Whitechapel lately — to be measured for a suit, perhaps?'

Gordon's eyes narrowed as he met the other's gaze. 'I don't understand the question.'

But knowing Foxy of old, Wally was certain that his gut feeling had been correct. 'I know you're hiding young Barry here.' He noted the surprised look on the other's face. He prodded Foxy in the chest. 'I don't like it when anyone interferes in my business. You of all people should know that.'

'You mean like when young Gerry Pike turned over the two banks on your patch!' Foxy couldn't hide the note of triumph in his voice.

And then Wally Cole knew for sure that Foxy had been meddling. His expression was thunderous as he stared at the promoter. 'You'll pay for this, I promise.'

'Pay for what?' Foxy couldn't hide his grin, which only infuriated the villain more.

Wally turned and stormed out of the building.

* * *

Shortly after, Jackie was reunited with his brother. Mickey had put a note through the door of Jackie's house telling him where Barry was, and finding it later, he had driven over to the gym immediately.

No one could doubt the love the two had for each other when Jackie was taken upstairs to see Barry. The young lad threw himself into his brother's arms. 'Where have you been?' he demanded. Then, without waiting for an answer, told Jackie how he'd spent a night with Miss Bonny and then driven with Mickey to the gym.

'I've had lots to eat!' he proclaimed, 'and I've had sweets and comics.' He looked accusingly at his brother. 'You didn't come back!'

Jackie tried to explain. 'I wanted to but I had to try and find something for Mr Cole first. Unfortunately I didn't, and then I heard you'd run away. I didn't know where you were or I'd have come to see you.'

Barry looked at him with a sulky expression. 'I didn't like it there with that man. You should have come and taken me away!'

Mickey intervened. 'He couldn't help it, Barry. He had to do as he was told, just like you had to when you came here. Anyway, your brother's here now and you'll be able to go home.'

The lad looked around. 'I like it here. I think I'll stay!'

Laughing, Mickey said, 'Sorry, son, you have to go. We are now very busy and there would be no one to buy you comics or sweets any more.'

The boy's face fell. 'Oh, in that case I'll go with Jackie. He'll buy me some, won't you?' he asked, turning to his brother.

'Only if you behave. Now, thank Mr Gordon for having you, and then we'll be off.'

* * *

It was the night of Mickey O'Halleran's defence of his title and the excitement in the arena was palpable. Would the champ beat his opponent, Jake Forbes? Forbes was no pushover and Mickey knew he would have to box to the best of his ability to outpoint him.

As the fight was taking place late on a Saturday night, Bonny was unable to be present until after the show was over and hoped she would be there in time to see Mickey box. There were minor bouts taking place earlier in the evening, building up to the grand climax.

Giles Gilmore had laid on a car to take him and Bonny to the arena immediately the final curtain fell, knowing that Bonny wouldn't rest until she was seated at the ringside, and he wanted to ensure that his star was happy. He had been making overtures to those who mattered on Broadway about taking the production to New York. So far, the interest had been favourable and he was excited by the prospect.

At last the performance came to its conclusion and Bonny hastily removed her stage make-up, swiftly changed, climbed into the car with Giles and headed for the arena, her heart pounding. She felt more nervous for Mickey and the outcome of his bout than when she was waiting to go on stage and she would be glad when the whole thing was over.

Settling into their seats, Giles turned to Bonny and, seeing the tension in her eyes, patted her hand. 'Relax, Mickey will be fine.'

'I can't help worrying that he will be hurt. Boxing is a brutal sport, but it's Mickey's life.'

The trumpeters suddenly began a fanfare and a buzz went round the crowd as first Jake Forbes made his way to the ring, shadow-boxing as he went. The announcer, resplendent in evening dress, heralded Forbes's arrival over the microphone from the ring and the crowd cheered. Then, after another fanfare, Mickey was announced and the crowd got to their feet and cheered wildly.

Mickey walked sedately to the ring, waving to his fans as he did so, but once he was in the ring he shadow-boxed to loosen himself up, ready for the fight. He walked to his corner and looked down at Bonny. He winked and blew her a kiss. The flash of the many newsmen's cameras caught the gesture, which would make front-page news the next day.

The champion glanced around the ringside seats and saw Foxy sitting fidgeting in his seat, busily talking to the man beside him, and a couple of rows back sat Wally Cole. Mickey felt his hackles rise, thinking how the villain encouraged young Charlie Black to gamble. Mickey was convinced

Cole was behind the young boxer's death, although a verdict of suicide had been brought in by the coroner. Wally Cole returned Mickey's gaze, his expression cold and calculating.

The two boxers were called to the centre of the ring where the referee spoke to them. 'I want a clean fight, no low punches, and when I say break I mean it!'

The men walked back to their corners and the seconds left the ring. The bell rang for the first round . . . and Bonny held her breath.

It was a fight that would go down in the record books as memorable. Forbes was a canny boxer with a powerful left hook, which he used as often as possible But O'Halleran was quicker on his feet. The men were fairly equal in the opening rounds until Mickey pulled slightly ahead in the markings.

Bonny was exhausted watching. Her stomach was in knots as she watched Mickey duck and dive and prance around the ring. But she jumped to her feet with a cry of surprise, as did hundreds of others, as Forbes caught Mickey a sharp blow to the chin and the Irishman was knocked to the ground!

'One, two, three, four,' counted the referee.

Bonny thought she was going to be sick.

'Five, six . . .'

Mickey got to his feet to cheers that rang round the venue, echoing in every corner. Bonny sank back in her seat, barely able to breathe. Her relief as the bell rang for the end of the round was her saving grace.

'Are you all right?' Giles asked anxiously, seeing how pale she looked.

'No, I'm a nervous wreck! I thought Mickey had had his chips then, he took so long to get up.'

'He was waiting to get his breath back, that's why he stayed down.'

'Really? I thought he was in trouble.'

'He just caught a lucky blow; he'll be fine, just you wait and see.'

'I'm not sure I'll live long enough!'

It was round eight and Forbes was tiring. O'Halleran certainly looked the fitter of the two, despite being dropped to the canvas earlier. The champ was now scoring more points and suddenly his fist shot out and caught Forbes on the point of the chin. The boxer sank to his knees and the referee sent Mickey to a neutral corner.

Bonny covered her mouth with her hand and quietly kept count with the referee. 'Seven, eight, nine . . . ten!' She jumped to her feet, yelling at the top of her voice, which was drowned by the cheers of the other spectators.

The referee caught hold of Mickey O'Halleran's arm and held it aloft. 'Ladies and gentlemen, the winner — and still middleweight champion . . . Mickey O'Halleran.'

Bonny threw her arms around Giles and hugged him.

People of note, and other champion boxers, climbed into the ring to congratulate the winner. A microphone was put in front of Mickey and he was asked how he felt about the fight. 'Jake Forbes was a great opponent and I had to be on top of my game to beat him.' The two men shook hands. 'But I would like to dedicate this fight to my beautiful fiancée, Miss Bonny Burton!' He smiled down at her and threw her a kiss.

The crowd went wild! The press gathered round and cameras flashed, taking pictures of both Mickey and of Bonny, who was smiling happily, now she'd got over the surprise of the announcement.

The only person not pleased by the news was Giles Gilmore.

CHAPTER TWENTY-FIVE

Giles Gilmore, standing beside Bonny after Mickey's surprise announcement of their engagement, smiled as the cameras flashed, but inside he was fuming. Bonny Burton was his star! The biggest attraction on the West End stage. Now a major player in the musical theatrical world . . . His means of cracking Broadway itself! She didn't have time for romance! But with so many of the press around, he had to be careful what he said.

'Are you pleased for Miss Burton?' asked a reporter.

Giles smiled benevolently. 'I must confess, I am surprised, but of course I'm delighted for them both.'

Another man pushed forward. 'What about when they get married, won't that affect the show? Will you lose your star?'

'Oh, come along,' said Giles through gritted teeth, 'many stars of the theatre are married, why should it make a difference? Now if you'll excuse me . . .' He left the ringside and followed Bonny to Mickey's dressing room.

Mickey was sitting on a massage table having his boxing gloves removed. Bonny ran to him and, throwing her arms around his neck, kissed him. 'So now we are official!' she said, smiling.

'I thought it was about time, princess. After all, it will keep all those men away who lust after you.'

'Oh, lust? I like the sound of that.'

'Listen, darlin', I'm the only man to get near you, you remember that!'

'Why would I want any other?' She stroked his bruised face. 'You scared me to death out there when you went down on the canvas.'

'He caught me a lucky blow, that's all. The man was no pushover, but I'm still the champion, that's what matters.'

Giles spoke up. 'Congratulations on maintaining your title, Mickey, and on your engagement. May I ask if you are thinking of getting married soon? After all, Bonny is my star and I have a lot of money invested in her and her future.'

Mickey's eyes narrowed. 'Don't talk about her as if she's a commodity! She's flesh and blood, a human being, and her future is my concern also.'

'Now, you two!' Bonny intervened. 'This has been a big night for Mickey and me and we will have lots to talk about. For goodness' sake, Giles, we've only just got engaged — to the public's knowledge anyway. Mickey has just been through a tough evening and all we want to do is celebrate. The future will have to wait.'

But Giles was concerned. He had to make Mickey O'Halleran understand the seriousness of the situation. 'Well, I hope soon to have another reason to celebrate. I am making plans to take the production to New York after the run ends here. How do you feel about appearing on Broadway, Bonny?'

She was astonished. 'Oh my God! Are you serious?'

'Very. It's my life's ambition to have a show in New York and this is the one which will take us all there.' He turned to Mickey. 'Do you understand what a big step this is for Bonny?'

'And for you, Giles.' Mickey understood immediately how Giles needed his fiancée to fulfil his ambition. 'You need Bonny to star in it, or it won't be viable. I'm right, aren't I?'

There was no point in denying it. 'Absolutely! Everyone is talking about her talent. She's the biggest thing in the musical theatre at this moment and she could take New York by storm. How do you feel about *that*, Bonny?'

She looked somewhat dazed by the idea. 'I really don't know what to say, Giles. My head's in a whirl. What a night! Mickey won his fight, announced our engagement and now this! How on earth can I think straight?'

Mickey got off the table. 'Of course you can't. I'll have a shower and then we'll go to the Savoy for dinner. There, we'll talk about everything.' He looked pointedly at Gilmore. 'Thanks for looking in; I'll no doubt see you when I collect Bonny after her next performance on Monday. Have a good weekend.'

Giles felt his hackles rise at such a pointed dismissal. He also realized that the boxer was someone he would have to deal with when it came to Bonny and any new contract. She was legally his until the end of the West End run; after that he had no legal hold on her at all. Surely she wouldn't turn down such a great opportunity — would she?

Foxy Gordon had been listening to the conversations taking place with great interest. After all, he owned forty per cent of the production and Giles Gilmore would have to negotiate with him before he could take the show anywhere. That gave him a great feeling of power and satisfaction.

* * *

When Giles returned home, he called a reporter he knew and gave him an exclusive about his plans to go to America. The next morning, in the gossip column of the theatrical section, these facts were printed in black and white.

Wally Cole read the announcement and was furious. That little bastard Gordon would cash in again! Well he would certainly have to do something about that. Gordon couldn't scupper his plans and get away with it. Oh no! That wouldn't do at all. Anyone who crossed Wally Cole would have to pay in the end.

Mickey stood in his bath robe and read the column. Now their engagement was common knowledge, after last night's dinner he had booked Bonny and him into their favourite hotel, where they had had their own private celebration. Now he was waiting for their breakfast to be delivered and had started reading the Sunday papers.

'Bloody Giles Gilmore!' he muttered angrily. As he sat down to read the article, he realized that Giles had stolen a march on him and Bonny. By publicizing the fact, the papers would be all over her, asking her about the move to the States, and what could she say, other than she was happy about it? Therefore committing herself to the move before there had been any negotiation.

The waiter knocked on the door and wheeled in a breakfast trolley, which he stood before the window. Mickey tipped the man and, pouring a cup of coffee, woke Bonny. 'Here you are, sleepyhead.'

She stretched languidly and smiled. 'Well, Mr O'Halleran, you certainly gave a championship performance in bed last night!'

He chuckled. 'And you were a star too, darlin'. We are going to have such a good life together.' He showed her the article in the paper.

Bonny frowned. 'That's a bit premature isn't it? After all, there are no definite plans as yet.'

'He's just being clever. How do you feel about it, princess?'

Her eyes shone. 'Just imagine, Mickey. New York, Broadway! It's far more than I ever could have hoped for. Of course I want to do it. In any case, it would be for a limited time only.'

'Not if it's as successful as it's been here in London. You could be in the States for a considerable time.'

She frowned. 'I wouldn't want to be parted from you for too long. Could you come out there too?'

Shrugging, he said, 'That would all depend on my commitments here.' Seeing her look of disappointment he added, 'But I would spend as much time as I could with you, you know that. We could get married before you go, if you liked.'

'That would be lovely! I'd like a quiet wedding, Mickey darling, if that were possible. With just family and friends. I'm so sick of cameras being shoved in my direction whenever I walk outside. And a wedding is a private affair after all. Do you think that's possible?'

'It would be difficult with both of us being in the limelight; we would have to keep it secret, apart from those invited. We could try.'

'Well, we'll have plenty of time to think about it as the show seems destined to run and run.'

He smiled. 'Let's not worry too much today. Have your breakfast and then we'll go out for a walk. Put a headscarf on and I'll wear a hat, and with a bit of luck, we won't be recognized.'

They were fortunate. They spent the morning strolling through the parks, hand in hand, enjoying their privacy, and at lunchtime Mickey took them to a small restaurant in Knightsbridge. As soon as they sat down, and Mickey removed his hat and Bonny her scarf, they were recognized by the owner, who came over and gave them his undivided attention, but after paying the bill, they walked to the door of the restaurant and were met by a hoard of photographers.

Bonny turned and looked accusingly at the owner. 'How could you?'

He did have the grace to look abashed. 'It's good publicity for me, Miss Burton.'

'But don't you see? We'll never come here again now.'

Mickey looked livid. 'Once is enough for him, darling', he's got what he wanted!'

They fought their way through the reporters and for once Mickey was curt with them. 'Listen, you lot, it's Sunday, Miss Burton's only day off, for once give us some peace!' And he hailed a passing taxi.

Bonny too was annoyed. It had been so nice to be with Mickey, to have the privacy that now was impossible, but to have been used in such a manner really irritated her. 'The public are like vultures. Everyone wants a piece of you!'

Taking her hand Mickey said, 'As I've told you, darlin', it goes with being a star. You can't have it all ways.'

With a sigh she looked out of the cab window. 'I do know that, but in all honesty, I hadn't ever envisaged being famous. Being in a West End show was my ambition. The rest just happened.'

'Are you telling me you don't want success?'

'No, of course not. I just wasn't prepared for it, I suppose.'

* * *

Wally Cole was making his own plans. *Broadway Melody* would not be taking off to America if he had his way. He could not allow Foxy Gordon to make any more money out of his investment. Cole was aware that the show needed Bonny Burton to star in the production — after all, he could read, and the papers were full of her talent. After Gilmore's announcement, the critics were certain she would be a great success in New York. Without her — the show was just another musical.

* * *

It was Saturday night. *Broadway Melody* had been playing to packed houses and there wasn't an empty seat in the theatre for tonight's performance. It was the final number — of the dockside scene with the liner in the background, waiting to sail. Bonny danced her way around and on the luggage waiting to be loaded, and as the last case was put on the conveyor belt, Bonny pranced up the gangway, which was then hauled onboard. As usual, she stood on the deck and climbed on to a rail, waving, as the liner's funnel roared, announcing its departure. The machinery started rolling and the ship started to move . . . then there was a loud grinding noise. The ship shuddered violently. There were screams from the audience as Bonny was thrown from her perch, landing with a sickening thud on to the stage below. The curtains were hastily drawn.

Mickey O'Halleran rushed from his seat and ran backstage. Bonny was lying awkwardly, moaning with pain. He knelt beside her. Taking her hand he said, 'I'm here, darlin', please don't move.' He looked up. 'Has anyone sent for an ambulance?' he shouted.

'Yes, it's on its way.' The stage manager told him.

Tears trickled down Bonny's cheeks. 'What happened?' she asked.

'I don't know, sweetheart, but I'm bloody well going to find out!' He looked pointedly at the stage manager, who just shrugged.

'Then go and find out!' Mickey demanded. The man rushed off.

A stranger knelt beside Mickey. 'Can I help? I'm a doctor, I was in the audience.'

'Thanks, please take a look at her. I'm so worried. I'd be glad of your help.'

The doctor carefully examined Bonny. He spoke softly to her as he did so. But when he stood up, he looked anxious and took Mickey aside. 'She has definitely broken her leg. She will have to be X-rayed before we can tell if there are any internal injuries, but I'm afraid Miss Burton will not be dancing for the foreseeable future.'

CHAPTER TWENTY-SIX

Mickey climbed into the ambulance after the medics carefully transferred Bonny to a stretcher and lifted her into the vehicle. He took hold of her hand and squeezed it. 'I'm here, darlin', I'm not going to leave your side. We will get through this, together.'

She looked pale and drawn with pain. 'I'm so scared, Mickey.'

'You're going to be fine, princess. You do have a broken leg, but that'll mend.' He leaned forward and kissed her forehead. 'When I saw you fall, I thought you were dead. Don't you ever dare do that to me again!'

She smiled bravely. 'I felt the same when you went down in the fight.' She looked at him and spoke softly. 'Will I ever be able to dance again?'

'Of course you will! It'll take time, of course; you'll have to let your leg heal first.' He stroked her hand. 'Whilst it does, I'll spoil you rotten; you probably won't want to work ever again after a bit of the O'Halleran magic!' But he kept hidden from her the concerns that were whirling around in his head. Had she damaged her spine in the fall? Only an X-ray would tell them.

True to his word, Mickey insisted that he stay with her during her examination and when she went for an X-ray, where he did have to wait outside the room, but he was at her side when she was taken back to the ward and put into a private room to await the results.

* * *

Giles Gilmore had rushed to the hospital and was pacing up and down in the waiting room. Although he was concerned for Bonny, his hopes of going to America with the show were now in tatters. It was her name that was selling the production to the Americans. Without her, he had nothing! Her understudy would have to take her place at the Adelphi as it was, but although the girl was a competent dancer, she didn't have the personality or talent of Bonny Burton. The bookings would drop as a consequence, as would the takings. He eventually sat down, his hands to his head, dreaming of what might have been and worrying himself sick as to what would happen to the production during the time it took for his star to recover.

* * *

The door to Bonny's room opened and a tall man wearing a smart suit, entered. 'Miss Burton, I'm Nigel Matthews, your surgeon. I have the X-ray results.'

Bonny looked at his expression and her heart sank. She gripped Mickey's hand.

'It's good and bad news I'm afraid. You have cracked two ribs and broken the tibia in your left leg, but I'm afraid you've badly damaged your kneecap and that will take some skill to repair. I have to tell you that knees are the very devil to treat. However, the good news is that internally, apart from some serious bruising, you've not damaged any of your vital organs.'

'Will I be able to dance again, Mr Matthews?' Bonny held her breath.

He raised an eyebrow. 'Until we operate, it's difficult to say, but although you may be able to, to a certain degree, I rather doubt if you will have the freedom of movement that you have now.' He sat beside her. 'I've seen the show and know how strenuous some of the numbers are . . . I doubt you will have the ability to do that again.' He placed a hand on her arm. 'I wish I could bring you better news. I've seen how talented you are.'

'Or was!' Bonny's throat was choked with emotion. 'You are telling me my career is over as a performer.' And she burst into tears.

Matthews looked over at Mickey. 'I'm so sorry, Mr O'Halleran. I've scheduled Miss Burton for an operation, tomorrow morning. By the way, Mr Gilmore is in the waiting room.' He rose and left.

Mickey sat gingerly on the bed and took Bonny into his arms. 'There, there, darlin'. You let it all out.' He sat silent until her sobs subsided.

A nurse came in with a tray of tea and put it on the table at the bottom of the bed and quietly left without a word.

Mickey poured two cups and handed one to Bonny. 'Here, princess, you sip this. It's good and strong, just right for a case of shock, they say.'

'You had better go and break the news to Giles,' she quietly told him. 'It's only fair that he's kept abreast of the situation. After all, he has the show to think of.'

'Will you be all right?'

She nodded and sipped her tea. 'Go, Mickey, he needs to know.'

* * *

Gilmore looked up expectantly as Mickey entered the waiting room.

Mickey sat beside him. 'It's not good news, Giles. Bonny has a broken leg and two cracked ribs, but she's damaged her knee as well. The surgeon thinks this will limit her ability to dance in the future. But he won't be able to tell for sure until he operates tomorrow.'

Giles looked shattered by the news. 'Then Broadway is out of the question!'

Mickey's anger rose. 'But she's not in bad shape considering how far she fell, thank you for asking!'

The man flushed with embarrassment. 'I'm really pleased to hear that, honestly I am, but you must understand my position; I have the responsibility of this production on my shoulders. There's so much riding on Bonny. The success of the whole show depended on her. Now I don't know how the bookings will be affected and that means a lot of people could soon be out of work if the public don't come.'

Mickey was not without sympathy for Giles . . . 'Of course, I do understand, but you must also understand that, to me, it's Bonny who is most important. How do you think she'll feel, unable to carry on? Being a star was not paramount in her life, but dancing is. I just don't know how she'll react, that's *my* concern. But I also know that she'll fret about the show, knowing the facts. She'll feel responsible.'

'It's not her fault the mechanism failed!' Giles rose to his feet. 'I'm going back to the theatre. I've got the engineers looking into what caused the accident and I want answers.' He shook Mickey's hand. 'Give Bonny my love. I'll look in again tomorrow.'

Mickey stood up. 'Let me know the result, because if the accident is through some error, I want the man responsible.'

The threat in the boxer's voice was not lost on Gilmore. 'I'll let you know,' he said and hurried away.

* * *

At the Adelphi, the man in charge of the mechanical devices used during the production had made a thorough search with his head man. To their horror, they discovered the apparatus used to move the liner had been tampered with.

Down on their knees, they could clearly see a rod had been placed through the cogs, which would have turned a few times before juddering to a halt as it tore through the spindles.

'Bloody hell!' The chief engineer scratched his head. 'This was a deliberate act! Get the crew together; there are questions to be asked here. Bonny Burton could have been killed!'

But when the crew were assembled, one of them was missing.

'Where the hell is Jenkins?' asked the chief.

'Don't know, boss,' said one. 'The last time I saw him was when we were setting up the final scene.' The others agreed. No one had seen him since.

When Giles was given the facts, he called the police.

* * *

Harry Jenkins had left the theatre quickly after tampering with the mechanism used to move the liner. He was certain that no one had seen him slip the rod between the cogs but he didn't want to be around when it all went pear-shaped. Consequently, he had no knowledge of Bonny Burton's predicament when he arrived at Wally Cole's house. But Cole had been informed of the accident by one of his men who had been in the audience, knowing that this was the night that the show was to be sabotaged.

Cole passed an envelope over to Harry. 'You did a good job tonight. The girl who was the star of the show is in hospital, so Gilmore's dream of taking Broadway by storm is dead and Foxy Gordon won't be making a fortune after all! You'd better disappear because the Old Bill will be looking for you and I want no comeback, understand?'

Harry understood too well. He was a dead man if ever the police found him and discovered his connection to the villain. 'I've packed a bag already. I just have to go and pick it up from my room.'

'Are you mad!' Cole's eyes widened. 'It's the first place the coppers will look for you. You have enough money there to buy whatever you need, so get on your way. I don't want to see you ever again.'

Jenkins pocketed the envelope and walked out of the room without another word.

Cole lit a cigar and sat back with a satisfied grin. It had been a good night.

* * *

The following morning when Foxy Gordon read the paper he nearly choked on his cup of tea when he saw the headline. *STAR OF BROADWAY MELODY IN HOSPITAL.* He read on, his heart thumping.

The reporter wrote about the accident and the fact that Bonny Burton was to have an operation that morning and that the police were investigating the cause of her fall. He was shocked to read that they suspected it had been a deliberate act. Foxy lost his appetite. His hopes of making a fortune, down the drain! He picked up the telephone and dialled Giles Gilmore's number.

'What the bloody hell is going on, Gilmore?' he demanded.

'I've no idea.' Giles told him. 'All I know is someone has tampered with the machinery and I don't have a star any more! And frankly I can do without you bellyaching over the phone.'

Foxy was furious. 'Bellyaching! I've invested a lot of money in this production so I have every right to know what's going on. Do we still have a show?'

'The understudy will have to perform until I can find another leading lady.'

'But the public want Burton; they won't want to see anyone else.'

Don't you think I'm aware of that? I'm holding auditions from tomorrow, but the hopes of finding another Bonny Burton are few and far between. She was unique.'

'Are you telling me we could lose our investment?' Foxy's voice shook with anger.

'I'm telling you I'm doing my best!' And Giles hung up.

* * *

Whilst he waited at the hospital for Bonny to come out of the operating theatre, Mickey O'Halleran was wracking his brain as to who would have wanted to destroy the success of *Broadway Melody*. It had to be someone who had a personal grudge against Giles Gilmore. There was no other explanation. He was aware of Giles's past and the fact that people had been sent to prison on account of him. He frowned. His trainer, Foxy Gordon, was one of them. He pondered over the fact for a long time, arguing that the man wouldn't have done such a thing, but the more he thought about it, the more he wondered.

Bonny eventually was wheeled into the recovery room and Mickey was told to come back later when she regained consciousness.

'There's nothing you can do here, Mr O'Halleran,' the surgeon told him. 'We've set the leg in plaster and we will have to wait to see the result of the surgery. Go and take a break. Have a bath, get changed and have something to eat. You've been up all night and you look terrible! I don't want you as a patient too.'

Mickey looked at his crumpled clothes and agreed. But after he'd bathed and changed, he made his way to the gym to talk to Foxy Gordon.

Foxy was in his office when Mickey walked in. 'Hello, champ, how's your girl?'

'Still under the anaesthetic,' Mickey told him and sat down. 'Did you have anything to do with last night?' he asked abruptly.

Foxy looked astounded. 'No, I did not, how could you think such a thing?'

'Because I know you and because Gilmore got you sent to prison.'

'I've invested a bloody fortune in the production, you stupid bastard, so why the hell would I screw that up?'

Mickey was taken aback by this news. 'I had no idea.'

'I own forty per cent of the show. I wanted it to succeed, not fail. I could lose a bundle if it closes! I bet that pleases Wally Cole, no end!'

'Wally Cole? Why would he care?'

'He wanted to invest too. He didn't know I had any money in it, but I didn't want him moving in so I laughed at him, said he didn't fit the mould. He didn't like that.'

Mickey left the gym and took a taxi back to the hospital. He knew Wally Cole. He wouldn't have liked Foxy talking down to him and the two men already had bad blood between them after young Charlie Black's death. Mickey wondered if the villain had discovered Foxy's involvement after all. After he'd seen that Bonny was all right, he would make a few discreet enquiries of his own.

When he walked into Bonny's room, he found Rob Andrews sitting beside the bed. On the bedside table, a large bunch of flowers.

'Hello, Rob, what are you doing here?'

'I came to see Bonny, but she hasn't come round yet. How did the operation go?'

They both glanced down at the cage covered with a sheet, protecting the leg which was in plaster.

'The surgeon said they'd have to wait and see, but you might as well get used to the idea that Bonny won't be able to dance normally again. Her knee's in a bit of a mess and it will probably restrict her movement.'

'But they don't know that for sure, do they?'

'Now you listen to me, Andrews. I don't want you putting any pressure on Bonny when she is recovering. She'll have to take it easy and you of all people should know just how much dancing means to her. She is going to have a tough enough battle finding out just what she can do. So leave her alone!'

Rob looked at the Irishman, his jaw tight, trying to keep his temper. 'Don't you think I care about her at all?'

Mickey leaned forward. 'I think you care about her a tad too much. Back off!'

Getting up from his chair, Rob picked up his coat. 'I'm not getting into an argument with you in Bonny's sickroom. Tell her I was here, that's all.'

Mickey sat down and, taking Bonny's hand in his, whispered, 'I'm here, darlin', I'm here.'

CHAPTER TWENTY-SEVEN

The day after Bonny's operation, her parents and Mickey were sitting beside her bed when Nigel Matthews entered the room to talk to her. She asked them all to stay, needing their support.

The surgeon looked somewhat grave as he began. 'The operation went well, Miss Burton, but I have to tell you it is my belief that the injury to the knee will prohibit you from any *very* strenuous exercise, like the dancing you were doing up until your accident.' He saw the look of horror on her face. 'It doesn't mean you can't dance at all, after you've had treatment from a physiotherapist. But there will be a certain amount of stiffness in the knee, I'm afraid.' He looked down at his notes. 'Just how much, we'll have to wait and see. You will have to attend the hospital on a regular basis for a while so we can monitor your progress.'

'This is going to take some time, isn't it?' she asked.

'I'm afraid so. You will be in plaster for six weeks, then you'll start with the physio, but please, don't be disheartened — it could have been so much worse.'

As the surgeon left the room, Bonny looked at Mickey as her eyes filled with tears. 'My career is over! I'll never dance again.'

He held her hand. 'That's not what the man said, darlin', he said you just can't dance as you used to. Who knows what you can achieve in the future? But if you've already made up your mind you can't do it, then you'll never make it. Come on, princess, I've seen you battle with rehearsals, your feet bleeding with the effort. Don't you lose that fighting spirit — not now. Now is when you need it most of all!'

'Mickey's right, Bonny.' Frank looked at his daughter and his heart ached for her. 'You must never give up. If you do, you're not the girl I know.'

Millie stood up and said, 'We'll leave you and go and have something to eat, but we'll be back this afternoon to see you. Is there anything you need?'

Bonny shook her head.

When they were alone Mickey spoke quietly. 'When you can leave here, I'll take you away for the six weeks, build you up, spoil you rotten. Then we can face this battle together.' He smiled softly. 'We'll go to Ireland! I'll teach you to fish, take you to a real Irish pub, buy you Guinness; it's full of iron so it's good for you.'

But Bonny appeared not to hear a word he was saying; she just stared at the bottom of her bed and the cage that covered her leg.

'Look at me, Bonny!'

The sharpness in his voice made her look up.

'We are going to train as if we are going to tackle the prize fight of your life! I'll make your body strong, but it will be your job to train your mind. I can't do that for you. You must *want* to win — otherwise I'm wasting my time. Do you understand?'

She saw the worried furrows in his brow, the deep love he felt for her shining in his eyes.

Squeezing his hand, she took a deep breath. 'Yes, I do. I do understand and you're right, I can't let this beat me. I do want to win!'

* * *

Detective Inspector Joe Phillips was reading a crime sheet. 'Jenkins has quite a history,' he told his sergeant. 'Burglary, GBH — he got into a fight outside a pub and knifed a bloke, spent two years inside for that — and other misdemeanours. Well, we've got a warrant out for his arrest; let's hope we catch him soon.'

'We've got the train and bus stations covered, guv, and the ferries, and his picture has been sent round all police stations. We can't do more than that.'

But Mickey O'Halleran had a plan of his own. After leaving the hospital, he made his way to the Four Feathers — Wally Cole's local in the East End — and walked into the lounge bar. It was quiet, with most of the customers in the public bar, but the landlord recognized him immediately.

'Bloody hell! If it isn't the champ himself.' He held out his hand and shook Mickey's. 'What can I do for you, Mr O'Halleran?'

'Well, you can pull me half a pint of bitter, but I want some information. Do you know a Harry Jenkins?'

As the owner pulled at the beer pump he nodded. 'Yeah, he has been in here on occasion, but not regularly. Usually to have a word with Wally Cole, but he hasn't been in for some time.'

Mickey knew that his hunch was right. Cole was behind Bonny's accident. He felt his anger rise, but he knew he would have to be clever and not let his own animosity towards the villain make him do anything stupid. He would go and talk to Foxy Gordon.

Foxy listened carefully as Mickey unfolded his story. When the boxer finished, Mickey's eyes glittered with anger. 'I want that bastard! He's ruined Bonny's life and I want him to pay.'

'Listen to yourself! He might have ruined Bonny's life, but if you deal with him, he'll ruin yours as well!' Foxy put an arm around Mickey's shoulder. 'I understand how you feel and I'd probably feel the same in your shoes, but you are the champ! You have a role to play, and the public don't like their heroes mixed up in scandal . . . Remember Charlie Black? Remember how the publicity affected your girl? No, my son, this is my fight. I owe Wally Cole for what he did to young Charlie for a start, and now he's messed with my investment. You go and take care of your girl, I'll see to Wally Cole.'

'You're not going to do anything stupid, are you, Foxy?'

The trainer laughed. 'How do you think I got my nick-name, Mickey?'

The young man had to be satisfied with that, what else was he to do?

But when he was alone, Foxy Gordon fumed. 'Bloody Wally Cole, always interfering, but now he has gone too far.'

* * *

Rob Andrews walked into the hospital and made his way to Bonny's room. He was relieved to find her alone and pulled up a chair. 'Hello, Bonny, how are you?'

She told him what the surgeon had said, her face pale and drawn.

Rob longed to take her into his arms and comfort her but he knew she wouldn't welcome such closeness from him. To Bonny, their relationship was purely professional, and after they'd had dinner together that night so long ago, when he had let slip that he felt differently, she'd made her feelings very clear.

'That's rotten news and tough for you to hear, knowing how you love to dance.' He thought for a moment. 'But you know, Bonny, even if after your treatment your dancing is still limited, it isn't the end of the line for you.'

'I'll never dance on the stage again! Of course it's the end.'

'No, it isn't. Don't you see? You can help other beginners.'

She looked puzzled.

'You could always teach dancing. If what you say is true and you'll have enough use of your leg to dance a little, you could teach others who want to learn, those who love the world of dance as much as you do. Think about it, Bonny. It could be as rewarding as what you were doing, but in a different way.'

He watched her as she mulled over his words and saw her mood lighten somewhat.

'I'd never thought of that,' she admitted. She gave a grateful smile. 'Thanks, Rob. You've given me food for thought. How is the understudy doing?'

He shrugged. 'She's all right technically, but she lacks personality.'

'Why don't you let Shirley do it? She has bags of personality. She knows most of my numbers, so she'd only need a bit of time to perfect the routines. I'm surprised you didn't think of her before.'

'Well, we haven't had much time over the past two days. It's all been a bit of a panic, if I'm honest. I'll have a word with her after tonight's performance.'

'She's a real trouper, you know that, Rob. She won't let you down, you'll see. She sent me a card and some flowers. Thank her for me, please.'

As he left, Bonny leaned back against her pillows. She suddenly felt uplifted. Rob had sown the seed of an idea that she thought might be possible, and she'd given Shirley a leg up the ladder. Not only because she was her best friend, but because Shirley had the talent and always seemed to miss out of the big time. She felt tired, but strangely rested. She closed her eyes and fell into a tranquil sleep.

* * *

Wally Cole took the briefcase containing the money collected from the many shopkeepers who were forced to pay him for protection from his top man, Jimmy Knight, and climbed into his car.

'Do you want me to drive home with you, boss?' asked Knight.

'No, there's no need. I'll see you tomorrow early. There's some stuff I need you to take care of.' He drove away.

Twenty minutes later, he pulled into the driveway of his home, pulled on the handbrake, put the gear into neutral and switched off the engine. He leaned over to pick up the brief-case from the passenger seat with a smile of satisfaction. Today had been more than profitable. As he went to open the car door, he was grabbed from behind and a pad placed over his face. He tried to fight off his attacker, but the chloroform on the pad took effect before he could escape . . . and he slumped over the wheel.

* * *

Harry Jenkins had made it safely to the Isle of Wight, using the ferry from Southampton before the police were able to put a watch on the passengers. He had booked into a bed and breakfast in Cowes, thinking that with it being such a busy place it would be easier for him to mingle undiscovered with the tourists. He told the landlady that he was looking for a small place for his parents to live in for their retirement, which allayed any further questions.

At first he'd enjoyed wandering around, eating in cafes, walking around the marinas, looking at the shops, sitting on the front, reading the paper, but after a few days he became bored and started going into one of the local pubs. He liked a game of darts and was a good player, so there was always one of the locals willing to take him on for the price of a pint. And one evening there was a darts match, which he thought he'd go and watch.

When he entered the pub, the captain of the darts team approached him. 'One of our lads can't make it tonight. Would you help me out and take his place?'

Harry was only too happy to oblige. It wasn't until he stood at the oche to throw his first dart, aiming for the bulls-eye — to see if he or his opponent were to throw first — that he overheard a conversation about the visiting team.

'It's time we took these coppers down a peg or two,' one of the locals said, amid much laughter. Too late did he realize that he was surrounded by off-duty policemen. He threw the dart and missed the bull by miles.

He played badly and lost his match, much to the derision of his teammates.

'Blimey, Harry, what happened?' asked the captain. 'I was counting on you to win your game.'

'I've got a headache,' he replied. 'I'm really sorry; I won't hang around, if you don't mind. I'm off to bed with a couple of aspirins.' He bought the winner a pint of beer and hurriedly left the pub.

* * *

The following morning in Cowes police station, the match was the main topic of conversation. Ken Watkins, who had played Harry, was checking some papers and amongst them was a picture of a wanted criminal to post on the bulletin board with the others. When he glanced at the picture next to the one he had placed, he exclaimed, 'Bloody hell!'

Within minutes, two policemen called on the bed and breakfast accommodation, to be told by the landlady that the man they were looking for had checked out early that morning. Phone calls were made and the search for Harry Jenkins began.

* * *

Word reached Detective Inspector Phillips that Jenkins was on the Island and there was no way he could leave without the ferry. It would only be a matter of time before he was apprehended. Something that pleased Phillips greatly. But he was shocked to be informed later in the day that the body of Wally Cole had been fished out of the Thames in much the same place as the young boxer Charlie Black had committed suicide.

* * *

When Mickey O'Halleran heard the news about Wally Cole, he rushed round to the gym to find Foxy working in the ring with one of his trainees. 'Can I have a word?' Mickey asked.

Foxy called another lad into the ring to take his place and climbed out. 'What is it? Is there something wrong with Bonny?'

'No, there isn't. But Wally Cole was fished out of the Thames this morning.'

'So?'

'Did you have anything to do with it?' Mickey stared hard at the man.

'Don't be ridiculous! Whatever made you think that?'

'You said you'd see to him.'

Foxy mopped his brow with the towel around his neck. 'Well, now I won't have to. Someone else has done it for me. You go and worry about your girl and leave the rest of the world to take care of itself.' And he climbed back into the ring.

CHAPTER TWENTY-EIGHT

True to his word, when Bonny was able to leave the hospital, Mickey took her to Ireland. They booked into a hotel that nestled beneath the Mourne Mountains, which loomed dark and mysterious in the distance. They walked along the beach, threw pebbles into the water, drank Guinness in one of the local pubs, and later, when Bonny was feeling better, they went fishing.

For Bonny these were halcyon days, where she learned how to sit quietly so as not to disturb the fish, and how to relax and let the autumn sun wash over her. How to be without any pressure at all. It was a time of healing for the body and the mind.

They made love with much hilarity, due to Bonny's one leg in plaster, but their closeness and understanding grew as the days passed slowly by, until it was time to return to Southampton and the hospital.

Homeward-bound on the ferry, Mickey put his arm around her shoulders as they sat looking out over the sea. 'Well, darlin', you look well rested and lovely. You're fit now to face the next step. Are you ready for it?'

Bonny knew that once the plaster had been removed, the days ahead with the physiotherapist were going to be difficult. She was concerned as to the outcome — her leg would be weak and the going tough — and at the end of her treatment she would know just how much movement she had lost.

She sighed. 'Yes, Mickey. I'm ready.' She leaned forward and kissed him. 'But without you, I'd never have been able to face the future.'

'Listen, princess, with me backing you up and the luck of the Irish on our side, you'll be amazed at what you can achieve!' He chuckled. 'I'll certainly be pleased when that bloody plaster has gone. The number of times I've caught my shin on it in bed isn't funny. I'm covered in bruises!'

* * *

In Southampton, the post-mortem results had shown that Wally Cole had chloroform in his system and therefore his death was not from natural causes.

'So we're looking at a murder case,' Detective Inspector Phillips remarked as he read the report.

His sergeant gave a wry smile. 'Well, someone did us a favour, boss.'

'I'm inclined to agree with you, but nevertheless, someone has to account for it. We can't ignore the law or we face anarchy.' But there were no clues to follow at the scene of the crime. And any questions asked by various members of the force in the East End were met with blank expressions. No one knew anything, and if they did, they were keeping it within the realms of the underworld.

Jimmy Knight was making his own enquiries, but getting nowhere fast. He had suspected that Foxy Gordon might have been behind the demise of his boss, in retribution for the sabotage of the machinery in the production of Broadway Melody, but there was no proof of the matter.

* * *

During the time that Bonny had been in Ireland, her friend Shirley had taken over the lead in the show as Bonny had suggested and had done well. She'd had a good write-up in the theatrical columns, so the ticket office was once again doing business — not nearly as much as when Bonny had been the star, but enough to keep the production open.

The profits had also dropped, of course, which meant the backers were just about breaking even now. This did not sit well with Foxy Gordon. Until Bonny's accident, the potential return on his investment had looked good, but now he thought he could put his money to better use. He made an appointment to see Giles Gilmore.

The two men sat facing each other in Gilmore's office. The hostility in the air was palpable.

'I want my money back!' was Foxy's opening.

Giles's face was grim. 'I can't do that at this time. You know how the bookings fell after Bonny Burton had her accident.'

'That's not my problem.'

'I'm very much afraid it is. There is no way I can come up with that kind of money at this time. You wanted to be an angel; now you'll learn it has its ups and downs, just like any other business.'

'Not good enough, Giles.' Foxy got to his feet. 'I'll give you a month to find the money. After that, things will get rough! I'll file for bankruptcy and the court will call in all my assets to pay my debts. Then where will you be?'

* * *

Meantime, there was great excitement at Southampton's police headquarters. Harry Jenkins had been found sleeping rough on the Isle of Wight. Too scared to book in to a bed and breakfast, Jenkins had been kipping down at night in different places in an effort to evade arrest, but due to the vigilance of a member of the public, he had been found early one morning, sleeping on a beach under a bit of tarpaulin. He was now being sent home — under guard — to Southampton for questioning.

After six weeks in the open, Jenkins was in no mood to play clever. His resistance was low and he very soon gave the police all the details they required about his involvement in the sabotage of the machinery in *Broadway Melody*, at the behest of Wally Cole.

'Why did Cole ask you to do this?' asked Detective Inspector Phillips.

'He wanted to get back at Foxy Gordon, who had a financial interest in the show. Wally wanted to buy into it too but couldn't. Foxy taunted him about it. That's why.'

Phillips was furious. 'How very petty! Do you realize, you could have killed someone? Poor Bonny Burton has had her career ruined by you. She broke a leg and may never be able to dance again! Others in the cast also sustained injuries, though fortunately for you they were not serious.'

Jenkins looked crestfallen. 'I never meant for that to happen. She's a nice woman, always had a word for everyone backstage.'

'Not only that, but someone murdered Wally Cole.' Phillips's eyes narrowed. 'He was found near the same spot that the young boxer Charlie Black was discovered.'

Jenkins became agitated. 'I don't know nothing about that, sir.'

'Oh, I think you do.' Phillips leaned forward. 'You are in deep trouble, Jenkins. You are looking to serve some serious jail time. On the other hand, if you help us with our enquiries, it will be to your benefit.'

'In what way?'

'The judge will take into consideration your helping us when he comes to sentence you. After all, you were lucky that no one was killed in the theatre. You could have been facing a murder charge. As it is . . .'

Jenkins turned pale. 'What do you want to know?'

Shortly after, Jimmy Knight, Cole's top man, was picked up for questioning.

* * *

Bonny had had her plaster removed and was now having treatment with the physiotherapist, learning to walk using her greatly weakened leg. It was hard and painful, but Mickey insisted on being there to encourage her. It was a difficult time. Bonny tried her best but there were moments of great depression and frustration. She would try her hardest but would sometimes end up in floods of tears.

Mickey would comfort her at such times, but gently persuade her to try again.

'I can't do this!' she cried.

'Of course you can!' Mickey insisted. 'Come on, darlin', show me that fighting spirit! You have to come out of your corner swinging.'

'I'm a dancer, not a bloody boxer!' She glared at him, sweat beading her forehead.

He chuckled. 'I don't know about that, princess. At this moment, if I got too close, I think you could floor me with a hefty right.'

She had to smile because that was just what she wanted to do, hit out at him, although she knew he was only trying to help her. 'Oh dear, Mickey, am I ever going to get through this?'

He held her close. 'Of course you are. You just have to be patient. You are expecting too much too soon. Think back to Ireland and how we had to sit for ages waiting for the fish to bite. You have to use that patience now and stop beating yourself up. I think you are a wonder woman, but truth to tell, sweetheart, you're only human.'

And so she tried again.

* * *

Jimmy Knight was being difficult. He denied any part in Charlie Black's demise. 'The coroner said it was suicide,' he claimed. 'The stupid bugger was deeply in debt. He knew he couldn't pay and he topped himself. So why am I here?'

'Of course he paid his debt!' snapped Detective Inspector Phillips. 'He threw the fight and Wally Cole made a packet on the result. You know it and I know it. Cole got rid of him so he couldn't tell anyone about it. You were the instigator of his death.'

Knight just looked at the detective and smirked. 'Prove it!'

'I intend to. Take him back to his cell!' Phillips told the constable standing by. 'We'll get a search warrant for Knight's place, and Wally Coles' too,' he told his sergeant. 'Perhaps we'll find something there. Take Knight's car to pieces too. He must have taken Charlie Black to the Thames in something. And take a look at Cole's car as well. I don't like unsolved crimes on my books!'

With that, Phillips took out the reports on both deaths and started to read through them. There had to be something that he had missed.

CHAPTER TWENTY-NINE

Giles Gilmore was going over the financial status of the company, his frown ever deepening. There was the cost of hiring the theatre and the wage bill to be covered, quite apart from the enormous electricity bills and other charges incurred. The bookings were ticking over, covering his needs with little to spare. With careful management he could just about make it, but not if Foxy Gordon carried out his threat. Giles had already put his property up as collateral for the bank loan he'd needed to finance the production, so there was no spare cash to be had. Gordon had threatened to ruin him. Was this his plan? Giles felt he needed to talk to someone about his problem and he sent for Rob Andrews.

Rob came into the office and, seeing the worried look on Giles face, sat down, took out a cigarette and lit it. 'What's the problem?'

Giles told him of his concerns.

After listening, Rob sat thoughtfully in silence and then made his suggestion. 'Now that Bonny is no longer starring in the show, the run here will be limited.'

Giles had already considered this and nodded in agreement.

'Why don't we take the production on tour? The fact that Shirley is starring, and not Bonny, won't make such a difference in the provinces. The public will love to see a show that has been on in the West End. The bookings should be healthy.'

Giles liked the idea. 'There is only one drawback and that's the scenery. Not all the stages in the outlying theatres are as big.'

Rob shrugged. 'We can probably still use the flaps on the sides of the stage, but we might have to scale down the rest on occasion. I'm sure we can work it out.'

'It would certainly be a solution, but what about Mr Gordon?'

'That's up to you, Giles. If the man wants to make money, he'll probably go along with the idea, especially if you offer him some sort of bribe.'

'Like what?'

'You say he owns forty per cent of the stock, so sell him some of yours. Give him an incentive to stay with you.'

The impresario went berserk. 'Then he'll own more than I will! I can't have that.'

'It's your choice. I suggest you tell him of your plans first and see what he has to say. But Giles, do think seriously about it. Do you want to have to close at the end of our run here in London — or carry on?' Rob rose from his seat. 'That's all the advice I can offer. Good luck!'

Giles chewed over the alternatives and eventually, with some reluctance, lifted the phone.

* * *

Both the vehicles belonging to Jimmy Knight and Wally Cole were being stripped down and searched for clues by the forensic team, in a large garage space in Southampton. It was a tedious and frustrating procedure. The search for fingerprints and bloodstains was meticulously carried out. Panels and seats were removed and studied.

A cry came from a man searching the interior of Jimmy Knight's car. 'I've found a button still attached to a scrap of material here.' He then filed it away in a bag for further investigation. The only thing discovered in Cole's car was a small piece of the pad used to chloroform the murdered villain. But there were no fingerprints, other than Coles' and Knight's, both of whom often drove the car.

The button, however, found behind a seat in Knight's car, was matched to the woollen garment worn by Charlie Black when he was fished out of the river.

When Chief Inspector Phillips was told of this evidence, he was delighted. 'That puts Charlie Black in Knight's car on the night of his death. Bring Knight in!'

* * *

Knight, Cole's top man, was looking somewhat pensive when he entered the interview room, and the look of satisfaction on Phillip's face as he looked at the villain evidently didn't help to allay his concern. 'Sit down,' he was told.

Phillips pushed a large bag towards him and showed him the contents. 'Do you recognize this woollen garment?'

Jimmy shook his head. 'Should I?'

'Let me remind you,' the detective said. 'This was worn by poor Charlie Black the night he was pushed into the Thames. I say night because it certainly wouldn't have been done in daylight.'

'What's that got to do with me?' Knight was trying to brazen it out.

Philips showed him where there was a tear in the garment and a button missing. Then he tipped out the button, still attached to a scrap of wool, on to the table.

'As you can see, this matches.'

Knight looked watchful but remained silent.

'This was found behind the seat of your car, which places the young boxer with you.' He sat back and waited for a reaction.

Jimmy Knight had been living beyond the law most of his life and he knew the score. This evidence was irrefutable. At best he was facing a long term of imprisonment; at the worst, he could face the hangman's rope.

'I want to make a statement.'

* * *

Foxy Gordon puffed on his cigar with pleasure. It was a good day! Giles Gilmore had phoned him and wanted to discuss plans for taking the production of *Broadway Melody* on the road. He had explained the financial benefit of so doing and had asked Foxy to meet him later that day to discuss the matter. Foxy was well aware of his powerful position in the negotiations and was wondering how to handle the situation to his personal benefit. He wasn't averse to making money, and if this was going to be a profitable proposition — rather than Gilmore just insisting he keep his stake in the show — he would listen.

He walked out of his office and into the gym. Mickey O'Halleran was working out in the ring, with Bonny sitting watching. He strode over to her and sat beside her. 'How are you doing?' he asked, looking pointedly at her leg and the wooden crutch perched beside her chair.

She smiled at him. 'Not so bad, thanks, but it's taking longer than I thought. My leg is still weak and the knee throbs a bit.'

'I heard that Harry Jenkins, who caused the accident, has been arrested.'

Her smile faded. 'That man ruined my career; I don't think I'll ever forgive him!'

Foxy looked at her knowingly. 'He was just the instrument; Wally Cole was the man behind it all.'

'But he was found drowned in the Thames!'

Foxy leaned forward and squeezed her arm. That's right.' He winked. 'We always look after our own, my dear, and debts have to be paid.'

'That's an interesting observation, Mr Gordon!'

Foxy and Bonny looked round in surprise. Detective Inspector Phillips was standing behind their chairs. 'Perhaps you would like to come down to the station and elaborate on that.'

'Am I under arrest?'

'Not at all. Just helping us with our enquiries, that's all. Shall we go?'

As Foxy left the gym with the inspector, Mickey climbed out of the ring and walked over to Bonny. 'What was that all about?'

Bonny told him of the strange conversation that had taken place. 'Do you think Foxy had anything to do with that man's drowning?'

Mickey looked concerned. 'I do hope not.' But the more he thought about it, the more he had his doubts. There was bad blood between the two men after Charlie Black's supposed suicide. Foxy had been adamant that Cole had been behind it all. Had it been payback time?

* * *

In the interview room at the police station, Foxy Gordon sat facing Phillips and his sergeant.

'Perhaps you would like to enlighten us about the death of Wally Cole and the remark you made to Miss Burton,' the detective remarked.

'I'm not sure I know what you mean.' The trainer looked unconcerned.

'Don't play games with me, Foxy! Cole was murdered. He was chloroformed before he was tipped into the drink. Was it you who snuffed him out?'

Foxy chuckled. 'Whoever it was did us all a favour, if you ask me. Cole was a bad 'un. The world's a better place without him. Don't tell me you're sorry he's gone, because if you did, you'd be lying!'

'That's not the point. We are dealing with murder and that cannot go unpunished.'

Gordon just shrugged. When he was questioned about his whereabouts on the night in question, he of course had an alibi. He wasn't a fool; he'd covered his tracks very carefully. After further questioning, the detective had no choice but to eventually release him.

'I'm sure he was behind Cole's murder,' Phillips remarked to his sergeant, 'but how the hell I'm ever going to prove it, I'm damned if I know!'

'But at least we have the murderer of young Charlie Black. Jimmy Knight had the good sense to confess.'

'He didn't have much choice when faced with such damning evidence. But you're right, at least that's one more unsolved murder taken care of. I feel sorry for the parents. It was bad enough thinking their son committed suicide; now they have to face the fact the lad was murdered. And, of course, there's the trial for them to face. Poor devils.'

* * *

When Foxy strolled back into his gym, Mickey and Bonny were about to leave. The boxer stopped and, looking at his trainer, asked, 'Are you in any trouble?'

With a shake of the head, Foxy answered. 'No, son. Everything is fine. Off you go with your young lady and stop worrying.' But when he was alone in his office, he poured himself a stiff brandy. That had been too close for comfort. A casual remark had almost put a noose around his neck; from now on he'd be more careful.

CHAPTER THIRTY

During the following weeks, Bonny worked hard with her exercises, and at last she could feel the benefit. There was a certain stiffness in her knee, as the surgeon had predicted, but she learned to cope with it. On bad days, she limped slightly as she walked; on others, it wasn't so noticeable. She hired a room in a dancing school and began to practice, accompanied by records played on a small portable gramophone. It was tedious and, at times, difficult, but she persevered.

When he wasn't training, Mickey would go along and encourage her, trying to build her confidence. And one day, Rob Andrews appeared.

Bonny looked up as the door to the practice room opened.

'Hello, Bonny.'

'Rob! What on earth are you doing here?' They hadn't seen one another for some time.

'I heard you were working and I thought perhaps you could do with some help.' He removed his jacket, walked over to the gramophone, chose a record and put it on. 'Come on,' he said, 'let's try this. Follow me and let's see what happens.'

'The Lullaby of Broadway' was a gentle tune, and he started to tap out an easy routine, which Bonny followed.

Then he played another record, which had been the music to one of their Astaire–Rogers numbers, and she followed that, reliving their old routine.

For Bonny, it was like coming home, and her spirits rose as they twirled around like old times. At the end of the number, Rob looked at her and smiled. 'That was pretty good!'

Bonny grinned back at him. 'That was bloody marvellous!' But she rubbed her knee, which was beginning to ache.

'Let's take a rest,' Rob suggested and they both sat on the floor. 'It's going to take time, Bonny, but from what I've seen today, you'll be able to dance pretty well.'

'But not enough to sustain a performance.' She sighed. 'I have to accept that my days in the theatre are over.'

'Not necessarily.' He looked at her and then made a suggestion. 'You could always help me, teaching the chorus line when a new show goes into rehearsal and working with the speciality numbers. You could be a great help, and it would still keep you in touch with the theatre.'

Bonny could hardly believe what she was hearing. 'Do you think I could?'

'Well, from what I've seen today, I have no doubt about it. After all, you wouldn't be working constantly, dancing for hours on end as you did in the show. It would be just in rehearsals, and I'm sure during those times you could manage. Think about it. You'd be paid, of course, which would give you a living.'

'I'd have to discuss this with Mickey first,' she ventured, 'but it sounds good to me.'

'*Broadway Melody* will be going on tour soon, and my work is done with them now anyway. I've been asked to choreograph a new production and I could do with the help. We start rehearsals in three weeks' time.'

Bonny could hardly contain her enthusiasm. 'I'll let you know.'

'Right, then let's do some more work.' He stood up and pulled her to her feet.

That evening when Mickey took her out to dinner, Bonny told him of Rob's suggestion. She was animated and excited as she told him all the details. 'Don't you see, darling, it means I'll still be working in the theatre. My career isn't over, after all!'

Mickey was less enthusiastic. 'Yes, princess, I can see that it means a great deal to you, but . . .'

'But what?'

'Well, there's no good beating about the bush. You know as well as I do that Rob Andrews is in love with you. I'm not sure you working together is such a good idea.'

Bonny was furious. 'Oh, for goodness' sake! I worked with him long enough before. And yes I knew how he felt about me, but I made it very plain to him that you were the only man in my life and he accepted that. Our partnership was purely professional. As it will be in the future.'

'So you've made up your mind then?'

She glared at him. 'Yes, as a matter of fact I have. Rob has given me a great opportunity and I'm not going to say no, just to satisfy your ego!'

Mickey sat and stared at her. He knew how much this meant to Bonny and he saw the grim determination in the cut of her jaw, the fire of battle in her eyes as she looked defiantly at him. 'I love it when you're angry, princess. It's really sexy. Let's go home and go to bed.'

'Oh, Mickey!' She started to laugh. 'You are outrageous!'

He chuckled softly. 'No, darlin', just crazy about you, that's all. But if that man steps out of line even just a little — I'll floor him!'

'Oh, I'm sure that Rob is well aware of that, so you have nothing to worry about.'

'There's just one thing, princess. If you do find it is too much for you, I want you to promise that you'll have the sense to stop.'

Leaning across the table, she took his hand. 'I promise.'

* * *

Broadway Melody moved from the West End and started to tour the provinces. As Rob had predicted, the bookings were very healthy and the finances of the company improved greatly. But Giles had had to make a serious decision before he moved the production.

His meeting with Foxy Gordon had been long and heated. Demands between the two men had been passed back and forth. But eventually Giles had had to agree to make Foxy Gordon a partner in this particular production. It was the only way Foxy would agree to keep his money involved. Giles was devastated, Foxy elated. He felt vindicated after serving five years behind bars after Giles Gilmore had taken him and others to court for fixing a fight.

It was not quite the revenge he had planned — but it came a close second.

* * *

Three weeks later, in a hall hired by Rob Andrews, Bonny stood beside him and faced the members of the chorus they were to train. She felt unusually nervous.

'Good morning, everyone. I am Rob Andrews, your choreographer, and I'm sure you all know my assistant, Bonny Burton?'

There was a buzz among the dancers and someone started to clap, which quickly spread until the whole chorus line was applauding. Bonny was greatly touched and fought the tears that threatened at this unexpected show of approval.

Rob grinned at her. 'They didn't do that for me, I notice,' he teased.

Bonny looked at the smiling faces before her. 'Thank you all so much. You have no idea what that meant to me.'

Rob intervened. 'Don't let her fool you,' he advised the dancers. 'Our Bonny is as much a perfectionist as am I, so be prepared to work and work hard. Those who can't cut the mustard will be leaving!'

This soon sobered the atmosphere — and the hard work began.

* * *

The following weeks were some of the happiest Bonny had experienced. She had been convinced that her dancing career was over, but now she felt exhilarated. She was able to fulfil her role as Rob's assistant, although at the end of the day she felt exhausted and her knee ached, but she rested whenever she could, and as the days passed, she grew in strength.

Mickey was thrilled to see the woman he loved content at last, but he was now training for another defence of his title, so their time together was limited. But whenever he could get away, he would meet Bonny after rehearsals and they would spend time together at the flat she had rented.

Despite the fact she was no longer fronting a show, Bonny was still newsworthy, and as the fiancée of Mickey O'Halleran, privacy on the street was seldom an option. But, as a boxing champion, Mickey often made appearances at important events, to which Bonny accompanied him. The press often asked her, did she miss performing? At first she found this difficult to cope with, but as time passed she was able to truthfully say, 'Yes, of course I do, but at least as an assistant to Rob Andrews I feel that I am contributing, though in a different way.' And she came to accept this fact. Fame and her name in lights had never been her criteria, but the dancing had been the most important thing in her life, which she was still able to do, to a better degree than she had at first thought possible . . . until one fateful morning.

Rehearsals were going well. The chorus line was composed of dedicated dancers, and with Rob's innovative choreography, some of the numbers were spectacular. Bonny was showing the lead dancer one particular tricky step. She danced across the stage, leapt into the air and landed on her bad leg awkwardly, twisting her knee. She fell to the floor with a cry of pain.

Everything stopped. Rob ran forward and knelt beside her. He took one look at the pain etched on her face and called an ambulance.

As she was carried into the vehicle on a stretcher she caught hold of Rob's hand. 'Please, call Mickey.'

Mickey O'Halleran rushed to the hospital as soon as he got the call. Rob was waiting for him.

'What the bloody hell happened?' Mickey demanded.

Rob explained as best he could, but he was beside himself with worry. 'Bonny is being X-rayed at the moment. We'll just have to wait and see the result.'

Both men walked up and down, lost in their own thoughts. Rob was overcome with guilt, feeling he had pushed Bonny into working with him, and Mickey was livid with the choreographer, blaming him for putting Bonny in the position where she might damage herself. Neither man shared their fears with the other.

Eventually, Nigel Matthews, the surgeon who had previously operated on Bonny, walked into the waiting area, carrying the X-ray plates. His expression was grim. 'I don't have good news for you, Mr O'Halleran, I'm afraid. Bonny has torn the cartilage in her knee. The cartilage works like a shock absorber, so you can imagine how vitally important it is, and Bonny already weakened that knee when she had the fall earlier in the year.'

'Is there anything you can do for her?' asked Mickey.

'I can trim part of the meniscus, the cartilage, probably, but I'm afraid Bonny's dancing days are over.'

'Does she know?' The boxer's face was pale as he asked.

'Not yet. I thought I'd break the bad news to you first.'

'Then let's do it! Bonny will want to know as soon as possible.' He turned to Rob. 'I guess you'd better get back to work. You'll have to manage alone now.'

'I can't tell you how sorry I am,' Rob began, but Mickey was already walking away with the surgeon.

* * *

Bonny was propped up in bed in a side room, her heart beating wildly, waiting for the verdict, but deep inside she felt the news would not be good. At the sight of Mickey she held out her arms to him.

He rushed to comfort her. 'I don't know about you, princess. You're not safe to be left alone for a minute!' He kissed her and then gently sat on the bed, holding her in his arms as Nigel Matthews told her his news.

She listened and after, with a tremor in her voice, she said, 'I knew it wasn't good as soon as I did it. Oh Mickey, now my dancing days are really over.'

'I'm afraid so, darlin'. For once he was at a loss as how to comfort her.

'I am sorry, Bonny.' The surgeon looked at her with sympathy. 'But these things happen in life. Now we must try and get it sorted as best we can. I'll come back and see you later when I know when we can carry out the operation.'

Bonny's eyes filled with tears, her face pale and drawn. 'Oh Mickey, how can I face this? Never able to dance again! How can I live without that? Dancing is my life!' She started to sob. 'I never craved stardom. As long as I could dance I was content . . . and now . . .' She couldn't continue as sobs racked her body.

Mickey didn't know what to say. He'd never seen her like this. He just held her close until her sobs subsided. After all, he knew that one day he'd have to give up appearing in the ring, but that would be his choice. Poor Bonny hadn't been given one.

'Come along, princess, you have to take this on the chin. Life is a bitch but when it throws you a curve you either fight it or go under — and I refuse to let that happen. We'll get through this next while, *then* we'll have to make new plans.'

'But we did all this before! At least then I had a chance. Now . . . I have nothing!'

'What do you mean you have nothing?' Mickey said angrily. 'You have so much. You still have your youth; you have your whole life in front of you. It will just be a different one, that's all. At least you did achieve your ambition; many people struggle through life and never ever do.'

Bonny wiped her eyes and took a deep breath. 'You're right, of course. I just can't think straight. I know I'm lucky to have tasted success.'

Mickey cupped her face in his hands and gently kissed her. 'Those are the bravest words I've heard for a long time.'

'I'm not brave, Mickey, just being realistic. At least I'll still be able to walk; that's something.' She grimaced and tried to be cheerful for his sake. 'I'm not looking forward to more exercises with the physio though. They were more than tedious.' She looked at him and smiled ruefully. 'I used to get so bad tempered — remember?'

'Oh yes. I thought you were going to floor me on occasion. But darlin', that was your fighting spirit, don't ever lose that.'

'But what about after? What will I do then?' Despite her acceptance of the situation, Mickey could hear the uncertainty and fear in her voice. Beneath the bravado, his lovely girl was scared of the future.

'One step at a time, princess. Let's get you over the first hurdle before we plan what to do about the next one.'

* * *

Back in the practice room, Rob informed his dancers of the outcome at the hospital. They were all saddened by the news.

'Right!' snapped Rob, 'we owe it to Bonny to work really hard. After all, she's put in many an hour with you all. We have to show her just how good a teacher she was. When she's out of hospital, no doubt she will come and watch you. We can't let her down, so let's get cracking!'

* * *

But later that night, when she was alone, Bonny Burton wept bitterly for what might have been.

CHAPTER THIRTY-ONE

Detective Inspector Phillips, sat at his desk, pored over the report of Wally Cole's death and scratched his head. His gut feeling was that Foxy Gordon was behind the murder of the local gangster, but how the hell was he going to prove it? He didn't have any evidence at all to support his theory. Certainly no reason to get a search warrant for his premises. It was beginning to eat away at him.

Phillips avidly studied Foxy's statement then called his sergeant in. 'I want you to go to this club that Foxy Gordon used as his alibi and question everyone who Gordon said was there at the time he said he was playing cards, starting with the staff. Hopefully he slipped up somewhere.'

The sergeant looked doubtful. 'We were thorough the last time, sir, but we came up empty.'

'Then try again. Maybe you missed something. Take Jill Masters with you.' Philips had had a sudden idea. The last time the club was under scrutiny it had been done by a male team, but sometimes he found that his women officers looked at things from a different angle, which had many times been fruitful, and Masters had a good eye for detail. Maybe it would bring up something new.

* * *

Jokers Wild was a small select club in the City of London, with a license for gambling. It catered for those who took the game of cards seriously. They held bridge tournaments regularly, and there was a hard school of poker with big pots changing hands. It also had blackjack tables. The clientele were from every walk of life — from the aristocracy, the racing world and the wealthy, with more money and time on their hands than most . . . to some members of the underworld.

Although Foxy Gordon was against any form of gambling for his fighters, he himself loved to play poker, but he always made sure he played with the amount of money he could afford to lose. He would never fall into the trap of getting into debt for the turn of a card. He was far too smart an operator for that. It was his one relaxation and he had said he was playing poker at Joker's Wild on the night of Wally Cole's death.

Jill Masters was a very bright WPC with an ambition to be a detective, which was a very male orientated part of the police force. But she hoped that in time she would be accepted in this particular branch of the force. Detective Inspector Phillips had recognized her abilities, and whenever he could he helped her to establish herself. And now she was off with the others, to the Jokers Wild club.

It was about two o'clock when they arrived. Sergeant Beckett flashed his warrant card and told the manager he wanted to question the staff again.

This was not met with any great enthusiasm. 'You'll upset the clientele if they see my staff being grilled by the police.'

Becket looked coldly at him. 'Then I suggest we use your office, so no one will be aware of us doing our job! Just send the staff in one by one. Starting now!'

Jill Masters left the sergeant to do his work and wandered around the club, familiarizing herself with the layout. There was the main room, with a bar, a couple of roulette tables, two tables for blackjack, and another room where poker was played. At the entrance was a cloakroom for coats and a young pretty girl in attendance. The young police woman spoke to her. 'Have you been working in the club long?'

The young blonde smiled. 'Almost a year now.'

'Do you work the same hours every day?'

'No, we work shifts. It's better, really — less boring. The evenings are busier, of course, especially at the weekends.'

'Were you on duty the night of July the fourteenth?'

'I was. I remember it well as it was my birthday and I had wanted to change shifts so I could go out with my boyfriend, but the boss wouldn't let me. Miserable devil!' She grinned and leaned forward and said softly, 'I got my own way eventually though.'

Intrigued, Jill asked, 'Really, how did you do that?'

'About eight o'clock I pretended to be sick. I rushed off to the ladies and pretended to throw up. I rubbed all the rouge off my cheeks so I'd look pale and I told him I was ill. He had to let me go.' She gave a triumphant look. 'My boyfriend took me out to dinner.'

'Do you know Mr Foxy Gordon?' Jill asked.

'Yes, he's a regular here, loves his game of poker, never plays anything else.'

'Do you remember if he was here that night?'

'Yes, he was. I remember because he went into the gents just as I dashed into the ladies. As I came out I saw him leaving by the back door.'

Masters was immediately alert. 'Are you sure?'

'Positive! I was surprised because he seldom leaves the table. I know, because I have to serve the players drinks. I've often wondered how he managed to hold his water, if you must know.' The girl giggled. 'Mind you, he seldom has more than a beer. He once told me that drink fogs the mind and he wants a clear head when he plays.'

'Did he come back?'

The girl shrugged. 'I don't know because I was sent home.'

'Did you see him outside when you left?'

'Not really. I did see his car being driven away. As I left it was halfway up the road.'

'You're sure it was his?'

'Oh yes, it's bright red, you can't miss it.'

'You've been most helpful. Would you come into the station tomorrow and make a statement so I can write down everything you just told me?'

The girl looked worried. 'Will my boss find out I put one over on him? Only, I don't want to lose my job.'

'No, he needn't find out, trust me. But tell me, were you questioned about this before by the police?'

'I was off duty. I know because the other girl told me she'd been questioned when I came in for my shift. But I wasn't seen by any policeman.'

Jill Masters made her way to the office to tell the sergeant what she had gleaned from her conversation.

'Well done, but how did we miss this during our previous investigation?'

She explained how the girl had been missed. The sergeant swore beneath his breath.

* * *

Whilst this investigation was taking place, Bonny Burton was recovering from yet another operation. Nigel Matthews was pleased with the result, despite the intricacies of the surgery. Fortunately he was a gifted surgeon, who specialized in knee surgery. Now Bonny was wearing a heavy bandage, walking with crutches, and Nigel Matthews told her not to put any weight on her knee until further notice. In time she would have to see the physiotherapist for treatment and exercise.

Once she was released from hospital, she decided to go home to her parents for a rest. Mickey was busy training and unable to spend much time with her. It was his suggestion that she go home, as he was worried about her being alone, but he did take time out from his training to escort her home on the train.

At the station he helped her into a taxi and they headed for Bonny's parents' house.

Millie, her mother, fussed around the two of them, ushering her daughter to an easy chair. She kissed Mickey on the cheek and put the kettle on for a cup of tea. They all chatted for a while until Mickey had to leave.

'I'll try and come down at the weekend, darlin',' he said as he kissed Bonny goodbye. 'Now, for God's sake, be careful! Don't do anything foolish.'

She assured him she would be careful.

Her mother returned from seeing the boxer off the premises and sat beside Bonny. 'How are you, love?'

Bonny shrugged. 'I'm fine, Mum, but goodness knows what I'm going to do when I'm better. I can't dance any more — and that was my life!'

'Then you find something else. After all, Bonny, you're engaged to a lovely man, and when you get married you'll have plenty to do, looking after him.'

Bonny didn't look convinced. 'You're right, but for me that isn't enough. I need more. I need an outside interest. I can't stagnate by being just a housewife.'

Her mother bristled at this remark. 'Well, I don't feel I've stagnated looking after you and your father!'

'And you haven't, but that was your choice. It was enough for you — it isn't for me.'

'Then you are going to find the going tough, my girl.' She went into the kitchen to prepare lunch for the two of them, unable to find any words of comfort for her daughter, but she was concerned for her future and how Bonny was going to manage, being away from the theatre and her usual way of life.

Bonny got to her feet and hobbled over to the window. She wished she could lift this lost feeling. Her world would never be the same again, and without the capability to dance she didn't know how she was going to cope. She hadn't meant to upset her mother, but she was young, with her whole life in front of her, and she needed to be fulfilled! Being married to Mickey would be wonderful, but she needed more. Was she being selfish, she wondered. But no, she knew that to survive, she needed to find some kind of outlet or she couldn't function.

The following morning she made her way to the Palace Theatre where her career had begun to have a word with Sammy Kendrick, her old boss.

Sammy looked up at the sound of a tap on his door and was more than a little surprised when he saw his visitor. 'Bonny, my dear! Come in, do. Take a seat. How are you? I heard about your accident, I was sorry, what bad luck!' He gazed at her crutch and added, 'I had no idea you were still incapacitated. I thought you were helping Rob, training the chorus.'

'I was, then I twisted my knee and had to have another operation. My dancing days are over, I'm afraid.'

He was sympathetic. 'That's really tough, I am so sorry. Have you any plans?'

She shook her head. 'At one time I thought I might run a dancing school, but then Rob persuaded me to help him. Now even that idea has gone by the book.'

He looked thoughtful. 'Why do you say that?'

'Well, I can't teach, can I?'

'Perhaps not, but you could hire teachers and manage them. They could show the pupils what they want as far as the actual steps, but you could lay out the programme and oversee it.'

'Do you think it would work?'

'Why not? Good God girl, you've been through the training yourself, you know what's required, you just need to find the right teachers. Come on, Bonny! You're the most dedicated dancer I've ever had in my chorus. Of course you can do it!'

'Oh, Sammy! I'm so glad I came to see you; I was beside myself with worry. I knew there had to be an answer somewhere. I never ever considered using other teachers, how stupid of me!'

'Do you have the necessary funds for this?'

She smiled. 'Oh yes. I was paid well and I saved my money for a rainy day . . . Mind you, I didn't expect it to bloody well pour!'

'That's more like the girl I knew. If I can be of any help, anything at all, you just give me a call.' He helped her to her feet.

Bonny gave him a hug. 'I can't thank you enough.'

She walked down to the Above Bar, towards the Bargate, a medieval building in the town centre, and into the High Street, feeling that at last she had a purpose and the future was bright. She couldn't wait to tell Mickey of her plans.

CHAPTER THIRTY-TWO

When Mickey came to visit her at the weekend, as promised, he found Bonny in a good mood, and when she told him about her visit to Sammy Kendrick, and his suggestion, the boxer was delighted. 'That's great news! Of course you can do it. But you need to find premises first of all, then you can advertise for instructors. You need to think of a name and have cards and letterheads printed. When my fight is over I'll be free to help you.' He hugged her. 'Oh, princess, I can't tell you how happy I am for you. I know how much this will mean to you.'

She gazed fondly at him. 'You understand me so well! How fortunate is that?'

He chuckled. 'Well, darlin', I know I'm the love of your life, but so is dancing. I'm not too sure which comes first, to be honest!'

She grinned broadly at him. 'It does a man good to be uncertain so I'll not tell you!'

'You cheeky madam! This calls for a celebration, so let's go out for a meal and we can talk about it further.'

* * *

Bonny was so excited about her plans; she decided to return to her London flat with Mickey to enable her to start her search for premises, whilst he continued with his training. His fight was scheduled for two weeks hence. It was to be against his hardest opponent yet and he knew he would have to be at the top of his game to win, and Bonny wanted to be there to cheer him on.

* * *

Foxy Gordon watched Mickey sparring in the ring. He knew his fighter was fit and able, but he also knew that Black Jack Stevens, from Jamaica, was a canny boxer and eager to take the title. The boxer had a lethal right hook, which had laid out many of his previous opponents and he was quick on his feet. The fight was the most popular fixture of the year. All the tickets had been sold and the winning purse was worth a small fortune to the victor.

When the big night arrived, Bonny was sitting in the front row with Giles Gilmore and Felix the chorus boy. They were all on edge, awaiting the final big bout.

The trumpets sounded and Black Jack Stevens made his way to the ring. Bonny was worried when she saw the powerful build of the man. He was obviously very fit and looked as strong as an ox, and she felt her heart beating wildly with anxiety.

Mickey then appeared among rousing cheers. He waved to the crowd, climbed into the ring, looked at Bonny and, with a wide smile, winked at her. She smiled back and blew him a kiss. She didn't want him to know she was worried.

During the first two rounds, the two men sounded each other out, exchanging blows and counter blows. According to Giles they were about even in the marking. But as each round continued, the battle really began, both exchanging telling blows, and Bonny had no idea how it would progress. She was sitting on the edge of her seat and wincing with every blow to Mickey's face and body. She could see the power of the punches as she watched Mickey's reaction.

During the start of the fifth round, Black Jack seemed to get the upper hand and he put Mickey down on the canvas. Bonny cried out and then quickly covered her mouth with her hand. The last thing that Mickey needed was to see her concern. He got to his feet eventually before the bell. But Bonny jumped up when, in the next round, the tables were turned and Mickey floored his opponent.

She clung on to Giles arm. 'Is he going to get up?' she asked, fingers crossed as she waited.

'I'm afraid so. Look, he's just waiting and taking a rest, getting his breath back.' And on the count of eight, Black Jack rose to his feet, gloved hands up to his face, ready for the next onslaught.

Between each round, the trainers and seconds in each corner were working on their boys. Foxy worked on Mickey's face as the second rubbed him down. 'Watch that bastard's right hand, Mickey. He's getting ready to try and end the fight. I know, I've watched him before. This is the pivotal round for him. Be very careful, keep your gloves up. Protect your chin!'

The next three minutes seemed endless to those watching. Both boxers fought like gladiators, exchanging blows, rocking each other on their feet. Bonny could hardly breathe. Then, just for a second, Black Jack dropped his guard and Mickey, quick to seize his moment, landed a hefty blow on the point of the other man's chin. Black Jack staggered, then sank slowly to the canvas.

The hall erupted! People were on their feet yelling, whistling and jumping up and down.

'Eight, nine . . . ten!' The referee counted the man out and sent Mickey back to his corner. The seconds jumped in to the ring, one shoved some smelling salts under Jack's nose and the boxer got to his feet and walked unsteadily to his corner.

Bonny threw her arms round Giles neck and kissed him. He held on to her in case in her excitement she hurt herself.

'For goodness' sake girl, be careful,' he cried.

The referee stood between both men and the crowd fell silent.

The announcer climbed into the ring and over the microphone made his speech. 'Ladies and Gentlemen, I give you the winner, and still the middleweight champion . . . Mickey O'Halleran, the pride of Ireland.' The referee held up Mickey's hand and the crowd cheered.

The two boxers clasped each other for a moment and touched gloves, then Black Jack retired to his corner and Mickey, lifted on the shoulders of Foxy and his second, was walked around the ring.

Mickey waved to the crowd and blew a kiss to Bonny, who was exhausted with the excitement, but she waved back at him, thankful it was all over.

'I'm not sure I can sit through another fight like that again,' she confessed to Giles. 'I felt every blow that Mickey took. I feel like a punchbag!'

He laughed. 'Not as much as he does I'll wager. He'll be very sore in the morning.'

The three of them waited for a while then walked to Mickey's dressing room. When he saw Bonny, he lifted her off her feet, swung her round and kissed her thoroughly.

She put her hand up to his bruised face. 'Oh Mickey, I was so worried for you up there.'

He laughed. 'Once or twice I was worried myself, darlin', but I knew if I could keep with him, he'd make a mistake, and he did.' He put her down and with a sigh of relief, said, 'But I'm glad it's over. Now we can spend some time together.' He gazed at her and said softly, 'I've really missed you, princess.'

'Me too,' she told him.

'Wait until I get showered and dressed, then we'll go and celebrate. Foxy has booked a table for us all. I won't be long.'

Looking round, Bonny said, 'Where is Foxy?'

'I don't know. He was behind me as we left the ring. Don't worry, he'll be here soon. He's probably talking to some of the fans.'

But Foxy had been waylaid by a couple of the members of Wally Cole's Firm. They cornered him at the back of the hall and shoved him outside in the dark alleyway behind the venue, where they pinned him against the wall.

'What the bloody hell do you think you're doing?' he demanded.

'We like to pay our debts,' said one.

'What debts? Don't tell me you put your money on Black Jack to win?'

'Oh no, we put our money on your boy with Wally Cole, weeks ago.'

'Yes, pity he missed the fight, he would have loved it, but there you go, someone took care of him. But at least you can have his share of the winnings.' And he grinned at them.

They were his last words.

'Yes,' said one of the men, 'you took care of our governor and now we've come back to pay his debt.'

Foxy felt something hard pressed into his body, but before he could utter a sound . . . he was dead!

The man pocketed the gun and they walked down the alleyway and out into the street where they climbed into a waiting car.

* * *

Mickey left a message for Foxy to tell him that they had all gone to the restaurant he'd booked and to follow on when he was ready. He ordered champagne whilst they all chose from the menu. It was a really happy gathering. Mickey and Bonny were telling Giles of her plans for a dancing school and he was offering advice and help. It wasn't until they were eating desert that Mickey was called to the telephone.

It was Bonny who first noticed that something was wrong as Mickey walked back to the table. They were all laughing at a joke Felix had told them, but as Bonny looked up and saw the shocked expression on Mickey's face, she grabbed hold of Giles by the arm. He stopped talking, looked at her, then followed her gaze, as did the others. Mickey sat down.

'What on earth is the matter, darling?' asked Bonny.

'Foxy is dead! Someone shot him tonight after the fight.'

They all started talking at once.

'Shot? Where?'

'Are you sure?

'Is it true, not a mistake?'

Mickey shook his head. 'They have just found his body. I can't believe it. Who would do such a thing?' But as he pondered on this, he also remembered how he suspected that his trainer might have been involved with the death of Wally Cole. If his suspicions were correct, then Foxy had paid the ultimate price.

CHAPTER THIRTY-THREE

The murder of Foxy Gordon made the headlines in all the national papers. *POPULAR BOXING IMPRESARIO SHOT* read one. *MYSTERY DEATH OF FOXY GORDON* wrote another. Everyone was talking about it. The world of boxing was in shock. There was to be a post-mortem, of course, but there was no doubt as to how the man had met his death. The mystery was — who had pulled the trigger?

Detective Inspector Phillips was discussing the death with his sergeant. 'I reckon it was someone from the Firm in retaliation for Wally Cole's murder.'

'We'll never be able to prove it without the weapon, guv. And by now, it's probably at the bottom of the Thames,' Sergeant Beckett said, then added, 'but at least we can stop our search for proof of Gordon's involvement. Someone has saved the force a lot of man-hours.'

'I know, but I hate unsolved murders. We'll have to go through the motions and question members of the gang. We won't achieve anything, but we have to be seen to be trying.'

Mickey O'Halleran, on the other hand, was devastated by the sudden demise of his trainer. As he told Bonny, 'Everything I am, I owe to that man.'

Bonny looked thoughtful. 'You know, after Wally Cole's death, Foxy told me that he took care of his own. I've often wondered if he was behind it. What do you think?'

Mickey let out a sigh. 'I think he was. After all, he was convinced that the Firm was behind Charlie Black's death, and of course he was proved right when Jimmy Knight was charged with the murder. Then Cole was behind your accident in the show. There was a lot of bad feeling between the two of them. But murder . . .'

'What will happen to the gym, do you think?'

'At this moment, it's open, but in the future, I have no idea.'

* * *

Eventually the coroner brought in a verdict of unlawful killing and the body was released for burial. Foxy had no family and so it was Mickey who arranged the funeral.

'It's the least I can do for the man,' he told Bonny.

Foxy Gordon's funeral was like a local state occasion. Everyone who was to do with the boxing world turned out to pay their respects — and from the world of theatre too. After all, Foxy was an angel and had invested a great deal of money in Giles Gilmore's production, which was now on tour.

The hearse was filled with floral tributes, as was the car behind. The church was packed, and during the service various members of the boxing world spoke of Foxy and his successes. Then Mickey O'Halleran stood at the lectern. He spoke without notes.

'I am here today to pay tribute to a friend and mentor,' he began. 'When I first came to England from Ireland with dreams of becoming a champion, it was Foxy who listened to my ambitions, who took me on and began to train me. He was a hard taskmaster but fair. If you worked hard, he was pleased — but if you didn't you got the length of his tongue — which could be lethal!' There were a few chuckles from those who had worked with him.

'He had strict rules about the behaviour of his boys. You kept out of trouble, you didn't drink to excess and never when you were training, and you never gambled. Although Foxy himself loved a game of poker, he said that not everyone could keep control of their money as he did and so he forbade it. He said that if we were under his training, we were to uphold the good name of boxing as long as we were part of it.

'As you all know, he also became involved in the theatre and was a backer for Giles Gilmore's production, which gave him great pleasure, but his heart was in the fight game and there was no one to match him.

'I stand before you as a champion, but I would never have reached this pinnacle in my career without him. I owe everything to him. I am proud of my association of such a great man, and the day he died I lost not only my mentor, but also a very dear friend.' He walked to his seat and sat down, trying hard to control his emotions.

Bonny had heard the break in his voice and knew how deeply he felt the loss of Foxy Gordon. She caught hold of his hand and held on to it throughout the service. And after the final hymn, she walked with him to a nearby hotel for the wake.

During the time that people drank and ate from the buffet that Mickey had arranged, Mickey was approached by Foxy's solicitor. 'Tomorrow morning I would like you and Miss Burton to come to my office as I have the reading of Mr Gordon's will. Is ten o'clock suitable?'

Somewhat puzzled, Mickey agreed. Turning to Bonny he said, 'I can't imagine why he wants us there.'

'It's certainly a mystery — to me in particular. Well, we'll soon find out I suppose.'

* * *

The following morning, Bonny and Mickey sat in the office of the solicitor. There was no one else there and Mickey was wondering why they had been summoned. They were both given a cup of coffee and then the solicitor began. 'I'll skip all the legal jargon in the beginning and get down to the nitty gritty of the will, if that's all right with you?'

Mickey nodded his approval.

'Mr Gordon says here, "I have no dependents, but I look upon Mickey O'Halleran as the son I never had. He has worked hard to achieve his success and he has done it with dignity and charm and he has upheld the good name of boxing throughout his career. But as we all know, a fighter has one day to hang up his boxing gloves. I know of no other man who holds the fight game with such affection and pride as I do and I want him to continue to be part of it. I want the work of training up-and-coming talented young men to continue and I can't think of a better man to take on this task than Mickey O'Halleran. Therefore, I leave to him my gym and the money in my estate with which to continue my work. I also leave five thousand pounds to Bonny Burton towards the cost of opening a dancing school. I feel a certain responsibility for the accident which befell her and put an end to her dancing career in the theatre. I know she will be a success because she loves her work as much as I love mine."'

The solicitor looked up from the paper. 'That about winds it up. We'll have to go to probate, of course, which will take some time, but Mr O'Halleran, there is a substantial amount of money in the estate. More than enough for you to fulfil his request.'

Both Bonny and Mickey were stunned. Mickey groped for words. 'I had no idea. I mean, I've never even considered the way he felt about me. A son he never had!' His voice trembled. 'That is such a compliment.'

The solicitor smiled. 'Congratulations to both of you. I am sure you will use the money wisely to carry out his wishes.'

'Of course,' they answered in unison.

'I'll be in touch, Mr O'Halleran, Miss Burton. I'm sure all those working in the gym will be relieved that it's to remain open.'

Mickey beamed at the man. 'It's the first thing I'm going to do — pass on the good news. There are some really talented young men there who thought their dreams were over. Now they can relax.' He shook the man by the hand.

Bonny and Mickey took a taxi to the gym where Mickey gave everyone the good news, which was greeted with cheers and enthusiasm.

'I'll be in tomorrow to see you all, but I have some serious thinking to do. As you can imagine this has come as a complete surprise to me and I have to try and get my brain around it all.'

Several of the men came over to congratulate him and wish him well.

As they left the premises, Mickey took Bonny by the hand. 'We need to go somewhere quiet and talk about this,' he said. And they made their way to a nearby hotel, where they found a quiet corner to have a drink and discuss the future.

Bonny was still stunned by her good luck. 'Five thousand pounds is a small fortune!' she exclaimed. 'How very kind of Foxy.'

'He felt badly about your accident, as he was the one that Wally Cole was trying to get at. That's why he left you the money. Now you can look for a place in the city itself. You need to be in the centre of things to be successful and . . .' He paused. 'I think you should call it the Bonny Burton School of Dance!'

'I like the sound of that, but why?'

'Because your name is known, and your skills admired. Why waste the opportunity to use this kind of publicity?'

She thought about it, then realized that Mickey was right. 'But how are you going to run Foxy's gym and train for another fight? How will you find the time to do both?'

He slowly sipped his beer. 'I've always thought a champion should finish his career at the top of his game. There's nothing worse than seeing a winner slowly slide down the ladder of success. It's a very sad sight.'

'So, what are you saying?' Bonny held her breath.

'I'm saying that I am going to retire from the ring.'

She stared hard at him. 'Oh, Mickey, are you sure? You love what you do and you're good at it.'

'Yes, princess, at the moment I am, but this last fight was hard, it could have gone either way, and who's to say my next opponent won't beat me?' He took her hand in his. 'I want to go out of the fight game as champion, not as a has-been. Now Foxy has given me a task that will give me a great deal of satisfaction — bringing on new boxers. Teaching them to be champions.' He smiled softly. 'As *you* will train new dancers, to work in the West End theatres, who may become stars, as you were.'

Bonny threw her arms around him and kissed him soundly, much to the amusement of the others sitting in the lounge bar. 'Oh, Mickey! I am so happy to hear that. I thought I'd die watching you in the ring the other night. I thought that man was going to kill you!'

He burst out laughing. 'Thanks very much. I'd hoped you had more faith in me that that!'

'You know what I mean,' she chided. 'It breaks my heart to see you getting hurt. It's almost more that I can bear.'

'There is just one more thing I want to do before all this takes place.'

'And what's that?'

He gazed lovingly at her. 'I want us to get married. We have no reason to wait. If we do, we'll be so caught up in our new careers that we won't have the time. Will you marry me, Bonny darlin'?'

She looked at him, caressed his face and said, 'Of course I will.'

'How soon can you be ready to get married? Please don't say months!'

She laughed heartily. 'Don't be ridiculous! You forget, as a dancer I'm used to quick changes. How soon can you arrange a wedding?'

He looked at her with amusement. 'I know you want a quiet one with not many guests, just family and close friends, so I'll try and find a vicar with an opening in three or four weeks. Will that be all right?'

'Perfect,' she said and kissed him again. 'We had best go down to Southampton at the weekend and warn my parents.'

Mickey pulled a face. 'What will we do if your father refuses to give me your hand in marriage?'

'Elope!' She started to chuckle. 'As if he would. You are a hero to my dad after he took you to the pub; to tell everyone you are his son-in-law will give him the greatest pleasure. And Mum already has a soft spot for you.'

He leaned forward and whispered in her ear, 'I know all your soft spots.'

'Mickey! Will you behave!'

* * *

The Burtons were delighted with the news and they opened the bottle of champagne that Mickey had brought with him. 'How exciting!' Millie cried. 'We'll have to start the search for your wedding gown, Bonny dear. Are you having any bridesmaids?'

'We just want a quiet wedding, Mum, with close friends and family. I would like Shirley to be with me, but that's all. We hope to make it in about a month's time.'

'So soon?' Millie was horrified.

Then they both told her parents about the contents of Foxy's will and how they would soon be very busy. 'So you see, Mum, we don't have a lot of time.'

'But you'll be married from here — won't you?'

Bonny looked at Mickey.

'If we can find a vicar who has a space for us in that time, Mrs Burton, then yes, we will, but if we can be married sooner in London, then . . .'

Bonny's mother wasn't having any of that. 'Right, then I suggest that you and Bonny call upon the vicar of St Michael's church today, after we've had a bit of lunch. Then we'll know where we stand.'

Mickey winked at Bonny. 'Yes ma'am!'

Luckily, the vicar was able to accommodate them. I have time in four weeks,' he told them. 'We can call the first banns this Sunday, so I'll book your wedding for two o'clock on October the fourth. I expect you in church tomorrow morning to hear the first calling of your banns.'

'We'll be there,' Mickey promised.

Once outside, Bonny said, 'I thought we were going back to London this evening?'

'I couldn't refuse the vicar now, could I? And, if I'm right, the couple concerned have to be in church at least once to hear their banns read. Come on, I'll book us in to the Dolphin Hotel for this evening.'

* * *

Bonny had quickly bought a wash bag with soap and toothpaste and toothbrushes for their brief stay, and Millie had given her a nightdress, which was still among her belongings at home. When in the hotel room, she got undressed and picked up the gown. Mickey, who was lying on the bed watching her, caught hold of her and pulled her down beside him. 'You surely don't intend to put that damned thing on, do you?'

'Well, I was going to.' She smiled provocatively at him.

'What a waste of time, I'll only have to take it off again. Come here.'

He gathered her into his arms and rained kisses on her. He caressed her body as he whispered how they were going to be together for the rest of their lives. How he would love her and cherish her.

Bonny was carried away in a state of desire and love for this man who now climbed on top of her and slowly entered her.

Later, they lay curled up together like two spoons and slept.

And the following morning, Bonny, Mickey and her parents attended the morning service together. After, they walked along the waterfront and went into the Red Lion for a celebratory lunch before returning to London.

CHAPTER THIRTY-FOUR

The following four weeks were frantically busy for both Bonny and Mickey. He was busy setting up a programme for the gym and he insisted on covering the costs of the wedding and the reception after, to be held at the Polygon Hotel. The guest list had been made, but as time was short the invites had been conveyed over the telephone.

Giles Gilmore, on receiving his, insisted on buying Bonny's wedding dress as a gift, saying, 'You are still my star, darling, and I want you to look like one!'

He took her to all the most expensive shops in London until they found a dress that pleased them both. Bonny stood before him in a long ivory gown with a short train. It was simply styled, with a low neckline and fitted bodice that showed her neat frame to perfection. The rhinestones and pearls, which were scattered over the body of the dress, were delicate in design. She chose a short veil, held in place by a small crown made of diamanté.

As Giles said: 'You are going to be queen for a day so wear a crown! And I know exactly what sort of bouquet you must carry.' He arranged that too.

Shirley was thrilled to be asked as bridesmaid, and she and Bonny toured the shops for her dress. They chose a pale forget-me-not blue, which was ideal for Shirley's blonde hair, which would be adorned with a small diamanté tiara.

The girls enjoyed their time together, catching up on all the news. 'I owe you so much,' Shirley remarked. 'It was your suggestion to Rob that he let me take your place. I can never thank you enough.'

'Rubbish! You have the talent, you just were never given the chance, but I'm delighted that you have been so successful. I've invited Rob to the wedding,' Bonny told her friend.

'Is he coming?'

'He said he would try.'

'Mm, I wonder if he will be able to stand in a church and see you marry another man? I doubt it.'

'Oh, Shirley!'

'Don't "oh, Shirley" me! You know how he feels about you.'

'I know, but we worked so well together, and I am fond of him — but only in a professional way.'

Shirley looked at Bonny with a calculating gleam. 'Didn't you fancy him ever?'

'Of course! When we first saw him at the Palace Theatre, I thought he was a magnificent specimen. We all did, but that was all. When we started dancing together, it was the dance that was the most important — for me, anyway.'

'Well, love, you can't have a better specimen of manhood than Mickey O'Halleran! Women dribble over him when he steps into a boxing ring.'

'I do that when he's out of the ring, I can assure you,' Bonny said with a wicked grin.

'Enough! You'll just make me jealous. Come on, let's go and have a cup of tea. This shopping is thirsty work.'

* * *

The day of the wedding arrived, and despite trying to keep the event quiet, word had got out, and when the bride and groom emerged from the church after the ceremony there was a crowd of photographers waiting for them. The flashes from the cameras was blinding for a few minutes.

'Sorry, darlin', this wasn't any of my doing,' Mickey said.

Bonny glanced across at Giles, who had emerged with the others. 'No, Bonny, I promise, it wasn't me either. I knew you wanted a quiet affair, but you didn't stand a chance. This is your home town; it was bound to get out with the calling of the banns.'

Mickey allowed the press to get their pictures and then held up his hand. 'All right chaps, that's enough. You've got your pictures, now I ask you to leave us to enjoy our day.'

There were cries of, 'Good luck champ, Mrs O'Halleran. Congratulations to you both!' And then the press made way for the official photographer.

At the wedding breakfast there were about thirty guests and it was a happy affair. Frank stood up to make his speech as father of the bride, looking somewhat nervous, but his happiness was evident as he spoke.

'There can only be one man in this room who is happier than I am today and that's my new son-in-law. And so he should be, because he's getting a jewel of a girl for his wife. My Bonny has been the apple of my eye from the moment she was born. I and her mother have been so proud of her success, but even more so from the way she has overcome the difficulties that life has thrown at her. But, strong as she is, I don't think she would have managed to overcome them had not Mickey been at her side. Now they both are starting over again. I know they will succeed because they have the character to do so, but better still they have the love that binds them together. I give you a toast, Bonny and Mickey!'

Bonny was overcome by the sentiment from her father. He had never been one able to put his feelings into words until today, and for a moment she was unable to speak.

Eventually, Mickey stood up. 'Millie, Frank, I am indeed a proud and happy man. How could I not be with this beautiful girl as my bride? It's like being presented with the Lonsdale belt all over again! I would like to thank you all for being here and sharing this special day with us. Please raise your glasses to Mrs O'Halleran.'

The best man, a fellow Irishman and friend of Mickey, gave his speech, then read out the telegrams. There was one from Rob Andrews, who had not come to the reception: *Congratulations to you both. I wish you many long years together. Rob.*

Shirley glanced across at her friend and smiled. She had been right after all. Today would have been too difficult for Rob to attend and she couldn't help but feel sorry for him.

* * *

After a week's honeymoon spent in Paris, the newlyweds returned to London, where they set about looking for somewhere to live and premises for Bonny's dancing school. Mickey, of course, had to oversee the training programme he'd set up at the gym.

He was standing outside the ropes of the boxing ring, watching a trainee, calling out instructions, when he realized that everything in the building had gone quiet. When the two men in the ring also stopped sparring, Mickey wondered what on earth was going on . . . then he turned to look behind him. Standing in the hall were three of Wally Cole's gang.

Since the demise of their boss, the Firm was slowly losing their grip on the underworld. Other gangs were slowly moving in on their territory; it was a known fact. The Firm were fighting for survival.

Mickey jumped down and walked over to the men. 'What brings you here?' he demanded.

The biggest one of the bruisers smirked and spoke. 'We thought we'd look you up and make sure you weren't being bothered by any unwanted pressure.'

Mickey stepped closer and glared at the man, poking him in the chest. 'The only pressure inside these walls is from me to my men who work here. I won't accept any from outside — from anyone. So gentlemen, I suggest you leave . . . Now!'

The smile faded and the gangster scowled. 'Are you being stupid enough to threaten me, O'Halleran?'

'No, I'm making you a promise. Leave my premises now, unscathed, or your men will have to carry you out!' As he spoke Mickey was aware of movement around him. He looked over his shoulder. All his staff and trainee boxers were standing behind him. Some just stood, prepared, waiting for trouble; others had picked up chairs, cricket bats and any other object that would inflict pain.

The gangster took a step back. 'You'll be sorry you spoke to me like that!' he threatened.

Mickey was not dismayed. 'Don't come here again, and if anything happens to my gym or any of my boys, I'll come after you, you can bank on it!'

'And if the champ is harmed, we'll come after you!' one of the others piped up.

The men turned and walked outside, muttering angrily.

'Thanks boys,' Mickey said, 'I appreciate the support.'

'Listen, champ,' said one, 'we are lucky to have this place and you. Nothing is going to spoil Foxy's dream, you can bank on that!'

Mickey was deeply touched. So far he'd not been bothered by any protection racket and that was the way he was going to keep it, no matter what.

'Right, lads, let's get back to work!' As he walked towards the boxing ring, he decided not to tell Bonny of this encounter, as she would only worry and she had enough on her plate at the moment, but he would give the local police a call and inform them of the visit. It was better to be safe than sorry.

It was a wise move, as the constable sent to keep a watchful eye on the premises foiled an attempt to set fire to the gym a week later. The culprits were caught and the Firm was finally eliminated.

* * *

The following weeks were a busy time for both Mickey and Bonny, but eventually they bought a house in Primrose Hill and Bonny found ideal premises near Covent Garden for her school. She advertised for instructors and interviewed them, had the place redecorated and found a couple of good pianists. She had cards and paper printed, then started advertising for pupils. The school would open in a few weeks time. There was to be a grand opening, with Jack Buchanan cutting the ribbon, and many of theatre's glitterati promised to attend, thereby ensuring massive publicity.

The influx of pupils wanting to attend had surpassed Bonny's expectations, and she now had a waiting list — and to her great surprise Rob Andrews had promised to take on specialized classes, once a week, without a fee.

'After all, Bonny,' he said, 'I'll be keeping an eye open for talented dancers for my shows and what better place to look than here?'

She was at a loss for words.

When opening day arrived, happily the sun shone. The press coverage was good, and inside, trays of canapés and champagne were prepared, with waitresses ready to serve the guests. Bonny was walking up and down in an effort to calm her nerves and excitement, with Mickey on hand to help her.

Jack Buchanan arrived and greeted her warmly. 'Bonny, my dear, how well you look!'

'Oh, Jack, I'm so nervous.'

'What? An old trouper like you? Come on, Bonny, take a deep breath. It's show time!' And he led her outside.

He made a heartfelt speech before cutting the ribbon and declaring the Bonny Burton School for Dance . . . open!

Stars of the theatre entered the premises and milled around, talking to each other. There were interviews taken for radio stations and pictures that would fill the national newspaper the following day. Mickey too, as the reigning champion, was also interviewed about his new life. It was a huge success.

Rob Andrews was among the guests and at the end he walked over to Mickey and shook his hand. 'Sorry I didn't make the wedding, but belated congratulations.'

Mickey smiled warmly at him. 'Thanks, Rob, but we did get your telegram. Thank you for offering to take a weekly class for Bonny. That's really good of you.'

'She deserves to do well. After all, she's had such bad luck and she was so very talented. It's the least I could do.' He made his excuses and left.

When it was all over, Mickey, with his arm round his wife, walked with her all over the new premises, listening to her plans for the classes, until they arrived back at the front door, ready to leave.

He took her by the shoulders and looked into her eyes. 'Tell me honestly, princess, is this going to be enough for you?'

Puzzled she asked, 'What do you mean?'

'You achieved such heights in your career, which was so suddenly taken from you . . . Is this now enough?'

She noted the concerned expression in his face and leaned forward and kissed him softly. 'Considering what happened to me, I feel I'm lucky to be in a position to open a school. Then getting the money Foxy left me, which enabled me to be in the best location . . . How can you wonder if it is enough for me? Of course it is!'

He breathed a sigh of relief. 'Of course, and to add to your luck you're married to a handsome young Irish lad.'

'Ah well, my luck had to run out at some time!' She laughed loudly at the shocked expression on her husband's face. 'Come on, let's go home and maybe *your* luck will change!'

'You, Mrs, O'Halleran, are a hussy and I thank the good Lord for that!'

The two of them walked away, arms round each other, ready to take on any new challenge that life may throw at them, knowing that their love for one another would be enough to see them through the years yet to come.

THE END

ACKNOWLEDGEMENTS

With thanks to the late Rita Malton, who as an ex-professional singer gave me an insight to life backstage in the theatre.

And as always my love and gratitude to my daughters, Beverley and Maxine.

THE JOFFE BOOKS STORY

We began in 2014 when Jasper agreed to publish his mum's much-rejected romance novel and it became a bestseller.

Since then we've grown into the largest independent publisher in the UK. We're extremely proud to publish some of the very best writers in the world, including Joy Ellis, Faith Martin, Caro Ramsay, Helen Forrester, Simon Brett and Robert Goddard. Everyone at Joffe Books loves reading and we never forget that it all begins with the magic of an author telling a story.

We are proud to publish talented first-time authors, as well as established writers whose books we love introducing to a new generation of readers.

We won Trade Publisher of the Year at the Independent Publishing Awards in 2023 and Best Publisher Award in 2024 at the People's Book Prize. We have been shortlisted for Independent Publisher of the Year at the British Book Awards for the last five years, and were shortlisted for the Diversity and Inclusivity Award at the 2022 Independent Publishing Awards. In 2023 we were shortlisted for Publisher of the Year at the RNA Industry Awards, and in 2024 we were shortlisted at the CWA Daggers for the Best Crime and Mystery Publisher.

We built this company with your help, and we love to hear from you, so please email us about absolutely anything bookish at feedback@joffebooks.com.

If you want to receive free books every Friday and hear about all our new releases, join our mailing list here: www.joffebooks.com/freebooks.

And when you tell your friends about us, just remember: it's pronounced Joffe as in coffee or toffee!

Printed in Dunstable, United Kingdom

74453574R00159